TOO SAFE

Paperback ISBN: 9798986018096

This book is a work of fiction. Any resemblance to any person, living or dead, or any events or occurrences, is purely coincidental. The characters and story lines are created by the author's imagination and are used fictitiously.

Developmental Editing by Melanie Yu, Made Me Blush Books
Line Editing, Copyediting, and Proofreading by VB Edits
Cover Design © Silver at Bitter Sage Designs

Contents

To anyone who's ever experienced a world-shifting,
devastating, life-altering moment...
then refused to let it define them.

You deserve to live. You deserve to *thrive*.
This book is for you.

Content Warning

Too Safe contains content some may find triggering, including on page panic attacks, kidnapping, mentions of past abuse/child neglect, mentions of past sexual assault involving the heroine, death of a parent, and chronic illness. This is book one in a three-book series. It will end with a nauseating cliffhanger.

Prologue

"It was a long life, but I played it too safe."

Those were the final words my best friend—really, my only friend—uttered before she closed her eyes for the final time.

We knew it was coming.

A person doesn't transition to hospice care at ninety-six years old without having a decent idea of what's next.

She had been imparting wisdom on me all week, stumbling through the recesses of her mind, sharing anecdotes and advice, then sometimes pausing so long she'd fall asleep mid-sentence.

But then she'd have these moments of clarity.

She'd send a nurse to fetch me, then shoo everyone else away once I was by her side. She'd place her hand in mine, the translucent skin stretched thin over mangled, arthritic knuckles, and give the softest squeeze.

"Never leave the house without rouge."

"Gentlemen prefer women who drink gin."

"Always spray your pantyhose to prevent runs."

Alice was the first client in my chair after I accepted a job at a care facility in Cleveland. A dream job, it was not. The commute was awful, and I was required to be a one-woman operation. But I was desperate, and a full-time job with excellent healthcare benefits wasn't so easy to come by in the industry.

Plus, it had proven increasingly difficult to build and maintain a clientele without any sort of social media presence. Despite my love of balayage and color melting, I needed clients who didn't rely on social media, so I resigned myself to a life of shampoo sets and nauseating perms. Once a month, I even hauled in a little tub for pedicure day.

We were fast friends, Alice and me. She was the talker. And oh, did she love to spin a story. Her favorite memories became fable; the timeline of her life and all that she'd seen and done shaken up in a snow globe of confusion because of the dementia.

First dementia. Then cancer.

"We all die eventually," she'd say with a wily, toothless grin. She forgot to put in her dentures more often than not. "It took two diseases to finally bring me down."

There was a softness to her the last time she sat in my chair in the makeshift salon wedged between the art therapy room and nutrition services office. Her fire was dimming. The last of the little flakes in her snow globe were finally laying to rest.

That's when she made me make her a promise. She made me swear on her life, knowing she only had days left to live. The saucy broad.

"Don't let the fear you carry become so heavy you don't live."

She knew so little about me. About who I was outside the beige sponge-painted walls of the facility. About who I used to be. And yet her advice was poignant and spot-on.

"Promise me, sweet girl. I lived ninety-six years, but I didn't live nearly enough."

I'd nodded along with her stories a hundred times to appease her, so it should have been easy to shrug her off. But as I met her eyes in the mirror, the desire to live—to stop surviving and to really *live*—pulsed through my veins.

"I promise," I choked out, fighting back tears.

Solemnly, she added, "And don't forget: a stitch in time saves nine."

I ducked, letting my long, dark hair fall like a curtain around me to hide my smile as she slipped back into a monologue about the time she shared a Lucky Strike with Dick Van Dyke. I could repeat that story word for word I'd heard it so many times.

Alice died the next day.

Her estate lawyer called a few weeks later.

She had left me everything—her life savings and a shoebox stuffed to the brim with broaches and colorful costume jewelry.

By the time all her affairs were settled and the lawyer's office took their cut, I was issued a check for forty-two hundred dollars.

It wouldn't be much to some. It was everything to me.

Galvanized by my promise, I called my uncle and applied for the nontraditional student scholarship at Lake Chapel University he'd told me about a few years ago. I wrote my application essay about Alice, and from there, the pieces fell into place. I like to think she had a hand in how things have changed for me. Ever since I decided to move forward, everything feels like it's happening at warp-speed.

In the last week, I've accepted a full-ride scholarship, turned in the keys to my tiny basement apartment, and resigned from my job. Now I'm stretching my neck from side to side on a bus as it coasts down route seventy-seven. I'm wedged between the freezing window and a middle-aged man whose bald head I have to keep guiding back onto his shoulders as he bobs in his sleep.

Forty-two hundred dollars, a vow to my ninety-six-year-old friend, and a life that had stalled out before it even had a chance to begin.

How can a moment feel like a last chance and a fresh start at the same time?

Today is the first day of my next chapter. As much as it scares me, I'm hitting rewind on the story of my life. Starting fresh. Being brave and choosing to live.

For Alice. *For me.*

Chapter 1

Josephine

I grip the gear shift so hard my knuckles are white as I pull into the commuter lot and guide my car into my assigned spot.

Closing my eyes, I suck in a shaky breath. I can do this. I *am* doing this.

Now I just have to get out of the car.

My next steps should be easy. Pull the lever, push the door open, heave myself out of the car, and walk onto campus. My first class of the day is a short trek from here.

But as I exit the vehicle and squint into the bright, already-too-hot morning sun, an eclipse darkens my whole *new year, new me* mojo.

Poof.

All the positive self-talk that's been cycling through my mind is no match for the massive brute before me.

"You're a girl."

I'm taken aback by his words. I'm even more disarmed by the tan fingers wrapped around the open doorframe of the 2002 Honda Civic my uncle gifted me last week.

Uncle Sam is unabashedly proud of the car—a rebuild he's been working on since I officially committed to Lake Chapel University and to living with him this fall.

He joked that if I had to live in a junkyard, I shouldn't have a ride that looked like it belonged there. I fought back tears when he handed me the keys.

I'm not a crier, and yet I could *still* tear up thinking about that moment. I've already named her Honey.

Suffice to say, I'm feeling extra prickly when I lift my chin to meet the gaze of the guy literally manhandling my new car. I'm fully prepared to tell him off, but my words falter as I assess his hard-set jaw, perfect lips, and annoyingly high cheek bones. But it's his eyes that stand to be my undoing.

Onyx black, with almost no distinction between the iris and the pupil. It's like staring into the inkiest lagoon—one that's all but guaranteed to be hiding a monster.

Although he's at least half a foot taller than me, I remind myself he's no monster.

I've faced real monsters. I've survived real monsters.

If this guy thinks he can intimidate me, he's got another thing coming.

Pursing my lips and cocking one brow, I stare right back with all the attitude I can muster. When he makes no move to get out of my way, I peel each of his fingers off my precious car and scrutinize him again.

"Paws off my ride, asshole. And yes, although gender is a social construct and it's not appropriate to assume you know anything about a person's identity, I am, in fact, a girl."

I brush my poker-straight hair over my shoulder and plant one hand on my hip.

Though it seems impossible, his irises get darker. Then he scowls and turns to the guy leaning against a black G-Wagon a few feet away. His chin is tipped down, and his attention is locked on the tablet propped against his stomach.

"She's a girl?" the first guy growls, like I've offended him in some way.

iPad guy's head snaps up. He peers at me through a pair of nerdy glasses that give off a professor-meets-superhero-in-disguise vibe, assessing me from head to toe thoroughly enough that my cheeks flush. He's slimmer than his friend, but lean and sinewy in a way that tells me he's fast. And strong. He's probably got exceptional endurance, too...

I blink to clear my head of all the naughty ideas it's conjuring up about Peter Parker's doppelgänger. I have never had a thing for nerds. And yet—

"You're sure this is her?" the bossy one demands.

The big lug peers down his nose at me. His expression is measured at first, but then the smallest hint of a smirk teases at the corners of his mouth.

"You're sure this is...them?" he clarifies, aiming his question at his friend without taking his eyes off me. "Since gender is a social construct and all."

Clever.

Nerd boy snaps out of his trance long enough to nod, then he studies his iPad again.

"Yep. The make and model of the car match what's on file with the registrar's office. Want me to check the VIN, Cap?"

Cap. *Cap*?

Forget the dumb nickname—what the hell is Peter Parker looking at? They have *what* on file *where*? My uncle must have registered the car on my behalf. Guess that explains the parking pass that was hanging from the rearview mirror when he gave it to me.

I take in a long breath, working to control my unease as I look from *Cap* to his sidekick and back again. There's no way they know who I am. They couldn't. They didn't even know my gender until moments ago.

"So the recipient of the Crusade Scholarship is a girl," he concludes, finally removing his hand from my car door and cracking his neck.

And with that, he turns his back on me. Signaling, apparently, that we're done.

Except we're not. Because I can't leave well enough alone.

Half the eyes in the parking lot are on us, burning my skin with intense curiosity. No one here knows me. Not yet. And I'll be damned if I come off as weak—less than, like a victim—on my first day.

"Do you have any other catch phrases, Cap?" I sling my bag over my shoulder and shove past him, slamming my door harder than necessary.

I wince. *Sorry, Honey.*

Worth it, though. The massive man freezes where he stands and shoots daggers at me over his shoulder.

I take a calming breath and lock my car, then adjust my backpack. Squaring my shoulders, I spread my legs a little, taking a wider stance. Obviously, I'm no physical match for this guy, but I'll be damned if I let his size intimidate me.

"She's a *hot* girl," a low voice proclaims.

At the comment, I clench my fists and turn, ever so slowly, back toward the pretentious car and the other men lounging around it.

The prolific speaker is wearing a Lake Chapel Football T-shirt. It's about three sizes too big, and the sleeves are cut out, showing off bulky, tatted arms. His dark brown hair is longer in the front, hanging over his eyes a little, but it's cropped close at his temples so I can see the gauges in his ears. There's a glint of silver in his eyebrow and an intricate black and red tattoo spanning from his throat to the edge of his jaw.

He looks like he should be passing out MDMA at Warped Tour, not leaning against a swanky car in the parking lot of a higher education institution.

He's got the faintest smirk when I finally focus on his face. He checks me out unabashedly before biting his lower lip and giving me an almost-indistinguishable nod.

My anger dissipates on the spot, transforming into a different kind of heat as we check each other out in earnest.

"You're not so bad yourself, Emo Boy." I let my attention linger for a few more seconds. And linger, it does. That neck piece is something. I'd kill to see the rest of the design, the way it swirls down his chest under that ridiculous oversized shirt.

Focus.

Time to get to class.

"Should I be concerned that you're all so curious about my sex?"

Three pairs of eyes blow out before I rewind the words and huff at my inadvertent innuendo.

"Grow up," I admonish, rolling my eyes. "Sex, as in the biological distinction. *I'm a girl*, remember?"

Holding my head high, I step toward the G-Wagon that stands between me and the path that leads to the humanities building.

I can feel their eyes tracking my movement. It's this visceral, tingly heat that creeps along my skin and makes it impossible to suck in enough air to fill my lungs.

Just when I think I'm in the clear, my backpack catches.

A low *hmph* draws my attention up—and then up even higher—to a beast of a man who's leaning against the passenger door and staring at me. This guy's also wearing a Lake Chapel U football T-shirt, but with a fitted tech shirt underneath. It's way too hot for long sleeves, but somehow, he pulls it off.

"S-sorry," I stammer.

"Watch it, Ohio," he grunts, his words deep and drawn-out as he deftly adjusts the strap on my shoulder.

I shudder on contact but grit my teeth as his warning sinks in.

Ohio.

He knows where I'm from. I've been on campus for less than five minutes, and yet I'm showing up in some database, and these guys already know details about my life.

Breathe, I remind myself. *They don't really know anything.* They can't.

My eyes flit between the four men: The dark, scowling asshole. The iPad-wielding nerd. The huge, tatted emo boy. The gruff, gorgeous jock. They'd look like a ragtag team of misfits if they weren't presiding over the parking lot like they own the damn place.

Without another second of hesitation, I turn on my heel and take off at a clipped pace.

I'm here for a reason. I have a purpose.

I fish out my phone and pop in my earbuds, glancing at the time in the process—I only have a few minutes to spare. I've come too far to turn back now.

Chapter 2

Josephine

My anxiety notches up the moment I step into the lecture hall. I inhale for four counts before exhaling and surveying my seating choices.

The back row is already filled, but I wouldn't have wanted to sit there anyway. The front row is also unavailable, as are all the aisle seats.

Shit on a crumbly cracker.

I tried to get here early. Had I not been held up in the parking lot, I would have had prime selection. Now I'm going to be wedged into a spot smack-dab in the middle of class.

I home in on a single seat situated between a pretty blonde and a dude with headphones securely in place. Beelining for the seat, I slide my backpack off my shoulders and finally let out another long breath, then pull myself together mentally and ease into the swivel chair.

The blonde acknowledges me before I'm even fully seated.

"You're new."

It's not a question.

I remind myself once again that I'm safe and that no one here knows me. Then I angle the seat and face the girl on my left.

"Is it that obvious?" I ask, wrinkling my nose.

"It *shouldn't* be," she admits, flicking a lock of her curled golden hair over one shoulder. "But at least half the students on campus grew up in

Lake Chapel, so we tend to notice when a fresh face arrives in town." She cocks one brow and gives me a knowing look.

I bite down on the inside of my cheek to hide my grimace and pull out a notebook, then swivel back toward the front of the hall, anxious for the professor to get started.

"I'm Hunter, by the way."

I glance over at the girl again—Hunter—and eye her outstretched arm.

"Joey," I supply with a cool smile as I shake her hand.

"Joey?"

"It's short for Josephine," I clarify, batting down the panic clawing its way out of my chest.

Joey. Josephine. Jo. It doesn't matter what I call myself. None of it fits.

Hunter smiles like the Cheshire cat. "Now I understand why Crusade had his gilded underwear in a bunch in the parking lot this morning."

"Crusade?"

Hunter's perfectly arched eyebrows shoot into her hairline. "Decker Crusade? The leader of the four-man welcome committee who greeted you the second you pulled in?"

Crusade. As in the Crusade Scholarship? The one covering my tuition for the next four years? Good grief.

"You saw that, huh?"

"Everyone saw it, girl. Decker and his boys were probably the first people on campus this morning, just waiting for you. But now it makes sense."

"Not to me," I mutter.

"You go by Joey?"

"Yes."

Hunter grins, using her toes to spin her chair one way, then the other with so much giddiness I'm surprised she's not clapping excitedly like a little kid.

"I guarantee Decker thought you were a guy."

Obsidian black eyes and the prettiest scowl come to mind, along with the first words he uttered. "*You're a girl.*"

"That tracks," I confirm. "But why would he care?"

Hunter rolls her eyes and snickers. "Because he's Decker Crusade. QB1. The big man on campus, and a control freak to boot." She purses her lips and gives me a quick once-over. "I assume you're the recipient of the Crusade Scholarship?"

"Yeah, but..." I frown.

Hunter scoots her chair a little closer and leans in. "Crusade always makes a big deal about welcoming the scholarship recipient to campus. If all he had to go on was that your name is *Joey*, I'm sure he was expecting a guy."

Huh. I guess I assumed the scholarship was named after a dead person, not the quarterback of the football team.

"Are you a freshman?" I ask, more than ready to divert the attention away from myself.

Hunter plays with the jewel-encrusted *H* charm on the end of her necklace. "Technically, yes. I grew up in Lake Chapel. Graduated with Decker and the guys. They're all seniors this year, but I tried to take a gap year after high school."

"Tried?"

She grimaces. "It sort of turned into a never-ending adventure. I'm still questioning why I left Lake Como for this," she admits. "Now I'm the only twenty-one-year-old freshman on campus."

I scoff. "You're not the only one, actually."

"Seriously?" Her eyes widen.

"According to the admissions office, I'm a nontraditional student because of my age and circumstances."

Hunter leans forward, wearing a bright smile. "Nontraditional? That sounds like a fancy word to distinguish that you aren't from around here," she hedges.

She's not wrong. She's friendly and seems genuinely interested, but not in the nosy, holier-than-thou sort of way. Her questions have all been straightforward. Her smile is genuine and kind. And considering my last friend was a ninety-six-year-old woman with dementia who's now dead, I could stand to make a friend my own age.

Decidedly, I tell her the truth.

"I didn't graduate from high school. I got my GED, then went on to cosmetology school. My uncle lives down here, just across the lake. He told me about the scholarship a few years ago and offered me a place to stay if I applied. I was finally ready for a change, so here I am."

It's the thinnest version of the truth. But it's the most honest I've been with anyone in a long time.

"Wow. Good for you. Are you prelaw?" she asks, perking up.

I shake my head. "No. This class was one of the few still open that satisfied the math gen ed credit." Logic 200 *would not* have been my first choice.

"Fair enough. So what is your major?"

Great question. I hadn't even considered going to college until a few months ago. It's probably going to take a little time to figure out what I want to study.

"I'm undecided right now. I might want to go into social work? Or geriatric care?"

Hunter wrinkles her nose but doesn't comment beyond that.

"Here." She hands me her phone. "This is my schedule for the week. Do we have any other classes together?"

On her device's screen is a color-coded schedule. She's got two more classes than I do—political science and American history—for a total of twenty-one credit hours. That's intense. We don't have any other classes together, but we're both off on Fridays.

"So you're prelaw?" I confirm.

She shrugs one shoulder and flips her hair. "What? Like it's hard?"

I grin at the Elle Woods reference. I really do like this girl. I hope the feeling's mutual, and that we might grow to be friends.

The thought hasn't even faded from my mind before Hunter speaks again.

"Put your number in my phone," she instructs.

Apparently, they grow them assertive in Lake Chapel.

"Let's do lunch tomorrow. We can go to my favorite sandwich shop. It's right on the water. Do you like seafood? They've got the best crab dip."

I nod in agreement and add my cell phone number.

I may be focused on her phone, but that doesn't prevent me from sensing him the moment he enters the room.

Snapping my head up, I fight back a grin as the hot punk rocker from the parking lot saunters into the lecture hall. He has this lazy, relaxed vibe about him. He's in no rush. Totally at ease.

He climbs the stairs slowly as people around the room call out to him. I barely hear them. I can't stop staring at his neck. I want to study his tattoo. Learn it. Trace it. Follow the lines all the way down—

"Hot Girl."

I startle when he stops at our row.

He rests a hand on my desk, drawing my attention. I start at his fingertips and drag my gaze up his bicep and over his inked shoulder.

When I finally take in his face, he smirks. He obviously doesn't mind the shameless ogling.

"Are you a philosophy major, too?"

Huh?

"Pretty sure you're the only philosophy major on campus, Locke," Hunter teases.

He tilts his head and looks past me to my new friend. "Hunter. Hey. Haven't seen you around for a hot minute."

She blows out a breath. "Here I am," she declares half-heartedly.

"Welcome home," Locke says with a quick smile. Then he sets his sights back on me. "You got your phone on you?"

I nod in a way that's no doubt reminiscent of a bobblehead, forgetting where I am and why I'm here. All I see is him.

With a lift of his chin, he says, "Unlock it and give it here."

I reach into my back pocket and hand it over without taking my eyes off him.

"What do you need her phone for?" Hunter scoffs. "You can't just demand she give it to you. You've been hanging out with Crusade too much."

Locke arches his pierced eyebrow in amusement and studies Hunter. But then his sole attention is on me again, and a salacious smile takes over his face as he holds my device in front of him and inspects it. "She knows what I need her phone for."

Good grief. He may as well have just whispered the filthiest dirty talk in my ear with the way my body tingles in response to his words.

The magnetism between us is twice as strong now that he's standing over me, invading my space in the best possible way. His tatted fingers fly over the screen, then he sets my phone on my desk in front of me with a satisfied smirk. I don't even have to glance at it to know he texted himself and saved his number for me.

"I'll text you later," he promises. Then he's gone, turning to head to a seat somewhere behind me.

"Oh my gosh. What just happened? Joey!" Hunter chirps in my ear.

The professor flies into the lecture hall, a mess of papers tucked under one arm.

I'm still grinning as he calls the class to order.

A new friend. A potential hookup. The morning didn't start as planned, but things are already looking up.

Chapter 3

Josephine

Slowing to a glacial pace, I ease my car over the uneven curb of Sam's Salvage and Parts—my new home.

I learned to take it easy the day after I arrived, when I almost hit Scout, the junkyard's armadillo in residence. Sam warned me to stay out of her way, because not only is she territorial, but armadillos can spread leprosy.

I came to North Carolina for a fresh start, not to contract a bacterial disease.

Slipping through the back entrance of the shop, I ease the screen door closed behind me. I'm barely two steps into the building when my uncle calls out from the reception area.

"Hey, Jo. Welcome home! Come on up here once you're settled."

My natural response is to grit my teeth at the invitation, but I force my jaw to relax and let out a breath instead. He means no harm. If anything, he's going above and beyond to be supportive. I'm just not used to having anyone care about me, let alone someone who's aware of my comings and goings. This move is a big change for both of us.

With a sigh, I dump my backpack on the floor by my bed and turn to the set of plastic storage drawers beside it.

Sam picked them up in preparation of my arrival. They're all pink. Just like the duvet on the twin-size bed and the new fluffy towels stored under the bathroom sink. Pink *used* to be my favorite color—when I was nine. But I love that he tried.

Before I head out to greet him, I change out of my jeans and pull on a pair of leggings, then spin my hair into a messy bun. I plug my MacBook in to charge—one of the purchases I made with the money Alice left me—and feel a surge of satisfaction when the little chime indicates it's connected.

My room is tiny. If I stand in the middle and stretch my arms out, my fingertips graze the walls. But Sam rearranged the entire shop, his entire life, really, to give me a place to stay. *To give me a second chance.* It's not much to look at, but it's everything to me.

"Jo?" Sam hollers from the front office.

"Coming!" I call back, making my way past the living room/kitchen combo that's recently become Sam's room, too. He insisted I take the only private space when I moved in, opting to sleep on the couch.

He's out of town four or five nights a week anyway, acquiring storage units and scouring estate sales all over the eastern side of the country.

He's so good to me—too good, almost, in a way that makes me feel unworthy. But as he's reminded me time and time again, we're family.

Family.

The idea never meant much before. A half sister twelve years older than me and a mother who rarely mustered up enough disdain to remember she had a kid to take care of were the only family I had for a long time. It'll take time for me to trust that this thing with Sam isn't too good to be true.

"There she is," he drawls when I enter the front office. "There's someone I want you to meet. Jo, this is Jeannie. She's been my right-hand gal for almost twenty years."

I turn to the desk, where a middle-aged woman with tightly curled, bleach-blond hair is stationed.

"Hey, sugar. Good to meet you." She rises out of her seat and shuffles toward me.

My body tenses without my permission as she moves into my personal space.

"Welcome to Lake Chapel," she adds as she wraps her arms around me and pulls me into a suffocatingly tight hug.

I stiffen further on contact, which only seems to inspire her to squeeze tighter.

"I'm a hugger," she laughs, then finally releases me. The smell of cheap hairspray and stale cigarette smoke lingers in the space between us as she takes a step back but keeps her hands on my shoulders, holding me at arm's length.

"You're gorgeous." She turns to Sam. "She's gorgeous!"

Sam shakes his head, then runs his hand over his stubbled face. "Give the girl some space, Jeannie. Jesus."

"I'm just so happy she's here." She squeezes my shoulders once more, her affection coming on a little too strong. What the hell has Sam told her?

Shaking my head, I force the paranoia that goes hand-in-hand with my anxiety back to the recesses of my mind.

Jeannie plops into her desk chair again and spins to face me. "Sam says you're going to help with the cleaning? And the filing?"

I nod. That was our agreement. Sam's gone above and beyond to make all this happen for me, so before I arrived, I insisted that I help around the shop. And that was before he gifted Honey to me.

"I'll show you the ropes over the next few weeks. How to file invoices, where we keep the cleaning supplies. I'm here on Mondays and Wednesdays, but we'll let you get the hang of your classes before we set up any kind of schedule. Okay, sugar?"

I nod again.

"She's quiet, isn't she?" Jeannie asks Sam.

My cheeks flame in response. I know my reservedness can come off as rude or even bitchy, so I pull in a deep breath, searching for the right words so I can offer some sort of explanation.

"It's been a big day," I admit. Driving to campus. Finding my classes. Not to mention the run-in with Crusade and his boys.

My phone vibrates in my back pocket. I'm itching to reach for it, but that will only make me look ruder.

Turning to my uncle, I press my lips together, weighing my options. I'm not used to having anyone to answer to, and we're still trying to figure out our dynamic.

"Um, I thought maybe I'd get started on my reading for class. Then I could make dinner?"

His answering chuckle eases my discomfort immediately. Maybe we're more alike than we first realized. He has no idea how any of this is supposed to work, either. But we're trying.

"That sounds great, Jojo. I'll have Jeannie make a list of which days I'll be out of town this month for you. Eat around six?"

I nod, then turn to Jeannie. "It was nice to meet you."

"You, too, sugar! You just let me know if you need anything, okay? I'll leave my number here on the desk. You can call me anytime. Or text me if that's easier. I'm not so good with the texts, but I can try."

"Let the girl study, Jeannie," Sam scolds mildly. "See you in a bit," he adds with a knowing look in my direction, followed by a chin tip toward the back of the shop.

That alone gives me the distinct impression that Jeannie can talk a person's ear off for an hour when all they expected was a two-minute conversation.

Grateful for the reprieve, I head back down the narrow hall, finally fishing out my phone. I grin when the screen lights up.

Emo Boy: I'll see you Wednesday in class, right?

I smirk. And here I was assuming he'd act too cool or play hard to get.

Hot Girl: Maybe?

Three little dots appear instantly.

Emo Boy: Say yes. Give me something to live for, Hot Girl.

I snort. I love that he has no chill.

Hot Girl: Yes. I'll see you then.

Emo Boy: I want to see you Friday, too.

Biting back a smile, I make my way into my room and perch on the edge of my bed.

Hot Girl: Sorry. I don't have any classes on Friday.

Emo Boy: Sorry? Why are you sorry? That means you're wide open and can come to the party at my place.

I scoff. I walked right into that one. We're well beyond the point of inevitable. But that doesn't mean I still don't want to play the game.

Hot Girl: Send me the details. I'll consider it.

With that, I stash my phone under my pillow, still grinning. I really do need to get started on my reading. Especially now that I've got plans this weekend.

Chapter 4

Josephine

"Hey, girl!" Hunter's rushing out the garage door before I even put Honey in park.

I checked the address twice before pulling into the driveway. Her house is *huge*. It's one of those regal Southern homes with white colonial columns, a circle driveway, and two sets of stairs leading up to the front door.

Though I thought it was a coincidence that neither of us had class on Fridays, it turns out that LCU only offers classes four days a week. A perk I didn't even know about.

At lunch on Tuesday, Hunter invited me to spend today with her so we can get ready for the party together.

According to her, the party Locke invited me to at *his place*, which, as it turns out, is a lakeside mansion owned by Decker Crusade, is *the* place to be. She gave me tons of other scoop, too—on Locke and Decker, and on their roommates Kylian and Kendrick.

Pretty sure I learned more during Hunter's course on Lake Chapel 101 than I did in all of my classes this week combined.

"I'm so glad we're doing this!" She wraps her arms around me.

At her embrace, I make a concerted effort to not go stiff. I don't *not* like hugs. I'm just not used to the frequency and intensity in which they're doled out in the south.

"Slight change of plans for today," she says, spinning back toward the house.

We weave through a garage with six bays filled with cars, a few motorcycles, and even a boat.

"I thought we'd have the house to ourselves, but my stepbrother and his teammates showed up an hour ago." She glances back at me over her shoulder and rolls her eyes.

"Let me grab a few things from my room, then we can head out. I made appointments for us at the med spa. My treat!"

I open my mouth to argue but close it again the second we step inside. The sheer amount of noise in the house means there's no way she'd hear me anyway. We've walked into chaos. No less than ten guys are hanging around the kitchen. A few lean against the countertops, stuffing their faces, while the others kick a soccer ball across the hardwood floor.

No sooner does Hunter come to a stop, plant her hands on her hips, and huff, than the soccer ball is airborne and heading right toward us.

The ball whizzes by me, and I squeak in surprise, but Hunter catches it and pulls it into her chest. *Wow*. She's got great reflexes.

"Greedy! Get your goons out of the kitchen before they break something!"

Her cheeks are pink with anger as she holds on tight to their toy. When her scowl deepens, I follow her gaze and catch sight of one of the most gorgeous specimens of man I've ever seen sauntering into the room.

Good grief. Do they grow them differently here? Is it the lake water?

The guy smiles, biting the side of his lip as he regards Hunter, then he turns toward me. "Hey, sis. Who's your friend?"

Tension crackles around them, but she doesn't respond.

The room has gone quiet. The rowdy boys from moments ago are all hushed whispers as they watch Greedy and Hunter square off.

"I'm Joey," I offer, extending a hand. "I just started at Lake Chapel U with Hunter."

Greedy is already leaning forward like he's about to accept my hand, but as the last of my words leave my mouth, he pulls back suddenly, as if he's been burned. His gaze shifts from me to Hunter, his expression turning from one of curiosity to pure ire.

"The fuck? You met at LCU? Seriously?"

"Come on," Hunter urges, grabbing me by the hand without acknowledging her stepbrother's outrage. She tosses him the ball and hightails it out of the kitchen.

"You can't hide from me forever, Temi," he calls after us.

The kitchen is so quiet now I swear I can hear each guy breathing as we hurry past them.

Halfway to the second floor, Hunter finally slows, then lets out the biggest sigh. From there, it's like she's used up all her energy reserves. Her steps drag at a glacial pace as we climb the last dozen stairs or so. Her shoulders are slumped, and I swear I hear a tiny sniffle. I don't know what to do or say, so I follow behind her silently.

What just happened?

This isn't the girl I met on Monday or had lunch with on Tuesday. She's totally deflated. If possible, she slows even further when we get to a room at the end of the hall. She opens the door, revealing a gorgeous bedroom decorated in sage greens and soft grays.

Plopping on the bed, she huffs out another sigh.

I perch on the end of the mattress, giving her some space, but I turn to her so she knows I'm here for her. "You okay?"

Though I don't understand it, something significant happened in the kitchen. I don't want to meddle, yet I feel compelled to ask. Friends talk about things like this, right? I'm rusty with the girl talk.

When Hunter doesn't respond, I backtrack. "It's okay if you don't want to talk about it. I wasn't trying to pry."

"It's nothing," she says as she takes my hand in hers and squeezes. "At least, it shouldn't be. I'm almost certain Greedy and his dad assumed I was enrolling at South Chapel University when I moved back this year. Surprise."

My stomach flip-flops. Shit. I'm the one who gave her away. "Oh god. Hunter... I'm so sorry I said anything—"

"Joey. It's fine. I didn't set out to keep it a secret. Although it was fun guessing when they would actually figure it out." Finally, a small smile graces her lips.

But it's gone just as quickly as she rolls over on the bed and props her head on her hand. "My parents divorced during my junior year of high school. It was... god, it was awful. Messy. Hateful. All either of them cared about was getting the last word and a bigger piece of the pie. Not even two weeks after the divorce was finalized, we moved in here. My mom and Dr. Ferguson were married two months later."

Holy. Shit. I school my expression, trying to hold back a reaction and reserve judgment.

"Things were okay at first. I like Doc, and my mom seemed happy. But then..." She trails off and stares at something over my shoulder.

No one would ever call me an open book. Thus, I usually have no problem letting people keep information like this to themselves. But despite my best efforts, my curiosity gets the best of me. "Then?"

"I don't really know what happened. One morning, I woke up to a note on the kitchen table from my mom. She said she'd be in Europe for two weeks. I haven't seen her since."

Confusion clouds my thoughts as I watch her, waiting for clarification. "Your mom just left you? When did this happen?" I'm no stranger to the absentee parent situation. But I was under the assumption that things like this happened to girls like me, not Hunter.

She traces the stitching of her duvet and sighs. "Four years ago."

"Hunter," I gasp, my heart plummeting for her. "I'm so sorry. That's the shittiest shit I've ever heard."

So much for reserving judgment.

I backtrack again, toeing the line of indignant outrage and supportive friend. I hope. "Is she okay? Have you seen her?"

"She's fine," Hunter scoffs. "She FaceTimes on holidays. And she's always posting on social media. I spent the first two years after high school trying to track her down and meet up in Europe. I'm almost embarrassed to admit that it took me that long to realize she was avoiding *me* just as much as she was avoiding her own life."

"That really sucks," I lament.

She sits up, then turns to face me. "It really does."

"And Greedy?"

From their interaction downstairs, it's obvious there's more to his story.

Hunter presses her lips together, and for a moment, she looks like she's fighting back tears. With a scrunch of her nose, the expression passes. Then she meets my gaze and subtly shakes her head.

I get it. We've only known each other for a week. So rather than harp on the issue, I share something about myself. This is what friends do, right? It's okay if she doesn't want to spill her heart out to me. I still don't want her to feel alone.

"My mom was absent for a lot of my childhood, too," I admit. "Although she wasn't in Europe. She could be found trading out food stamps for booze and closing down the local bar."

"I'm sorry," she offers simply.

"Me, too."

There's a sad neutrality that comes with having to raise oneself. Knowing we have this in common makes me feel more connected to

Hunter. She may lead a charmed life, but she's proof that not everything gilded is golden.

"Okay, enough sad girl mama drama," she declares, rising to her feet. "There's a party tonight, and I booked facials for us this afternoon. You in?"

I grimace and consider lying, but Hunter has been so honest with me. She deserves the same in return.

"I doubt I can afford a facial right now, but I'll definitely tag along."

"Joey," she admonishes. "I already told you. It's my treat!"

Ugh. I don't want her to think I'm using her. And I don't want to make a habit of letting her pay my way. But she's already booked appointments for us, and it's obvious that what she really wants is to get out of this house.

"Okay. But just this once," I tell her. "And you have to let me do your makeup for the party to repay you."

"Perf. I was already planning to ask you to since yours is always flawless."

Hunter parks along the street in a quaint little downtown area, then breezes into the med spa like she owns the place. The waiting room is pearly white, save for the vibrant green grass wall behind the front desk. A hot pink neon sign reads *Lake Chapel Radiance*, and new-age music plays softly in the waiting room.

"Checking in?" a receptionist asks.

Hunter handles the details while I look around. Near the edge of the reception desk is a brochure and price list, but I can't bring myself to investigate how much a place like this charges.

But next to the brochure stand is something I'm much more interested in looking into. It's a sign that reads *Help Wanted*.

I not-so-patiently wait for Hunter to finish chatting, then catch the receptionist's eye.

"Are you hiring?" I ask, pointing to the sign.

She gives me an appraising once-over. "We are. Have you ever worked in the beauty industry?" she asks with a saccharine smile.

Hunter steps back up to the desk, shoulder to shoulder with me, and takes it upon herself to answer. "Joey has her cosmetology license and years of salon experience."

Salon experience is a bit of a stretch, given my makeshift setup at the hospice facility.

"I'm licensed in the state of Ohio," I clarify. "I just moved to the area."

"Oh." The receptionist's censure is quickly replaced with mild interest. "We're hiring an assistant position, so you might be overqualified. It's mostly prepping and cleaning treatment rooms, taking out the trash—"

"I'm interested," I interject.

Paying for my own gas is a must. And I'd like to earn enough to occasionally go out to lunch with Hunter. I want the freedom I'm used to when it comes to supporting myself.

Sam's done so much for me already. But I can't accept much more than what he's given me thus far. I'll feel more like myself if I can earn my own money. Plus, I'm only taking two in-person classes this semester, and this little downtown shopping area is halfway between the junkyard and campus.

"I'll get you the new client paperwork, along with an application. Hang tight."

Hunter links her arm with mine as the receptionist leaves the waiting room. "You're a little go-getter, aren't you?" she teases.

I smile to myself and think of Alice. I'm not usually a go-getter. But I did make a promise. And I fully intend to see it through.

Chapter 5

Josephine

Hunter puts the car in park, then flips down her visor to check her makeup one more time. It's perfect. It better be, considering I spent more than an hour acting as her one-person glam squad. And I was happy to do it. She has the best products money can buy, and we had a great day together.

We're more similar than I ever would have imagined. People look at her and see a pretty face and a life of privilege, access, and connections. She's judged for what those who encounter her think they know about her. We're two sides of the same coin in that regard. They have no idea she's genuinely kind, freaking brilliant, and has the dirty sense of humor of a twelve-year-old boy.

"Ready, hot stuff?" She caps her lip gloss and rolls her lips, then pops a smooch in my direction.

"Where are we supposed to go?" I ask, unbuckling my seat belt and scanning the lines of cars ahead of us and behind us. The sign at the entrance of the parking lot read *North Marina*, and even though it's dark outside, it's clear there are no houses in the vicinity.

"You don't know where we're going?" Hunter gives me a thoughtful look.

I arch one brow. "You said the party was at Crusade's."

"*And* you have no idea where that is. Shit. I'm sorry. You're too damn easy to talk to, girl. I keep forgetting you're not from around here."

With that, she climbs out of the car. So I follow, still waiting for answers.

"Decker lives on the lake," she explains, locking her car and tilting her head, indicating I should follow.

I know that. He lives in a lakeside mansion along with Locke, Kylian, and Kendrick.

"Like, *on* the lake," she emphasizes when I say nothing. "The Crusade Mansion is a lakefront property on a private isle. Please tell me you don't get sea sickness." Spinning so she's facing me, she cringes.

A few other people get out of their cars and move in the same direction. In the dark, the whir of motors and the slosh of water are the only clues I get before the ground beneath my wedges transforms from concrete to wooden planks.

"Hunter," I warn, grabbing her arm and halting her in her tracks.

She falters slightly on her heels and turns to face me.

"How, exactly, are we supposed to get to this private isle?"

She grimaces apologetically, thumbing over her shoulder. "On that?"

I peer around her and watch as a sleek vessel in chrome and black and red slows on approach. The thing is massive. I guess it's a boat? Or maybe it would be considered a small ferry? Even in the dark, it looks expensive.

Do these people realize that it isn't normal to travel by luxury watercraft to a party? Because the whole vibe of this small crowd is nonchalant. Casual. Like this is an everyday thing.

"Is this okay? I didn't even think to mention it—"

Letting out a laugh at the audacity of the whole thing, I interlace our fingers. "I mean, I guess it's fine? I've never been on a boat, so I don't know."

"Seriously?"

"I'm from Ohio," I counter.

"But don't they have lakes there? Isn't there a *Great Lake* there?"

Yes, but her idea of the pothole-speckled roads and the dilapidated manufactured homes where I spent the first twenty-one years of my life is so far off base it's not worth explaining.

"So what happens now?" I ask, ignoring her original question as a boy in a white polo with a popped collar hops off the boat, grabs a length of rope, and spins it into an intricate knot.

"The only way to and from Crusade's is by boat," she rushes out, probably because my eyes are practically bugging out of my damn skull. "But it's just a fifteen-minute ride across the lake. Promise. And they always have two boats running, taking people back and forth. The boats literally run all night and well into the morning for anyone who stays over."

We queue up behind two large jocks as a whole crowd of tipsy girls gets in line behind us. The guy who secured the boat to the dock gives a bro nod to the jocks, indicating they can get on. Climb aboard? Hoist the anchor? Drop trou? I have no idea what it's called when someone steps onto a boat.

He then offers his arm to Hunter, who searches my face before accepting. "Is this okay?"

I love this girl. I've never had a friend like her. Despite spending all day getting ready, her concerned expression makes it clear she'd ditch the party in a heartbeat if I wasn't comfortable with this.

But surprisingly, this *is* okay. I have more than my fair share of fears—I'm terrified of storms, and I fear being held down or waking up in a strange place that isn't a bed—but open water and boats aren't an issue. At least, I don't think they are. There's only one way to find out for sure.

"Let's go, bitch."

We grin at each other. Then she steps onto the watercraft, and I deftly follow when Mr. Polo Shirt holds his arm out for me. The boat sways slightly, rocking as more people join us. Five minutes later, we're seated along a plush, heated bench and zipping across the dark lake toward a row of enormous houses adorned with lights.

Hunter squeezes my hand, and I squeeze back, holding back a squeal. Our hair is whipping around us, uncontrollable and free. It feels like we're flying, soaring toward something indescribably exciting. The night's possibilities are limitless.

It's in the air, and it's all around me. This is what *living* feels like.

Chapter 6

Josephine

The party is more night club than college get-together. Compared to what I'm used to, at least.

Trap music pours out of the speakers in the expansive living room, bleeding out onto the decks and patios through the wide-open floor-to-ceiling windows. People are everywhere—filling each room, perched on every surface. Red and purple lights strobe in time with the beat. Scantily clad girls with sculpted, fluffy brows and sleek hair grind against each other while boys with bulging muscles straining under their popped collar shirts leer at them like predators and sip from red solo cups.

The whole scene gives me the ick. But I guess it's to be expected when pretty girls and privileged boys are thrown together in a blender and the switch is flipped.

"This is ridiculous," I yell to Hunter over the music.

She grins. "They do this every week. Usually on Saturdays after football games. Wait until you see the production that goes into Shore Week."

I arch a brow in question, but before I can ask her to elaborate, she goes on, "Our biggest rival is South Chapel University, located on the other side of the lake. That's where my stepbrother goes to school. It's not the most important game, but the rivalry is decades old, so everyone goes fucking crazy. Parties, pranks, and the annual charter cruise."

Seriously? I can't imagine something bigger and wilder than this.

"Like I said—ridiculous."

In response, all I get is a smirk. Then she's bopping her head to the music and straining up on her tiptoes to survey the crowd.

"Come on." She grabs my hand and pulls me toward the kitchen. "I need a drink, then I want to dance!"

I let her pull me toward the massive kitchen island that's covered with every type of alcohol imaginable. Tito's. Belvedere. Jameson. Jack Daniel's. The sheer quantity is astounding.

There are just as many bodies in the kitchen as in the living room-slash-dance floor. I can't move an inch without rubbing up against someone. I find myself muttering "excuse me," then eventually "excuse *you*," when a few jerks shoulder past like I'm not an actual person.

When we finally find a free spot along the bar, I snag a sealed water bottle and crack it open, then take a much-needed gulp and survey the scene. Hunter sidles up to the island beside me and reaches for the Tito's and a fresh cup from the stack. I focus on her cup, unblinking, as she mixes a drink and lifts it to her lips. Satisfied, I prop one hip against the cool quartz countertop and look around, soaking it all in.

A crowd has gathered around a table, playing a drinking game I can't see from where we stand. Cheers erupt from the group every minute or so—cheers, then a rowdy LCU chant everyone here knows but me.

A girl in a skin-tight black leather dress has climbed onto the island and is sloppily dancing, an open bottle of vodka gripped in her perfectly manicured hand.

Off the kitchen is a wide staircase that curves after the first few steps. The bottom is stanchioned off with red velvet rope, and on either side of that, two of the largest men I've ever seen—with necks the size of my thigh, I swear—stand guard. They're significantly older than anyone else here and dressed in matching black T-shirts.

"What's that about?" I ask Hunter, tipping my chin toward the men in black.

She scoffs. "I told you—Decker Crusade requires control in all things."

I snort. How domineering must a man be to hire security and string a velvet rope across a staircase at a party? If I wasn't seeing it with my own eyes, I wouldn't believe it.

A moment later, fingertips brush against the bare skin of my hip in a warm caress, sending a prickle of awareness up my spine.

I jolt from the contact and snap my head around. Only when I see that it's Locke do I let out an exhale and drop my shoulders.

He leans in so close that the warmth of his exhale washes over my neck before he speaks, igniting the smallest flame in my belly.

"Hot Girl," he murmurs, his voice so low it's almost a taunt. "Didn't know if you'd make it tonight."

I take him in slowly, momentarily distracted by the bit of extra detail of his neck tat peeking out from the V-neck he's wearing. I bite down on my lower lip to keep myself from doing something epically embarrassing... like sticking out my tongue and tracing the ink-stained hollow of his throat right under his Adam's apple.

Jesus, Joey. Get a grip.

I school my expression and drag my focus back to his face. "Aren't you happy to see me?" I deadpan, planting one hand on my hip.

The grin that breaks out on his face is too much. I have to avert my eyes to stop myself from grinning right back.

"Fucking ecstatic."

A crash on the opposite end of the island startles us. I wince when I take in the scene. Island dancing girl is half hanging off the edge of the bar, her open bottle pouring out on the countertop. Someone else rushes to help her, thankfully.

"Want to ditch this scene?"

I side-eye the man in my space and note the wanton look on his face, confirming what I expected. He's not asking a question so much as he's offering an invitation.

He's looking at me like he wants to devour me. The lust pulsing through my veins only amplifies the way the mutual attraction zings between us. I absolutely want to ditch this scene and be alone with him—naked, ideally, so I can explore his ink.

But I'm not about to come off as an eager beaver.

Cool. Calm. Collected. That's all I'll allow myself to give.

"You've gotta be scene to be scene, Emo Boy," I retort, arching an eyebrow.

He practically growls at me in response, and I swear to god I feel the vibrations in my clit.

The bantering ceases with the shaky exhale he blows out as he eyes my tits pushed up in the sheer tank top Hunter loaned me. It's two sizes smaller than what I'd normally wear, but it's doing all sorts of great things for my cleavage. Good to know this little exchange is affecting him as much as it is me.

I clear my throat, and when his eager hazel eyes meet mine, he doesn't even bother looking embarrassed. He inclines his head ever so slightly, and that one single motion is enough to have me pushing off the counter.

Then he's turning on his heel and stalking out of the kitchen, knowing damn well I'll follow.

Pausing, I meet Hunter's gaze. "You good?"

A salacious smile splits her face at the exchange she just witnessed. "Oh, I'm great. You two have fun now," she teases.

"I'll still need a ride home," I assure her as a blush creeps up my chest and heats my neck. "And if I'm not back in thirty minutes—"

"Joey," she chides. "You're good. We just got here, and I'm not in a rush to get home. I won't leave without you. Pinky promise. Go fuck shit up and have fun. But if the rumors are true about Nicholas Lockewood"—she waggles her brows—"you're gonna need more than thirty minutes."

Chapter 7

Josephine

Locke is turning to look for me just as I catch up. Grinning—with that shockingly white smile that looks almost comical against the severity of his ink—he snags my hand and pulls me along behind him.

We pass the stanchioned staircase, and I can't help myself. I tug on his hand, though it doesn't stop his movement.

"Don't you live here?" I ask his back. "I thought maybe you wanted to show me your room."

A hint of a grimace passes over his face before he shakes his head and expertly weaves us through a group of partiers in our path.

"Not worth the hassle," he mutters just loud enough for me to hear. Then he quickly amends his statement. "*Them*. They're not worth the hassle." He nods at the beefed-up security dudes who are scowling at nothing.

"Hmph. You don't know whether I'm worth the hassle either, Emo Boy. Not yet."

He peers over his shoulder with hooded eyes. "I'm about to fuck around and find out."

He pushes open a random door and pulls me inside behind him. And before I have time to get my bearings, he's shoving me against the closed door, circling my throat with his hand, and squeezing ever so slightly.

Fuck.

He presses his lips to mine, sending a zap of electricity through me. My toes tingle when his tongue dips into my mouth. He feeds me the tip as I greedily drink him in, my hands landing on his waistband and finding purchase on the hem of his T-shirt.

Pulling him closer, I run my fingertips along his lower abs, eliciting the sexiest shiver from him.

"Hot Girl," he groans into my mouth, fisting his free hand and knocking it into the door beside my head. "I knew this mouth had to be good for more than dishing out sass."

Before I can come up with a witty reply, he's diving back in for more. He kisses like he wants to consume me. And I'm desperate to match his energy, slipping my tongue into his mouth for a taste, then nipping at his lower lip.

His lips leave mine, and for a moment, he leaves me bereft. But then he kisses down my neck, sucking on the skin between my collarbone and throat until I throw my head back, breathless.

"Kissing isn't the only thing this mouth can do." Panting, I brush my hand down the front of his jeans. I have to bite back a gasp when his hard length just. Keeps. Going.

"What the fuck are you hiding in there?" I demand, gripping what has to be at least ten inches of dick.

He chuckles against my neck, then bites into my flesh and sucks. Hard. I buck my hips and grind against him, more eager than ever to get intimately acquainted with his body.

"I'll show you mine if you show me yours," he murmurs, tracing the waistband of my jeans until his fingers stop below my navel. Deftly, he undoes the button. Then he pulls back and searches my face. "Yeah?"

I swear to god my pussy clenches. I fucking love a man who understands consent.

"Hell yeah," I confirm, shimmying out of my pants so fast I have to throw out an arm and steady myself using his shoulder so I don't lose my balance.

Once I've extricated myself, Locke grips my bare hips and lifts me effortlessly, carrying me two steps before setting me on a ledge.

Without taking his eyes off me, he takes a step back, reaches behind his back with one hand, and pulls his T-shirt off over his head.

My mouth drops open as I take him in. I go practically cross-eyed trying to look everywhere at once. His neck tattoo blends seamlessly into an intricate, detailed chest piece that covers his pecs and both shoulders.

The briefest hint of a smirk lifts his lips as I shamelessly ogle him. Then the man drops to his motherfucking knees.

Both hands caress my inner thighs. A moment later, the tease of hot breath hits my already-soaked, needy cunt.

"Fuck yeah," he murmurs reverently before he licks the entire length of my pussy.

His tongue is warm, lapping at me with languid caresses. With one hand, I grip his hair, pulling on the ends in encouragement.

Apparently, he's in no hurry. He continues to lick me with measured strokes that I'm fucking positive he's using to intentionally edge me.

"Locke," I groan, tilting my hips to try and get him where I want him.

Below me, he smiles wickedly against my cunt, then places a featherlight kiss on my clit.

"Say it again," he husks, meeting my gaze through long, dark lashes.

This guy. Acting like we have all the time in the fucking world when there's a party raging on the opposite side of the door.

"Locke," I scold. "Stop fucking around and lick it like a good boy. I want to come, then I need to see what you're packing."

That's all it takes.

On the next breath, he spears me with his tongue. Then he does it again. And again. And again.

The steady tongue fucking continues, ratcheting my need even higher, until he runs the tip over my clit, then quickly nips at the coiled bundle of pleasure. Closing his lips around me, he sucks, providing the perfect force that ignites my nerves.

His mouth sends me higher and higher. I'm lost to the all-encompassing pleasure shooting down my spine.

He's an expert at teasing, but he's a fucking master of steady, consistent pressure where I need it.

"I'm close," I whimper, grateful he's holding my thighs open as my muscles tense in anticipation.

There's nothing like that moment when the pleasure crests and the orgasm is *right there*. Excitement floods my veins as the telltale tingle starts in my toes. I revel in the joy—in the ecstasy and anticipation—in the buildup that's almost as sweet as the actual release.

"I'm going to come," I pant.

And like the good boy he is, he changes nothing about what he's doing. Just peeks up at me and keeps the perfect tempo.

Electricity shoots through me as my core clenches in ecstasy. I can hear myself moaning, feel my body convulsing. But the world around me is fuzzy and soft, like the wispy edges of a fluffy cloud. I pulse rhythmically as I come, and Locke mercifully releases my clit to lap up my release.

If the sounds echoing in the dark room are anything to go by, I'm drenched because of that orgasm—*fuck*—and I swear to god fresh arousal surges through me as I watch him where he's perched between my legs, slowly, languidly licking me from ass to clit.

"Fuck yeah." I preen, throwing my arms over my head as he softly fucks me with his tongue.

I realize too late that the wall behind me isn't a wall at all when I knock over a container and send its contents spilling all over the floor.

Locke freezes, then chuckles when he looks up and meets my horrified gaze.

"What the hell?"

"Decker's nuts," he grunts. He doesn't wait for a response before spreading my folds open and going back in for more.

I grip his hair and pull him off my cunt.

"Decker's *nuts?*"

What the hell is that supposed to mean?

"Cap's a health food freak," he offers, hopping to his feet like a lithe jungle cat. He wipes his mouth with the back of his hand, then grins wickedly and crowds my space.

I should be totally entranced, lust drunk and more than eager to return the favor. But I'm rattled by the mention of Crusade.

I peek around him and discover a mess of almonds scattered all over the counter and floor. Leaning forward, I glance behind me, noting for the first time the shelves filled with dry goods and food.

"Are we in a pantry?"

Locke hits me with another salacious grin, rubbing his thumb back and forth over his bottom lip. "This is where I keep all my best snacks."

"You're ridiculous," I laugh, hopping off the counter and brushing a few stray almonds off my discarded pants before pulling them back up.

"Ridiculously horny," he counters, angling in to capture my lips in a hot, sloppy kiss. "And already craving another taste," he murmurs into my mouth as he fiddles with the jeans I just buttoned.

"Nuh-uh." I pull away and scrape my nails down his bare chest. "Your turn."

I spin, trading positions. Or rather, he lets me guide his body backward. Then I push him against the counter I was just propped on. I pepper his chest in kisses, wishing for more than the dim track lighting in this pantry so I can properly appreciate his chest piece.

Sinking to my knees, I sweep my hair over one shoulder and ogle him as he pushes down his pants.

He pulls out his cock, already stiff in his hand, and gives it a few lazy strokes. I tip forward, kissing along his hip bone the same way he teased me.

I fully intend to lick a path along his happy trail. But I falter when my tongue passes over something warm, smooth, and distinctly metallic tasting.

I crane back and squint, then tilt my head to search his face.

"Pubic piercing," he supplies without prompting. "Wait 'til you feel it on your clit the first time you sink down on my cock."

Fuck. Me. Literally. Please. Like, right now.

I'm torn between sucking him into my mouth and rising to my feet so I can climb him like a tree. I've never even heard of a pubic piercing, but there it is—a barbell affixed above the base of his dick. I can only imagine what it feels like when he's buried to the hilt.

My thighs clench with desire. I'm consumed by a fiery heat that's going to take so much more than one encounter to quell.

Focusing my attention on the task at hand, I wrap my lips around him and hollow my cheeks. Then I get to work, enthusiastically bobbing on his cock, working him deeper and deeper until he hits the back of my throat. I gag but swallow again and will my throat to relax. I'm still inches away from his piercing, but I've got my target squarely in sight.

"Fuck yeah, Joey," he murmurs, weaving a hand through my hair.

The way he says my name only spurs me on more.

I pop off and grin up at him, fully prepared to deep throat him again.

But then the space is flooded with light. Blinding, disruptive light.

"What the fuck, man?" Locke barks out while cupping the side of my face to shield my eyes.

An indistinguishable grunt sounds behind me.

Locke's cock is in my hand, and my mouth is less than an inch from the tip. It's beyond obvious what we're doing.

In my periphery, a shadow overtakes the harsh light, drawing my attention. I glance up and just about fall over and die when I meet the eyes of the gorgeous, gruff jock who also lives here. He's the one who called me Ohio.

Kendrick, maybe?

We lock eyes, and his scowl remains firmly in place as he glares down at me. Finally, *fucking finally*, the side of his mouth tilts up. He gives me a barely there smirk, essentially dismissing me as he reaches over my head and grabs something off a shelf.

I watch, horrified, as he rips open the corner of a protein bar with his teeth.

"Cap's looking for you," he tells Locke in a low, even drawl. His voice is a deep bass, all smooth and sexy in a way that makes my pussy clench.

Which makes this whole scenario all the more horrifying.

He ducks out as quickly as he appeared and slams the door closed behind him.

Locke puffs his cheeks and sighs, muttering something that sounds like *unbelievable* under his breath.

He regards me with disappointment, offering a hand to help me to my feet. "Time's up, Hot Girl."

Once I'm upright, I gape, equally confused and pissed off at the interruption as he puts his dick back in his pants.

"That's it? Crusade sends for you, and we're done?"

His eyes soften, and he loops his arms around me, pulling me into his still-shirtless chest. He's so fucking solid. The comfort of his skin against my cheek pisses me off even more.

Pulling back, he cups my jaw, then he dips in for a slow, tender kiss.

"I'm nowhere near done with you," he murmurs against my lips, kissing me again and igniting another round of sparks between us.

A sharp knock on the door jolts us out of it.

"To be continued," he promises on a sigh.

I'm dizzy with lust while simultaneously all sorts of cranky from being cock blocked by Decker Crusade.

Locke wraps his hand around mine and pulls me toward the door. But I take one extra second to swipe my arm along the counter, sending more almonds flying along the floor.

Take that, Nut Cap.

Chapter 8

Josephine

I roll over in bed, pulling the quilt tighter around me and reveling in the sense of calm. My room is mostly dark thanks to the blackout curtains. Dark and deliciously chilly. The window A/C unit hums constantly. Even though it's September, North Carolina humidity is no joke.

Cozy. Rested. *Safe*.

A drawn-out, lazy yawn escapes as I squeeze my eyes shut tighter. I haven't felt this good in a really, *really* long time.

I should spend some time reading for class today, but the idea of a lazy Sunday is tempting. Or maybe I'll use the fancy gym on campus. But not until I appease my rumbling stomach.

The kitchen is stocked with a carton of eggs and a fresh loaf of bread, if I'm not mistaken. So first things first—if Sam's up, I'll make breakfast for the both of us.

I roll out of bed and throw on a crewneck over my tank top, then twist my hair into a messy bun. Snagging my phone from the charger, I hastily make my bed and creep into the hallway.

My uncle's voice carries down the hall from the front office, confirming he's awake and already at work. Until I moved in, I had no idea how much goes into running a salvage yard. The man works from morning 'til night when he's in town. Then there are the overnights and multi-day trips. I don't think he has any hobbies; he simply doesn't have the time.

Pulling the eggs and milk from the fridge, I set to work on breakfast.

As the frying pan heats, I pull my phone from my back pocket and check my messages. There are several from Hunter—a mix of memes and pictures from last night, along with a text from an hour ago.

Hunter: Girl. Last night was so fucking fun! And you hooked up with Locke! Gah! Let's do lunch tomorrow after class. Love you.

Butter sizzles and pops in the pan as I type out my response.

The next text has me grinning just as wide. The time stamp shows it came through in the middle of the night—a few hours after Hunter and I left the party.

Emo Boy: My cock's been rock-hard just from the memory of you on your knees. I need to see you again ASAP.

He can name the time and place, and I'll be there. I intend to take full advantage of our mutual attraction. Like he said to me last night: I'm nowhere near done with him, either.

I add the eggs to the pan and start scrambling, then shoot off more texts to both Hunter and Locke.

"Someone's in a good mood this morning," my uncle quips as he plops down onto the couch across the room.

"Are you hungry?" I ask over my shoulder. "I'm making eggs."

He holds my gaze and regards me for a moment before nodding. "Sure. I won't ever turn down a homecooked meal." He smiles wider. "Did you have fun last night?"

Sam made it clear when I moved in that he had no intention of keeping tabs on me or playing the role of overly concerned guardian. I even have my own entrance in the back, so I can come and go as I please. But I'm still not used to the care he shows or the interest he has in my life and happiness. It's kind of… nice… to not feel so alone or invisible.

"I did," I confirm. "I hung out with my friend Hunter all day, then we went to a party."

"Crusade's?"

I still at the reminder—*fucking Decker Crusade.*

"Mm-hmm," I confirm as casually as possible as I plate the food. "You know him?"

Sam chuckles quietly and rises to his feet to meet me at the two-person table.

"Do I *know* him? No." He snags the pepper shaker and aggressively coats his eggs. "But Decker Crusade is a local celebrity. Soon to be national celebrity, if the rumors are true."

"Rumors?" I ask a little too quickly. I stuff a huge bite of food in my mouth to mask my eagerness.

A smirk plays at Sam's mouth. "Supposedly, Decker Crusade is going to follow in the footsteps of his father. Word is the South Carolina Cougars plan to snag him as their first pick in next year's draft."

I can barely contain my eyeroll. "His dad plays football, too?"

Sam gawks at my apparent lack of sports knowledge. "Thomas Crusade is a sixteen-time Pro Bowler with seven rings. He's the crown jewel of Lake Chapel."

None of that holds meaning to me. But now I have a better understanding of how Decker Crusade can afford a lakeside mansion on a private isle.

His holier-than-thou asshole vibe makes more sense now, too.

"Thomas has got one, maybe two years left in him, tops. People reckon he's just waiting for Decker to be drafted before he passes the torch and retires."

I nod and chew, mulling over the interactions I've had with Crusade up to this point. I had no idea he was such a big deal. Maybe that's why he comes across so prickly and rude? If he's used to women fawning all over him, then our encounter likely came as quite the surprise.

I don't think I've ever even watched an entire football game. So if he expects me to be impressed with his mere existence, he'll be sorely disappointed.

My phone vibrates on the table, inspiring an instant smile as I eagerly reach for it to see whether Hunter or Locke replied.

Rather than one quick vibration signaling a text message, though, the device continues vibrating, and the screen is alight with an unfamiliar phone number.

"Hmm, eight-two-eight is from around here, right?" I ask as I stare at the digits.

"Yep. That's a local area code," Sam confirms.

I rise to my feet as I answer.

"Hello?"

"Is this Josephine Meyer?" The female voice on the other end of the line is curt.

"It is." I shift from hip to hip, fidgeting in confusion.

"This is Marilee from Lake Chapel Radiance. I received your application for the assistant position. Can you come in for a working interview tomorrow?"

Excitement washes through me as the pieces fall into place. Hell yes. But I swallow and school my giddiness to keep from sounding overly enthusiastic.

"I'm interested in the position, but I have class in the morning. Could I come by in the afternoon?"

Thankfully, the change of plan isn't an issue, and Marilee, my potential new boss, confirms the time and the dress code before we end the call.

Grinning, I drop back into my seat and meet my uncle's questioning stare.

"I applied for a job at a spa near campus. They called to set up an interview. I'll still clean and help around the shop," I rush to add. That was part of our agreement—I would help out around here in exchange for room and board. "But earning some extra money would be nice."

"Jojo," he admonishes, his expression softening.

Emotion prickles behind my eyes at the nickname. No one has called me Jojo for years.

"You came here for a fresh start. Whatever you want that to be, whatever that looks like, I'll support you. Just make sure it doesn't interfere with school. Don't take on more than you can handle," he cautions.

I turn my head to hide the tears welling in my eyes.

A fresh start. A second chance. I wouldn't be here without him. I'm endlessly grateful for this new beginning, and I intend to make the most of every opportunity.

Chapter 9

Josephine

I'm pulling a heap of fluffy white towels from the dryer when I'm bumped with just enough force to send me stumbling. But before I can collide with the industrial appliance, I catch myself and spin in search of the offender.

A gorgeous redhead dressed in all white side-eyes me from a few feet away as she disposes of a handful of needles in a sharps container.

"Oh. Sorry, hun. Did you need something?" she purrs, her voice sticky sweet and almost childish. I think her name is Staci. Yep. Staci, with an i.

She's one of the nurse estheticians at Lake Chapel Radiance. Her face is made up to perfection, and her hair is perfectly coifed. Clients probably use her plump, filled lips and taut, smooth forehead for inspiration.

"No. I'm good," I concede, proud of myself for picking my battles and passing on this one.

Marilee hired me on the spot after my working interview on Monday. The schedule is surprisingly perfect—the spa is busiest in the afternoon and evenings, and my two in-person classes are both in the morning. The pay is nearly double minimum wage, and some of the nurses share their tips.

The job is ridiculously easy, too. I check people in. Get them tea, wine, or champagne. Prepare the procedure rooms, then clean them afterward. And I take out the trash and do the laundry.

My primary objective is to be discreet—which Marilee couldn't stress enough during my interview—and to blend in. Lucky for me, going unnoticed is a specialty of mine. The solid black uniform (nurse estheticians wear all white, and assistants and support staff wear black) makes it even easier to put my head down and focus on the task at hand.

The hours will cut into my study time a little, but I can't pass up this kind of money. Plus, I like being busy. Putting in a solid day's work feels good. Familiar. There's dignity in the ability to provide for myself. I'm grateful for the exhaustion each night, and I've had no problem completing my homework this week while still finding time to hang out with Hunter.

I'm focused on folding the freshly laundered towels and trying my best to stay out of Staci's way when a pair of male voices carry down the hall.

It only takes a moment to recognize them.

Popping my head out of the back room, I peek down the corridor and grin at Locke's and Kendrick's backs. Giddy, I fight back a girlish squeal that is so out of character I surprise myself.

I told Locke about my new job, although I have no idea how he knew I'd be working today. And I don't remember mentioning the name of the spa, either.

I bounce excitedly on my toes as I fold the last towel, then take off after the guys. Locke and I have plans to meet up on Friday night, which means avoiding the inevitable party and another interruption on Saturday night.

Near the back entrance, the guys are talking to a man in a white coat over broad shoulders. I bite the inside of my cheek and do my best to school my expression as I continue my trek toward them, watching as each of them shakes hands with the man. Kendrick hands him something, then they turn to leave.

Fishing my phone out of my pocket, I double-check to make sure I don't have any texts or missed calls from Locke. I click open our text thread, but the last message from him was from this morning. Confusion clouds my mind, and I pick up the pace, hoping to catch them. By the time I reach the door, the man in the white coat has ducked back into a procedure room, and the hallway is empty.

I push through the heavy door and call out as I step into the thick evening air. "Locke!"

Both men freeze in place the second my voice rings out across the small lot.

Kendrick's head whips around, his eyes boring into me with an intense, predatory glare.

Locke turns around slowly, and when he's facing me, he swallows thickly.

I hurry to catch up. "Hey." I grin, slightly breathless, as I glance back at the exit to make sure no one followed me out. I only have a minute before I have to get back in there, but I can at least—

"What the *fuck* are you doing here, Ohio?"

Stomach plummeting, I blink rapidly and scramble to make sense of his question.

"I—I work here," I stammer. Defensiveness creeps up my spine, so I pull myself up straighter. Squaring my shoulders, I return Kendrick's glare. "What the fuck are *you* doing here?"

"Joey, don't," Locke warns, shifting from foot to foot.

Don't? Don't what?

All the joy coursing through me a moment ago saps out of me when I register the dread in his eyes. Instead of the confident smile I expected from him, his face is drawn, and his brow is furrowed. That's when it clicks. Locke isn't here for me.

I'm still trying to make sense of the situation when Kendrick takes a menacing step forward, getting right up in my face.

"You saw *nothing*," he growls.

And now my hackles are raised.

Is this sourpuss pissed off that I caught him at a medical spa? Is he worried I'll tell people he likes to indulge in expensive-ass facials? I have no interest whatsoever in Kendrick's business. Up until a minute ago, I thought he was accompanying Locke to see *me*.

Blinking away my annoyance, I turn to Locke. But he looks like he wants to be anywhere but here.

"What the hell is going on?" I demand. "Why are you here?"

In response, Kendrick swears under his breath, pulls out his phone, and pounds out a message with far more aggression than necessary.

"Dude," Locke tries, snapping out of whatever mental anguish he was just experiencing. He swipes at Kendrick's phone, but the other man recoils and dodges the attempt without even glancing up. "Kendrick. Seriously. It's fine. She didn't see shit. She didn't even know we were going to be here, did you, Joey?"

I look between the men, utterly confused. Shaking my head, I answer. "No. I didn't see either of your names on the schedule."

Kendrick's head snaps up, and he bares his teeth. Shit. Another strike for Joey.

"You *actually* work here?" he challenges.

I stare back, frowning. Why the hell is he being so hostile? Cold and grouchy is one thing, but this reaction is totally unexpected, and frankly, unnecessary. Glancing back at the door, I crack my knuckles.

"Look, I have to get back in there before they notice I'm gone."

Kendrick scoffs, his tongue in his cheek as he shakes his head. "This isn't gonna fly, Nicky." His warning is for Locke, but he doesn't take his eyes off me.

My cheeks heat under his glare, and I take a step back.

He's clearly pissed off. And yet I still have no idea what I did to contribute to his big bad mood.

"Kendrick," Locke practically pleads. "Don't do this."

His words are coated in emotion. Queasiness sets in when I realize he's desperate.

For what, I have no idea. And maybe I don't want to know.

Kendrick's phone dings, startling me.

And to think I was excited. When I spotted them, I assumed they were here to visit me. Now I can't shake the impending sense of dread swirling around us in the humid night air.

Kendrick glances at his screen, then nods once to Locke. "It's already done."

With that, he turns and stalks over to his car, leaving Locke and me staring at each other.

Before I can formulate a question, Kendrick lays on the horn. Locke whips his head toward the car, then looks back at me. His face is pained, his expression filled with remorse.

"Fuck. I'm sorry, Joey. I'm so fucking sorry. I'll call you."

And just like that, he's gone.

I stand in the parking lot, dumbfounded. When I finally remember where I am and what I'm supposed to be doing, I hurry back into the building, holding back tears.

What the hell was that?

"There you are," Marilee admonishes when I numbly make my way to the front desk. "Where did you disappear to?" she demands.

I mumble something about taking out the trash, but before I've finished the sentence, she's hurrying off down one of the halls.

"I need you to clean up the Rejuvenation suite," she calls over her shoulder, and then she disappears through an open doorway.

I work on autopilot to clean the room she directed me to. It's one of the largest in the facility, and it's typically used for couples or small groups. I go through the motions of sanitizing the surfaces and tidying the space. I glove up and carefully dispose of the needles on the tray, then check the mini fridge to ensure it's fully stocked.

I'm nearly done when I reach for a bottle of disinfectant and knock a manilla folder into the sink. I'm still a trembling mess from that parking lot face-off.

"Shit," I huff out, gathering up all the papers. I quickly rearrange them in what I think is the right order, glancing over the documents to confirm. But my attention snags on the name at the top of the file: *Kendrick Crusade.*

Except....

Kendrick's last name isn't Crusade. It's Tyler, or Taylor, or something along those lines.

Isn't it?

Of their own volition, my hands flip open the second file. I'm not even surprised when I see *Nicholas Crusade* at the top.

I know with absolute certainty his last name is Lockewood.

Why the hell were they here, and why did they feel compelled to use pseudonyms? Bad, obvious ones at that?

I've just set down the files when the door to the suite flies open.

"Ah, there they are," a man mutters. And it's not just any man. It's the doctor in the white lab coat. The one who was talking to the guys before they snuck out the back door.

"Almost done in here?" he asks, making me jump. I peek up at him, but he's not even looking at me. He's making a note in one of the guys' files. "I've got another appointment in thirty minutes."

"Yep, all done," I squeak, my voice shaky and hollow. I slip out of the room before the doctor has a chance to look up from the files, desperately hoping he didn't bother to look at me and that I can avoid being pulled into the middle of whatever bullshit is going on here.

Fighting back angry tears, I take off toward the back room.

I don't understand any of it, but the one thing I know is that I have too much self-respect to let someone disregard me and treat me the way Locke just did. I don't need any sort of defined relationship, but I do need to share mutual respect with the person I'm hooking up with. If he thinks he can meet up with me in secret, then blow me off when he's with his friends? Then fuck him.

Hot Girl: Don't bother calling me later. Or this weekend. Or ever.

I stash my phone and snatch the full hamper from the corner and get started on another load of laundry. For the first time all week, I glance at the clock and do the mental math, counting down to when I can leave this place and crawl into bed.

Chapter 10

Josephine

There's a distinct flavor of shame that comes with misreading a situation so badly. Honestly, I'm not surprised that Locke turned out to be a spineless asshole. But I am disappointed in myself for thinking he might be different.

Because I know better. I fucking know better than to trust entitled jocks who have never wanted for anything. I let myself get distracted by the gauges and his pop punk vibe, when in reality, he's nothing more than a prick in disguise, walking around pretending to be something he's not.

I squeeze my closed eyes tighter, banishing all thoughts of his gorgeous ink and ripped physique. On a deep exhale, I force away the sadness, trying to convince my mind to settle so sleep will come.

Hunter and I have plans to go to the gym early tomorrow—before it's crawling with hungover coeds like it is most Friday afternoons.

On my drive home, I called her and filled her in. She made all the outraged *tsks* and asked all the expected supportive friend questions. She didn't seem particularly surprised by the encounter, though, which makes me cringe even more. I knew better. She knew better... and yet.

Instead of letting me dwell on it, she changed the subject and insisted we figure out plans for the weekend. I'm beyond grateful for the distraction.

I swipe away an angry tear—an angry, indignant, pissed off tear, because that man-child doesn't deserve my heartache—then flip my pillow over. Resting my cheek against the cool fabric, I make a promise to myself. When I wake up in the morning, I'm done. No more tears. No more thoughts of... what was his name again? Oh. Right. Nicholas Lockewood. One night is all I need to get over him. I never even got under him in the first place.

Resolved, I hug the quilt around me a little tighter, willing my brain to relax. I've never been a good sleeper, yet I'm a grouchy, emotional mess if I don't get enough sleep.

Finally, after I flop over one more time and adjust my quilt so it hits my chin just right, the first wave of drowsiness settles around me, and my body releases all the bullshit and disappointment it's been gripping like a life preserver. A stillness washes over me, coaxing me into a relaxed state as my breathing slows.

I'm on the precipice of unconsciousness when a noise jostles me out of my sated drowsiness. *Fuck*. The interruption is jarring but far away. Definitely from outside. I wouldn't have even heard it if I had my sound machine turned up a bit louder.

It's probably just a raccoon or Scout. Another charming thing about armadillos, in addition to their bad attitudes and ability to spread leprosy? They're nocturnal.

I blow out a long, frustrated breath.

I almost had it, dammit. And being woken up on the brink of rest is the worst. It sends a shot of adrenaline surging through my veins every time, and that means it'll be another half hour until I can lull myself back to sleep.

Grinding my molars, I roll over and start my settling-in routine again.

Except another noise comes from out in the yard. And this time, I swear it's a voice.

Sitting up, I check the time on my phone: 1:17. It's too late for buyers to stop by, and Sam's supposed to be out of town until Monday anyway.

I hear it again. A murmur. Or maybe the low hum of an engine? *Shit.*

A pit of dread in my gut urges me to get up—to get ready—to *flee*. But I'm sure that's an overreaction. There's a perfectly reasonable explanation for the clatter out in the junkyard in the middle of the night. Right?

My breath is loud and erratic in my ears, the blood in my head whooshing like a metronome turned all the way up.

My feet hit the floor as the door to my room cracks open.

Someone's inside. Shit.

I'm running for the door in an instant, because that's obviously the smartest move in this situation. Instinct takes over, and I slam my shoulder into the solid wood, forcing it shut. Pain blossoms on the right side of my body, radiating from arm to hip. I bite back a whimper when the door cracks open again, despite all my weight leaning into it.

Before I can slam myself against it again, the door is open several inches.

What the fuck, Joey? Think!

A low, masculine chuckle shocks my system. I stagger away, and in what feels like slow motion, the door swings open to reveal the enormous frame of Decker Crusade.

I blink rapidly, confusion the only real reaction I can muster at the sight of the man before me.

He says nothing at first. Just crosses his arms over his chest and inspects me from the doorway. As if he didn't just barge into my bedroom in the middle of the night uninvited. As if *he's* annoyed with *me*.

"Get your shit. You're coming with us."

A laugh sounds in the distance. A shrill, maniacal laugh. It takes me several seconds to realize the noise is coming from me.

Heaving a deep breath and forcing myself to calm down, I shake my head. "You are out of your goddamned mind, Crusade. Get out."

Though I would have assumed it impossible, his scowl deepens further, and he takes one big step into my tiny room. Awareness tickles up my spine at his nearness. Saliva pools in my mouth, and my palms break out in a sweat. The visceral reaction my body has to this man... *fuck*. I could tell myself it's because he's purposely trying to intimidate me. But that would only be a partial truth.

It's then that I notice Locke behind him.

And now the *us* makes sense.

My eyes dart from Decker to the guy who jilted me earlier tonight. Of course their surprise visit is connected to my run-in with him at work. I should have seen it coming.

Another step from Decker has me retreating deeper into my room. I almost laugh again when my calves connect with the frame of my bed. The space is truly nothing more than a glorified closet. And now that a huge football player has forced himself inside, I swear the walls close in around us.

"We can do this the easy way or the hard way. You can either grab your things and come willingly or..."

He doesn't finish the sentence, but he cocks one eyebrow, letting the threat linger.

He clearly hasn't thought through this stupid idea if he thinks he can barge into my bedroom in the middle of the night and demand I go quietly.

A small smile teases my lips. "I'm not going anywhere. Especially not with you, Crusade."

I pull in a big breath, holding it in my diaphragm as I prepare to scream.

But as I open my mouth, he takes another step forward. "Save your breath, Josephine. We know your uncle's not here."

A squeak escapes before I can clamp my mouth shut. Outraged and slightly embarrassed, I peer over Decker's shoulder to look at Locke.

His shoulders are slumped, and his attention is fixed on the floor. Because he's a spineless, gutless bastard—but he's not getting off the hook that easily.

"What the fuck, Locke? What is this?"

Pained eyes meet mine, disarming me and almost making me believe he's upset. *Almost*.

"I'm sorry, Joey. Just get your things. It'll be easier if you—"

"No!"

I stomp my foot, but I immediately regret the childish impulse when Decker's lip twitches. The asshole's expression has transformed into one of mild amusement.

We stand there, a foot apart, glaring at one another, for several seconds. Eventually, his patience snaps, and he grabs for my upper arm. When his fingertips graze my skin, I duck away from him. Decker has the size advantage here, but he obviously didn't expect me to see the move coming. And the cocky bastard probably didn't anticipate that I could slip out of his grasp.

Spinning, I beeline for my bedroom door, not even bothering to look at Locke as I shoulder past him. Once I clear him, I sprint toward the front office, only to make it three strides before smacking into a solid mass.

A solid, warm mass.

One that grips my shoulders and steadies me on my feet.

"Ohio," Kendrick grunts, the nickname both a jab and a blatant disregard.

Without another word, he turns me around and pushes me toward my room.

I dig my heels in, but my bare feet find no purchase against the linoleum flooring. He'd surely have no problem lifting me and carrying me to the intended destination if he wanted, but he lets me stumble all the way there.

"Hands *off*," I huff out when he stops in front of a glaring Decker.

"You've caused enough trouble for one day, Josephine," Decker says from the doorway of my room. "Get your shit and let's go."

I glare back, fuming. There's no fucking way I'm going anywhere with him. Not now. Not ever.

My resolve must be obvious in my expression or my posture, because before I can make a move, Decker assesses me up and down, then darts a glance at Kendrick. "Grab her."

I'm hoisted into the air and over his shoulder on my next breath.

By the time I suck in a lungful of air to scream, we're out the door.

"Put. Me. *Down*!" I shout, beating on Kendrick's back with each word. The big lug doesn't even flinch as I do my worst.

Protest as I might, it's not good enough. It's never good enough. But I refuse to give up.

He carries me several feet, then heaves an SUV door open and tosses me into the back seat.

I clamber across the bench seat to the other side, only to be met by Locke, who's climbing in and sitting down.

"Move!" I demand, scrambling over him. Big hands wrap around my waist and haul me back to the middle.

"Sit down, woman." Kendrick is already in the car, sandwiching me in place.

Decker climbs into the driver's seat, and it's then that I notice the other one—Kylian. He's slumped over in the passenger seat, focused on the iPad in his lap. Always with that stupid iPad.

"What the fuck is happening right now?" I demand, my voice panicked and shrill. I'm freaking out, but I choke back the trepidation.

Sure, I'm stuck in a car—which is now moving—with four men I barely consider acquaintances.

The situation is dire. But maybe it's not hopeless. They don't want to do me physical harm. At least I don't think they do. In fact, Decker and Kendrick seem more annoyed than anything.

"Where are we going?" I try as Decker pulls out of the junkyard and onto the main road. My question is met with cold, hard silence, as if no one even heard me. "Someone better tell me what's going on," I grit out through my teeth.

"I grabbed your purse and your phone," Locke offers quietly, as if he did me some sort of favor.

"Should I say thank you?" I spit. "Thank you for blowing me off, then snatching me out of my bed like the goddamned football fuckboy mafia?"

"That'd be a good band name," Kylian murmurs so softly I almost don't hear him, still tapping away at the tablet propped on his thighs. "Football Fuckboy Mafia."

Decker smirks, one hand on the steering wheel as he navigates the SUV onto the highway via an on-ramp I recognize from when I rode to the marina with Hunter.

"We're clear?" Decker asks, his eyes focused on the road.

"Sam's handled" is Kylian's response.

Bile surges up my esophagus. He's *handled*? What does that mean? They wouldn't hurt him, would they? I still don't even know what crime I committed in the eyes of Decker Crusade to justify this... this... *kidnapping*.

"Someone better answer me," I seethe. I have nothing to follow up with, but I grit my teeth and turn to the boys on either side of me. They're both ignoring me. Kendrick looks bored, and Locke looks pained, but neither one will look at me.

"Where the *fuck* are we going?"

Finally, Decker's onyx irises meet mine in the rearview mirror.

"We're going home, Josephine."

"I *was* home," I sass back as adrenaline courses through me and panic sets in.

Sure, I've lived with Sam for less than a month. But the shop, my room, my car, *Honey*—I was more at home there than I've been anywhere for a very long time.

Chapter 11

Josephine

A barely there mist coats my skin as I will my body not to shiver. I grind my teeth obstinately, refusing to show signs of weakness.

This is survival mode. A setting I know all too well.

I'm on a boat. Against my will.

I dig my fingernails into the dense, spongy material of the life vest. I feel ridiculous with it strapped across my chest over the thin tank top I wear to bed. But with the way Kendrick shoved my arms into it, I get the impression that it isn't optional. After he carried me caveman style to the car, I wouldn't put it past him to hold me down and force me into the safety device if I tried to fight him.

The vessel isn't as large as the ferry boats that cart people from the marina to the isle, but it's big enough that all five of us fit comfortably on it.

Not that there's anything comfortable about this situation.

Decker parked his G-Wagon in the lot where Hunter and I parked last weekend. Then they marched me down the same dock I willingly walked along last Saturday. When Decker said home, he meant *his* home.

But *why*?

Why did these assholes wake me in the middle of the night and physically remove me from my room? Why did I let myself be taken?

Most importantly: why the fuck did I ever think getting involved with the likes of Nicholas Lockewood was a good idea?

I glare at him across the boat. He's seated next to Kylian on a cushy vinyl bench identical to the one I'm sitting on. Apparently, my glare isn't as threatening as I intend, because he reads it as an invitation.

He crosses the watercraft and approaches me. His steps are tentative, whether because of the speed and swaying of the boat or because of the daggers I'm shooting him, I don't know.

"You have to be freezing," he murmurs, propping on the edge of the bench beside me. "Here." He pulls off his Lake Chapel U hoodie and holds it out to me.

"Fuck. Off. Lockewood," I snarl.

He recoils like I've struck him. *Good.*

But instead of retreating like I hoped, he doubles down.

"This doesn't have to be the end of the world, Joey. If you don't act like a victim—"

"Fuck *off*!" I screech, my voice shrill and desperate.

All eyes snap to me.

They don't want me to play the victim? Maybe they shouldn't have forcibly removed me from my bed. They don't get to be the bad guys, then insist what they did wasn't that bad. I won't be gaslit by Nicholas Lockewood or any of these other entitled assholes.

Victim. I hate that fucking word.

I swore to myself I'd never be a victim again. So I won't. But they don't know that yet.

Shuddering from the chill, I close my eyes and rest my cheek on the side of the overstuffed armchair. I curl my arms around my legs, thankful now that I was too tired to change out of my leggings and into my usual sleep shorts after work.

I've been in here for what feels like hours. Not that I actually know how much time has passed since I don't have my phone. Though I'm pretty sure Kylian was fiddling with it when they escorted me inside.

I gave up physically fighting them when I got off the boat and almost face-planted on the dock outside Decker's house.

I'm desperate to get away, but I'm not suicidal.

Now that I'm here, I have to be smart. The only way off this hellish isle is by boat, according to what Hunter implied last weekend. But there's a dense, woodsy swamp behind the house that *must* lead somewhere.

I sneer at the memory of the last time I was in this place. Was it really just a week ago? When I willingly—excitedly, even—showed up, hooked up with Locke in the pantry, and rolled my eyes at Decker's overbearing antics?

I underestimated him, that's for damn sure.

A soft knock on the door has me scrambling to sit up. I won't let them catch me lying down, feeling sorry for myself. I refuse to let them see me as a *victim*, as Locke so eloquently put it.

Kylian steps inside first, focus glued to the device in his hand, per usual. The light reflects in the lenses of his glasses, making his eyes glow a Caribbean blue that momentarily mesmerizes me.

I shake myself out of it when Decker follows. He stalks into the room like he owns the place. Which I guess he does.

Sitting up straighter, I catalog his every move. As much as I hate his stupid face, I can't deny that he has this presence about him. He commands attention. Awareness dances up my spine when he's near, and even when I fight against the urge, I can't seem to look away.

That's how it is between predators and prey, isn't it? I'm transfixed. Watching his every move. Waiting for him to strike.

Kendrick saunters in behind them, his signature bored expression firmly in place. I've yet to see him look anything but unamused.

Locke is last. His face is screwed up in distress like he's going to be physically ill. And again, he's making a point to look everywhere but at me.

That's all I need to know about what's about to happen.

"What's the plan, big guy?" I rise to my feet and crack my knuckles, then roll my neck a few times. Preparing for battle but feigning a casual demeanor, like I haven't a care in the world.

"What you saw—" Decker starts.

"I didn't see *shit*," I seethe. Hands bunched into fists, I push down the urge to charge and shove him in his stupid broad chest.

So much for keeping my cool.

"What you saw," Decker repeats sternly. He pauses and scrutinizes me. Probably gauging whether I'm going to interrupt him again.

When I cross my arms under my chest and glare, he continues.

"Could affect a lot of people in a lot of ways. And that's a big fucking problem."

My chest squeezes at the implication, but then I scoff.

"Nobody gives a shit if you like to get facials or chemical peels," I counter, looking from Kendrick to Locke, then finally back to Decker. Truth be told, I have no idea what services the guys were in for. I've worked at Lake Chapel Radiance for less than a week.

"Is that what this is about?" I throw out my arms in a display that I'm sure comes off as childish. "I'm a spa assistant, asshole, and I've worked there for all of four days! I don't even know the scope of what they offer yet, and I have no idea what sort of procedure or treatment they were there for."

Decker examines me coolly, and Kylian looks up from his device. When no one says anything, I continue my defense.

"I was in the middle of my shift when I spotted Locke." I omit the part where I idiotically thought he'd shown up to see me. I drag my gaze to him and add, "I thought I saw a *friend*."

A thick fog of awkwardness passes between us. Awkwardness mixed with agony on his part. But I refuse to read too much into his emotional state. He's done literally nothing to help me tonight. I don't owe him shit.

"I called out to them," I jut my chin toward the two men, "then I followed them out the back door to the parking lot. I stupidly thought maybe they didn't hear me. I just wanted to say hi. I *saw* nothing. I *know* nothing. Just because I work at—"

"Worked."

My eyes flick up to Decker's. "Excuse me?"

"You *worked* at Lake Chapel Radiance. You don't work there anymore, Josephine."

Bile rises up my throat again, but I choke it down. I can't fall apart. *Not yet*. My uncle said Decker Crusade is a local celebrity. A known figure around town. I have no doubt that if he wanted me fired, the med spa would do so without hesitation.

I'm powerless in this moment. Powerless and going numb around the edges. Blinking, I suck in a steadying breath. I can't succumb to the hopelessness threatening to consume me. I refuse to go down without a fight.

"You can't tell me what I can and cannot do."

A cruel smile teases the corner of his lush lips.

"Oh, but I can. I protect what's mine. And as of tonight, you're a liability. I don't believe a word you've said, *Josephine Meyer*." He spits out my name like it's a curse. "You're not as innocent or unaware as you'd like us to believe. So here's what's going to happen."

He takes a step forward, and I instinctively shuffle back until my calves brush against the chair behind me.

His next words come out soft and melodic, like he's whispering sweet nothings in my ear.

"You'll stay here, with us, for the foreseeable future. You'll be accompanied to class, and you'll come to our games. You don't leave this isle without an escort. You don't tell a soul about what you saw. You don't so much as move a muscle without running it past one of us. You'll resign from your job. You'll make up excuses your uncle will believe. And you'll do *exactly* as I say."

His tone leaves no room for argument. Hot, indignant tears press behind my eyes without my permission. But I fight against them—will my body to reabsorb them—as I step forward to stand toe-to-toe with this despicable man.

"I *have* to work," I hiss.

I don't know why, out of all the bullshit that just spewed from his mouth, that's the point I cling to. But I won't backtrack or back down now.

His lip quivers into a hint of a smirk. "Then you can work for me."

Outrage swirls inside me as my coping mechanisms battle for dominance. The numbness continues to spread, yet I can't stop now. I haven't survived the last handful of years, haven't made it this far, to go down without a fight.

"You can't keep me here. That's essentially kidnapping. I'll call the police."

A chortle sounds behind Decker. "Tell my father hello when you call in to the station," Kendrick says smoothly. "And that I'll get with him after the game tomorrow."

"Your father is a police officer?" *Of course* he is.

I peer around Decker's huge body to glare at the three stooges who have been all but silent throughout this exchange. Kylian is fixated on the screen of his iPad—surprise, surprise. Locke is focused on his feet.

But Kendrick is staring right back at me, his bottom lip caught between his teeth. He's more animated right now than I've ever seen him.

"My pops *is* the police. He's the sheriff." Then he adds, "And my uncle's the county commissioner."

I close my eyes, mentally scrambling for a way out of this. I know better than to try and reason with them. My pride won't allow me to beg.

Shit on a crumbly cracker.

Opening my eyes and exhaling, I regroup. Surely my uncle will be able to help me. Except he's out of town, and the guys somehow knew that when they showed up tonight. Sam has made it clear from the beginning that I'm allowed to come and go as I please and that he's not there to keep track of me.

There's Hunter, but she's only known me for a week. There's no way I'll involve her in this. Or ask her to put her neck on the line for me.

I don't have anyone else. I don't know anyone else here.

Every part of me hates the idea of relenting to Decker's demands. My survival instincts are screaming *run*. But I have nowhere to go. I don't even know how to get off this damn isle unless it's on one of their boats. Maybe that's an option. Or maybe I could swim for it? Either way, that isn't going to happen right now.

I need to know what I'm up against. And I need time and information to gain that knowledge and formulate a plan.

So I close my eyes and ask, my question coming out whisper-thin.

"How long?"

Silence follows.

And it just keeps going. The tension in the room is sharp, crackling with every inhalation. Finally, when I open my eyes, I'm met with Decker's most pointed look yet.

He stares down his nose at me, pupils blown out and indistinguishable against the dark onyx color of his irises. Blinking, he gives a subtle shake of his head, as if snapping himself out of some sort of reverie.

Finally, he smiles. It's not a cruel smile, but it's smug and full of self-righteousness.

He thinks he's won, but the games haven't even begun.

"Until the end of the season."

Confusion has me searching the guys in the room. But then the meaning of his announcement strikes me. He means football season. Because, apparently, the world revolves around Decker Crusade and football.

"Then, if you've proven to be trustworthy and we haven't had any issues, we'll revisit our arrangement."

Our arrangement.

As if he asked my consent or gave me any semblance of choice. It's the word choice that does it. Without conscious thought, I'm mouthing off again.

"Fuck you, Crusade. I may not be able to fight you right now, but I refuse to lie down like a doormat and let you walk all over me. I'll make every moment of cohabitation as hellish as possible. You'll rue the day you kidnapped me and forced me onto your stupid island."

Decker rolls his lips and arches one eyebrow. "Rue the day?"

He's teasing me. After all this, he has the fucking audacity—

"It's an isle," Kylian murmurs without looking up from the device in his hand. As if he can't resist correcting me.

But his little correction is just the reminder I need. This glorified prison *is* an isle. It's not completely surrounded by water, just mostly. And that means there has to be another way out of here.

I made a promise to Alice.

The reminder of how far I've come, along with the tiny taste of freedom I've experienced over the last month, is all it takes for the pressure to build up behind my eyes again. This time, it's so intense I worry that if I blink, the tears will flow.

I push past Decker, ignoring the other men behind him, and beeline for the door. No one moves to stop me, which makes me feel even more pathetic and weak.

They know they've got me. I'm trapped. Backed into a corner. Stuck on this godforsaken isle.

Storming into the hall, I squint against the intense sunlight streaming in from the floor-to-ceiling windows. I know my way around well enough from the party, and I'm sure I'll have plenty of time to explore in the coming days. Hell, the coming weeks if Decker gets his way. But I can't stop moving right now. I need air. I need space. I need to be alone.

I rip open one of the sliding glass doors, letting it ricochet on its rubber runner, not bothering to shut it behind me.

Still fighting back the tears, I jog down the stairs of the deck and over the perfectly manicured yard toward the lakeshore. When my feet hit the sand, I push harder, forcing myself into a sprint that lights my calves on fire and sends a pang of awareness up through my right hip. But I don't stop or falter. I keep going—keep pushing—until my feet hit the landing that juts out into a dock.

Once I reach the end of it, the farthest physical point from Decker and his merry band of assholes, I collapse.

My knees hit the wooden planks. My head drops into my hands. And finally, mercifully, I let the sob that's been threatening to rip through me for the last several hours break free.

Chapter 12

Locke

Decker's out of his goddamned mind.

He's like a brother to me, but this has to be the most ill-conceived, harebrained idea he's ever had.

"You can't keep her here against her will," I grit out again, bracing my hands on the edge of the stone countertop until the un-inked skin around my knuckles turns so pale it's translucent.

It's the argument I've been issuing for hours. The one the guys clearly don't understand. Or maybe they do, and they're choosing to ignore it.

"We voted," Kylian states matter-of-factly.

That we did. Three to one, the group elected to force Joey to live here until further notice.

We've been making decisions this way for years. First as friends on the middle school football team, then through high school, and since we became roommates. It's Decker's house, and he's our captain on the field, but he leads in a way that's democratic and inclusive.

Most of the time.

But this girl has them all bugging out and on edge. Ironic, since I'm the only one who really knows her.

I'm sick over the whole thing. Joey doesn't deserve this.

I only met her a week ago, but a deeper part of me *knows* her. And I believe it when she says she has no idea what kind of treatments Kendrick and I received last night. Or why.

It's Kendrick's fucking fault this is all happening now.

His reaction when she followed us to the parking lot was over-the-top. I don't know what's gotten into him. I've never seen him so viscerally angry toward someone for no apparent reason. On the field, sure. The guy carries the record for most rushing yards in our division, a title that requires an unstoppable tenacity and bullheadedness. Now, his hotheadedness paired with the lack of information we can dig up on the girl have created the perfect storm.

"She'll be fine," Decker mutters, scowling at his phone. He's trying to come off as unaffected, but I know him too well. He's twisted up because he can't figure her out—there's no easy answer in this situation. There's very little he can't control. But apparently, Joey Meyer is an exception. "She'll be more of a nuisance than anything," he adds.

"What is *wrong* with you?" I fume.

That gets his attention. His dark eyes are on me in an instant, swimming with anger as his jaw tics incessantly. It's one of his few tells—that damn jaw tic.

"What's wrong with me? What's wrong with *you*?" he counters. "You're the reason we're mixed up with this girl. If you had just kept it in your pants—"

"She doesn't know anything!"

It's what I suspected all along. And Joey hasn't backed down from that claim. But the situation escalated when Kendrick shot off a text to the group chat last night.

"I don't believe that. Even if it's true, she has *access*. Would it be worth it? Do you want to spend senior year in the stands? *If* they don't expel you and ban you from campus? Do you want Kendrick to be kicked off the team, too?"

Fuck.

I hate it, but he's right.

Joey isn't a threat. I'm certain she has no idea why we were at Radiance. But if shit got out...

Kendrick and I have both received peptide therapy since high school. The treatment does wonders for my rheumatoid arthritis, and Kendrick's lupus has been in remission for almost two years. If it stays that way, he's got a real shot at going pro.

But peptides are classified as a banned substance by the NCAA, meaning our football dreams would be dashed if our visits to Dr. Kline at Lake Chapel Radiance were to be uncovered. Between a discreet doctor and Kylian's computer wizardry, we've kept it under wraps for years. Honestly, I sometimes forget that what we're doing is against the rules. We have our routine down to a science, and the risk of being caught has always been negligible given who we are.

Until her.

I blow out a long breath, glaring at Decker with as much disdain as I can muster. He meets my gaze and holds it. As much as I want to keep fighting him on this, I won't. He knows it. I know it. So after several tense seconds, I drop my head in defeat.

"Look, if we could find some fucking information on her, it'd be different." His tone isn't as hard as before, his words an olive branch.

We all turn to Kylian, but he just shrugs.

"I'll keep digging. If you all get to know her better while she's here, maybe you'll uncover information that'll help."

Decker nods but side-eyes me again. As much as he likes to be a bossy asshole, he tries to lead by consensus. I know he wants my agreement.

I still don't like what we're doing. But I understand his reasoning.

With a subtle dip of my chin, I relent.

He sighs, crossing one arm in front of the other in a stretch, obviously itching to get into the gym and work through some of this tension. We all are after the fucking night we've had.

"That's what this is about when it comes down to it. Kylian can't find anything about Josephine Meyer from Blakely, Ohio. No records. Nothing on social. Maybe it's a coincidence. Maybe we've stumbled upon the last remaining twenty-one-year-old without any sort of online presence. But something about her doesn't add up. I don't trust it."

That's the heart of what has Decker so paranoid.

Out of thin air, a new girl shows up in Lake Chapel. She's a nontraditional student and the recipient of the Crusade Scholarship. She's already been to the house. She and I have texted every night this week. Then we just randomly run in to her after our treatments? Even I can see how unlikely the coincidence is.

Decker determined she's a threat. It's the only logical conclusion, even if it doesn't track with what my gut's telling me.

I can't even fault him for it. He's always been our protector, and he's a damn good leader. Between his dad's celebrity status, what happened to his mom, and what he's destined to be, Decker has every reason not to trust people.

Everyone has an angle. Everyone wants something from him. Everyone except the guys in this room.

There's nothing I wouldn't do for Decker, Kylian, or Kendrick. And I know without a doubt the feeling is mutual.

My hands are tied.

I don't agree with him. In fact, I'm fucking pissed at how over-the-top this whole thing is.

But Decker is my brother. I owe him for so much. I trust him. I love him.

If this is what he deems necessary, then I won't fight him on it.

Even if it means losing Joey's trust and blowing up the sizzling connection between us I wasn't anywhere near done exploring.

Fuck.

Every time I start thinking about her as a threat, I forget that she's just a girl.

No, not just a girl. A woman. A woman I was fucking lucky to be intimately acquainted with last weekend. A woman I desperately wanted to get to know even more.

She's got to be so pissed, and there's no doubt a lot of her rage will be aimed at me. At least I'll have plenty of opportunities to make it up to her now that she's staying at the house.

I'm not giving up. If she's living here, we're bound to be forced to spend time together. I'll find my way back into her good graces. Even if we don't pick back up where we left off in the pantry last weekend, I'm sure she could use a friend.

Pushing off the island, I turn toward the windows, searching for the woman who's held my attention for the last week. Guilt clogs my throat when I spot her slender frame huddled at the end of the dock.

"I'm going to check on her," I announce.

"She's gonna push your ass in the lake."

I glare at Kendrick, but he's not wrong.

"I'll go," Kylian offers, shocking the shit out of me. "I have to give her phone back anyway."

Chapter 13

Josephine

A prickle of awareness dances up my spine a few seconds before a long shadow veils the end of the dock.

I don't know which one of them it is, nor do I care. The crash from the adrenaline and anxiety that have churned through my nervous system all night has finally started to dissipate, and a bone-tired weariness is settling in its place.

I'm all out of fight.

He sits beside me on the rough boards of the dock, and I finally brave a glance over.

Kylian meets my gaze through his glasses, but his expression is unreadable. I have no idea if he's out here as a messenger or a spy—as a friend or a foe. He's not as hard as the others, but he rarely looks at me. He's usually engrossed in whatever's happening on his damn iPad, so I haven't had a chance to truly assess him.

He's looking now.

Gulping past my hesitation, I pull my knees into my chest and wrap myself in a hug. My body aches, and I'm desperate for a hot shower and a long nap. Except both seem like faraway possibilities, given my current situation.

After a few minutes of quiet, I finally break the silence. "Can I ask you something?"

He nods, shifting slightly so he can face me.

"What does Decker think I saw?"

His eyebrows shoot up over the rim of his glasses and into his hairline.

"What?" I scoff. "If you're convinced I already know something, what does it matter?"

"Fair point."

He's quiet for a moment, looking from me to the lake, then back again.

Pressing my lips together, I do my best to mask the eagerness I feel. I'm desperate for something to go on here.

Kylian keeps his gaze set on the lake when he speaks. "Nicky and Kendrick need treatments that aren't approved by the NCAA."

The nickname—Nicky—is adorable. I can't focus on that shit right now, though. Nicholas Lockewood could have intervened at any point over the last several hours, but he didn't. He's not a knight in shining armor. He's a wolf in sheep's clothing. Or maybe he's just a sheep, going along with what Decker tells him to do.

"And?" I prompt, when I realize Kylian's watching me. Like he's waiting for me to connect the dots. "I don't think I even know what NCAA stands for."

"You really don't know anything, do you?" His voice is soft, bordering on sympathetic, the words seemingly kind.

I can't help but roll my eyes.

Kylian considers me, then subtly nods. "Nicky and Kendrick need help to feel their best. What works for them is considered a banned substance, so if the powers that be find evidence of their treatments, they won't be able to play football."

Football. This is about fucking *football*?

"I'm sure I sound like a broken record at this point, but I don't even know what a 'banned substance' is or why it matters. Is it like doping?" I glare at his profile.

He doesn't look away from the water. "Technically, yes."

Now I'm intrigued. "Aren't they drug tested?"

Kylian's lip quirks up ever so slightly. If I wasn't so focused on him, I'd have missed it.

"Regularly. By Crusade Labs."

I can't stop the *tsk* that escapes. Of-fucking-course.

"And let me guess. It's easy to fix the results of a drug test when your name is on the building?"

"Or when your friend is a tech genius," he adds, tapping his finger on his temple.

I sigh and drop my chin, fighting my fatigue.

But Kylian keeps going. "The good doctor used to come to the house. But the paps started coming around again when Decker turned eighteen. He was worried someone might figure out what they were doing."

"Paps?"

"Paparazzi," Kylian clarifies. "Local media and bloggers, mostly. The occasional tabloid. But everyone's got a camera in their pocket these days, ya know?"

I do. I really fucking do.

"Why would paparazzi care?"

Kylian's brows shoot up again. He's looking at me like I'm a moron. And maybe I am. Decker is undoubtedly attractive. He's all male in that testosterone-fueled kind of way. I had no idea being a football player on a college team could come with such notoriety.

"Decker Crusade can't take a shit without someone posting about it online. Kendrick, too, nowadays."

I scan the shoreline with that admission. So not only am I trapped on an isle, being held semi-prisoner in a mansion, but I'm also at risk of being photographed?

"Relax, Jo," Kylian murmurs. "We have a ton of security around here. You won't see them, but they're always there. Plus, the paps are used to seeing women at the house. They won't care about you."

"Charming." His dismissiveness grates against my nerves.

"Honest," he quips.

I take solace in that, hoping like hell he's right.

"Speaking of... Security will know to watch for you. If you try to run or escape in some way... they'll know. *We'll* know. There will be consequences. It won't be worth it."

I crack my knuckles quietly in my lap, inwardly seething.

With a groan, I drop my head and push the heels of my hands into my eyes. This whole situation is a nightmare I didn't even know was possible. Stupid hormones being attracted to Locke in the first place. Stupid heart being all girly and thinking he was trying to visit me at work last night. Stupid, stupid, stupid.

"Ya know, a lot of girls would kill to be in your shoes."

I don't bother lifting my head when I snap back at him. "To be kidnapped with nothing more than the clothes on their back and forced to live with four men they barely know?"

"No. To have the undivided attention of half the Lake Chapel U offensive line."

I roll my eyes so hard they hurt. The audacity and the attitude. These assholes really think that highly of themselves. They could all use a healthy serving of humble pie. And I want to be the one to dish it up for them.

"I guess I'm not like most girls," I retort, internally cringing at the sentiment. I hate that kind of thinking: the way society pits women against each other to perpetuate patriarchal norms. I've experienced firsthand just how nasty it is to be on the receiving end of a calculated, tactical smear campaign from another female. I shudder as I shove down the memories.

"I won't argue with that. No social media presence and a complete immunity to Decker's charms. You really aren't like most girls I know..."

My anxiety blasts off into the stratosphere, and my spine snaps straight. "You tried to look me up on social media?"

Kylian side-eyes me. "Yes. I also went through your phone and search history."

I fight back the tears pressing against the back of my eyes and resist the urge to jump into the damn lake just to escape this moment. If he found—

"I had to be sure you weren't a rat or a spy," he explains. "It was the only way to assure Decker that you're harmless. You can have this back, by the way."

He holds out my phone, and relief smacks into me on the next breath.

"I swapped out the SIM card but transferred over your contacts and apps," he continues, but I'm barely listening now. "There's a location tracker on it, but that shouldn't be an issue since you'll be here or with one of us all the time."

"Are you kidding me?" I fume, rising to my feet and gripping the phone in my hand.

"No," Kylian replies coolly. He stands and brushes off his jeans, then glances over to where I'm shooting figurative daggers at him. "Oh. That was a rhetorical question, wasn't it?"

This fucker. And here I thought maybe he was less of a threat than the others.

"Do you think you're being funny right now?" I snap.

Kylian tilts his head slightly, his face screwed up in puzzlement. "I assure you I don't."

"Do you think this is a game?" I push, my anger getting the best of me as I unleash it on him. I have no doubt Decker was the one who came up with the terms of my captivity, but fuck Kylian for being complicit. Fuck all of them for thinking they can trample all over my life—my hopes, my dreams, my fresh start—because of a simple misunderstanding.

He scratches at the back of his neck, revealing a hint of ink on the underside of his bicep. I drag my attention back to his face and scold myself for being even momentarily distracted. Living with these guys and keeping my hatred firmly in place will be a major test of willpower.

"Look... Locke and I worked really hard to get you that," he juts his chin toward the phone in my hand, "and to talk Decker down from more of his, shall we say, creative ideas to keep tabs on you."

I choke down the sense of dread bubbling up from my gut. I've gone toe to toe with Decker Crusade twice in the last two weeks. If only I weren't so damn affected by him. It's clear that he's intense, to put it lightly, and that he's willing to go to extreme measures to get what he wants.

"Come on," Kylian encourages, starting back toward the gargantuan structure they all call home. "The phone thing doesn't have to be a big deal."

Easy for him to say...

"You'll have your own room and access to the whole house. I can link you up to my Amazon account for anything you need, and if you add your food requests to the tablet in the kitchen, our housekeeper will pick it up on her weekly trip to the grocery store."

I'm frozen on the end of the dock, my feet unwilling to follow. As if my refusal to walk back into the mansion makes any difference to my current situation.

Kylian stops several feet away from me and turns back, holding out a hand.

I close my eyes and say a silent prayer, although I don't know who I'm praying to or what to even ask for.

Just not this.

When I open my eyes, nothing has changed about my surroundings or my situation. But I'm exhausted and mentally out of fight. I need to regroup, get my head on straight, and figure out my next move.

"The season is just starting, Jo. It's up to you whether the next fourteen plus weeks are miserable or enjoyable."

"Fourteen *plus* weeks?" I gape.

"Twelve regular season games and two bye weeks, then playoffs and a bowl game. Lake Chapel University is expected to take it all the way this year."

Chapter 14

Josephine

I shuffled behind Kylian as he gave me a quick tour of the house. The kitchen, media room, living room, and gym are all on the main floor, as is the master suite, which is Decker's room, apparently. My room is on the second floor, in the same hallway as Locke and Kendrick and a few other guest rooms. In my stupor, I didn't think to ask Kylian where he slept.

My room is fine—nice, even. One wall faces the lake, and the view is undeniably gorgeous. The décor is all powdery blues, deep purples, and shimmery golds. There's a feminine touch to the design that I would admit to liking if I wasn't so disgruntled about my new living arrangements. Or concerned about who typically uses this room.

Kylian mentioned the paparazzi are used to seeing women at the house. So. Yeah. It's fair to assume that this is where said women might stay.

Do any of the guys have girlfriends? Who should I be prepared to run into or even cohabitate with?

My head is swimming with questions. Questions, the fog of exhaustion, and the groggy pull of sleep after my unexpected all-nighter.

Yawning, I trudge into the en suite bathroom, then blink at the pristine space. The room is huge—bigger than my bedroom back at my uncle's, with an enormous vanity, a high-tech walk-in shower, and a gorgeous soaking tub.

The comparison to my place with Sam jolts me back to reality. I haven't tried to text or call him yet, because honestly, I don't know what I'm supposed to tell him. I disappeared, but I can't tell him where to or why or when I'll be back. He probably couldn't help me even if I *did* feel comfortable divulging details. He's already done so much for me, and I don't need to mix him up in what is turning out to be another act in the shit show that is my life.

That's something else I'll have to figure out. But that's a problem for tomorrow, after I've gotten some sleep.

I shower on autopilot, which is a shame, because the water pressure is fabulous, and the temperature stays scalding hot the entire time. I get a smug bit of satisfaction about using up all the hot water before I remember who I'm living with and just how rich he must be to afford a fancy-ass bathroom like this. *Attached to the guestroom.* There are probably a half a dozen more like it here, too. I doubt this is the type of place that runs out of hot water.

Begrudgingly, I dry off and admit to myself that, under different circumstances, that might have been the best shower I've ever taken.

Just like the bed might be the comfiest I've ever had the privilege of lying on.

There's a Lake Chapel U crewneck in the closet, along with several pairs of sweatpants and T-shirts. Pulling on clean sweats feels wonderful but does nothing to ease the lethargy threatening to pull me under.

I lock the bedroom door—another small mercy; the lock actually works—then close the blinds, shrouding the room in darkness. Then I crawl into the annoyingly comfortable bed, resolved to let myself rest. A quick nap will help me get my head on straight so I can figure out my next move.

I wake with a start, groaning as I blindly pat the bed in search of my phone. Blinking the sleep out of my eyes, I practically leap off the mattress when the screen lights up with the time.

It's just after seven, meaning I've slept the entire day away.

I've got multiple missed calls from Hunter, which is almost enough to send me into a panic spiral. What the hell am I supposed to tell her?

After several minutes of contemplating my phone, I decide a text is the safest bet.

Joey: Hey girl. Sorry I've been MIA all day. I got caught up with something and totally lost track of time.

That's all true. I have no idea where the day went—I never sleep that soundly, especially in a new place. Stupid comfy bed and fancy blackout curtains.

Hunter: Phew! I'm happy to hear from you. I was starting to worry! No big deal. We still on for the party at Crusade's tomorrow?

If she only fucking knew...

Joey: Yes, for sure. Let's meet at the party. I have a few things to take care of first.

Like figuring out how to explain my new living arrangements, for starters.

Hunter: Perf! My stepdad's making me go watch my stepbrother play tomorrow so I won't be at the LCU game. But I'll see you after!

Fuck. I had almost forgotten about the football game. The game I'm required to attend, according to Decker, the bossy fucker.

If the guys have a game tomorrow, then, with any luck, maybe they'll be at practice tonight.

I creep toward the door and unlock it silently, then open it just an inch. I hear nothing. Though I wish that meant that I'm alone, I don't trust it. The trouble with mansions? They're so damn big it's impossible to get a sense of who may be where in the house.

I can't ignore the rumbling in my stomach much longer. I spent a good chunk of my childhood in a constant state of hunger, especially on weekends or when my mom would lock me out. I haven't gone without a meal since I was old enough to get a job and take care of myself, but that doesn't stop the hunger pangs from hitting hard, especially when I'm feeling so emotionally strung out.

I decide it's worth the risk of running into the guys to scrounge up food. My optimism grows as I tiptoe down the winding staircase and enter the huge kitchen. It's empty, and the house is quiet.

Grinning to myself, I practically skip to the fridge but freeze when the clinking of silverware and soft murmurs waft in from the deck.

"Josephine."

I grip the handle of the refrigerator tight as my teeth snap together. And to think I was obtuse enough to assume I was alone for one brief moment...

"Come out here and join us."

I cautiously pad my way over to the sliding glass door and peer out. There is an absolutely massive spread of food covering the table, and the guys are all here.

Decker, Kylian, Locke, and Kendrick. Sitting around the table and enjoying a meal, as if they didn't kidnap a woman and upend her whole life this morning.

"Sit," Decker says. It's a one-word command. The kind one would give a dog.

I scan each seat—there are four empty chairs at the table, each next to one of the four men.

Resigned, I settle for the one next to Kylian. It's the closest to the door, so it makes sense from a practical standpoint. And he's the only person who's offered even a shred of kindness to me today.

Once seated, though, I immediately regret my choice. Because I'm unexpectedly close to Decker at the head of the table, and right across from Locke.

Shit.

I'm so focused on the two of them that I'm startled when a glass of water appears in front of me. Blinking, I take in the hand that set the cup on the table and follow it up a muscled arm as Kendrick turns and sits back down without looking at me or even acknowledging the gesture.

I clear my throat, hoping my words don't waver, then offer a quiet thank-you. With a relatively steady hand, despite the situation, I bring the glass to my lips and take a long drink of water and sigh when I set it back down.

"Eat," Decker commands.

Glaring, I whip my head around to face him but bite my tongue, nevertheless. I'm starved. And this spread looks amazing. I know better than to bite the hand that feeds me—literally.

"Can you pass the potatoes?" I ask Kylian after putting a few pieces of grilled chicken on my plate.

"Sure thing, Jo."

His words are soft, comforting in a way. When I smile at him, I'm caught off guard by the sincerity in his sapphire eyes.

"I came up to check on you earlier, but you were asleep," he murmurs quietly.

I open my mouth to ask how he knew I was asleep—my door was closed and locked, after all—but think better of it and snap my jaw shut again. Honestly, I don't want to know.

"We always eat together on Friday nights, Josephine," Decker says, like he's royalty speaking to a peasant. And I suppose, in a twisted way, he's not that far off. "Family dinner is at seven. You'll be expected to join us. Don't be late again."

I side-eye him as I cut into my food. "And if I'm not interested in participating in your little family dinners?"

"It's not a request." His glare is so piercing I swear it's singeing the skin on the side of my face.

Good. Maybe his face will get stuck like that. I fully intend to elicit that glare over and over again in the coming days. I'm still out of my depth, but I'm committed to my plan. If Decker Crusade wants to make my life a living hell, I'll reciprocate with all I have.

"So I can't leave the isle without an escort, I have to eat with you on Fridays, and I have to attend all your games." I finally turn to face him. "Any other non-requests, Cap?"

His eyes dilate slightly. Because of my alleged cooperation? Or the nickname he thinks he recognizes?

Either way, he smirks. "That's it. For now at least. Glad to see you're falling in line."

Now it's my turn to smirk. "You bet, Cap. Or should I say *captor*, since you took the lead in the equivalent of human trafficking today?"

His smug smile is instantly replaced with a scowl.

Beside me, Kylian chuckles under his breath.

Yep. I needed that nap. Because now the games can really begin.

Chapter 15

Josephine

After an annoyingly restful and indulgent night's sleep, I wake up on Saturday morning to the sounds of an apparent pregame ritual. The bass from the music coming from downstairs is so intense it's rattling the windows facing the lake. I hoped to avoid the guys all day today, honestly. Kylian is taking me to the stadium at noon. I assumed the others would be out of the house early.

I freshen up in the bathroom, using the fully stocked toiletries in the vanity, then twist my hair into a high ponytail. I reach for the crewneck I wore last night but pause, arm outstretched, assessing myself in the mirror.

My thin tank top is tight against my tits and just a bit too short, showing off a stretch of tanned stomach. I'm wearing a pair of LCU sweats rolled low on my hips. With a grin, I find a tube of lip gloss in my purse, then spot my meds hiding below it. Thank god Locke grabbed my bag for me during his contribution to my middle-of-the-night kidnapping. Small mercies and all that.

I'm determined to beat Decker at his own game and make him regret the day he decided to keep me against my will.

Giddy at the notion of making the guys flustered, I practically skip down the steps. Below, it sounds like Locke singing along to the song, amping himself up and screaming the chorus.

As soon as my feet hit the landing, the music pauses, and four pairs of eyes sear into me with so much intensity I almost turn around and run right back up the stairs.

Frozen, I look from man to man. My ruse worked—I've clearly disarmed them, based on the way they're all gawking at me. What I wasn't counting on was how my body would respond to their heated stares.

My traitorous nipples pebble beneath the thin fabric of my top as my heartbeat hammers an erratic rhythm in my chest. With a thick swallow, I push away thoughts of my physical reaction, then let out a shaky, breathy laugh.

"Uh, hi. Good morning."

That snaps them out of it.

A new song blares through the speakers, and Kendrick turns to open the fridge. Decker scowls at me a moment longer, then stalks around the kitchen island to join Kylian, who's got two devices propped up in front of him. It takes Kylian a few extra seconds to blink back to the present and turn to his screens again.

Locke is the only one still looking at me. He offers me a thorough assessment from head to toe, followed by a sly, almost shy smile as I approach him.

"Are you hungry? I made eggs," he murmurs, picking up the spatula from beside the stove. "Just scrambled, since I don't know how you like them."

My stomach rumbles before I can respond.

I haven't really decided what to do about Locke. It's utterly pointless to continue to ignore him while we're living under the same roof. Kendrick barely looks at me. And I cringe every time Decker says my name. I could stand to use another ally around here—especially one who knows how to cook.

"Thanks, they look great," I eventually reply.

Locke's eyes light up, and he scoops a huge serving onto a plate. "Salt and pepper are on the table. How do you like your coffee?"

Hmm. What are the chances they have fancy creamer in their mega-stocked fridge—

"Josephine," Decker grunts.

It takes every ounce of willpower I possess not to roll my eyes.

"Yes, Cap?" I reply, my tone sticky sweet.

"These are yours. For the game." His eyes are narrowed on me as he holds up a black bag and a lanyard. "It's a media pass and a camera. You'll be expected to take pictures." He holds up the lanyard so the badge attached to it sways. "The pass will let you onto the field so you can sit on the bench with Kylian."

"You're on the team?" I ask Kylian, not bothering to mask my surprise.

Decker scoffs, then claps a big hand on Kylian's back. "He *is* the team."

I have no idea what that means. Whatever. I'm sure Kylian will explain things once his beloved captain takes off for the stadium.

"All right, boys, wrap it up. We've got a game to win. We'll leave in five."

With that, Crusade grabs a shaker bottle and pops in his earbuds, then turns and heads out of the kitchen. Kendrick follows wordlessly.

Locke remains, quietly washing the pan. Turning to me, he leans back against the counter. "You'll be at the game?"

He just heard Decker explain where I'll be sitting and what I'll be required to do. Maybe Locke thinks I'm a flight risk—spoiler alert: I am—or maybe he's just trying to make small talk. Either way, I nod in response.

"I'll be there," I confirm sourly. Then I add, "Thanks for breakfast. Good luck today. Go, uh, Lake Chapelers?" I'm a full-time student, so I should probably know what the school's mascot is, but I've been a little busy being kidnapped and strategizing my escape to look it up.

Kylian laughs beside me as Locke smirks and walks out of the kitchen. "We're the Lake Chapel Crusaders, Jo."

The bench we're sitting on practically vibrates as fans scream on every side of us. The band plays, adding to the pandemonium as the Lake Chapel Crusaders ravage their opponents on the field. The energy is something I've never experienced before. The whole stadium is pulsing with excitement: One heartbeat. One purpose. It's mesmerizing and intoxicating at the same time.

Me? I still don't really know what's going on. There are a lot of rules, and the guys are only on the field sometimes, when Kylian says we have possession of the ball.

Here's what I do know:

Decker is the quarterback, which means he's involved in all the offensive plays.

Kendrick is a running back, and he ends up with the ball about half the time. He's scored twice so far today, and, according to Kylian, he keeps getting downs, whatever that means.

Locke's position is guard. He's taken hit after hit from the guys trying to get to Decker. He hasn't let anyone through yet.

It's the person I'm parked next to who surprises me most, though. Now that I'm watching him in action, Decker's comment about Kylian makes sense. He *is* the team.

Kylian is juggling two tablets and wearing a headset. Every time a play occurs on the field, he types furiously on one of his iPads, and the whole screen of numbers and figures recalculates. He scrolls through—clicking and tapping faster than humanly possible—then calls out random nonsense into a headset.

It's fascinating to watch him work. He's locked in and laser-focused. It's like his brain is in another dimension, totally unaffected by the chaos and pandemonium around us.

The coaching staff and team give him a wide berth, so we have an entire bench to ourselves. Beside me, it's just Kylian, his devices, those fast fingers, and his calm, confident murmurs into the mic.

I can't stop watching him. The skill he possesses is insanely sexy. It's obvious Kylian was meant to do this, whatever this is.

"It's stats," he tells me when I ask him to explain it between the first and second quarter. Because in addition to being a wizard with his various spreadsheets, he can also carry on a conversation with me.

"The coaches make the final play calls. But I update our stats in real time, calculating the probability of success associated with each play. More and more professional teams are deferring to stats for play calling. Decker's convinced I'll land a job with him or Kendrick next year when they're drafted."

The team runs off the field at halftime, but Kylian stays put, so I stay seated, too. I assume he's still deep in his spreadsheets when his words catch me off guard.

"If you need to go anywhere or do anything... I'll help. Just ask, and I'll help."

Emotion clogs my throat. I have to remind myself that he's partly to blame for why I'm stuck at the Crusade Mansion, though.

"Why?" I ask with a shaky breath.

He doesn't answer right away. In fact, so much time passes, I'm convinced he's not going to answer me at all. The roar of the crowd kicks back up as halftime ends and the team rushes back onto the field.

"You're not alone in this, Jo," he says, cupping his mic so his words don't carry. "I'll help," he repeats.

I don't have time to reply before the start of the third quarter.

Chapter 16

Josephine

"People are already here?" I ask as I take in the scene. Kylian is easing the speed boat up along the dock as a ferry unloads a few dozen partiers.

The Crusaders won their first game, and apparently, it's time to celebrate.

"Yep," he answers evenly as he climbs out of the boat. His eyebrows pull together as he uses some kind of fancy knot maneuver to secure it to the dock. Does everyone just know how to drive watercraft and make those crazy boating knots around here?

Kylian offers his hand to assist me off the boat, his expression softening when he catches sight of me.

"Don't worry about your room. No one's allowed upstairs without approval."

I lift my hand to my mouth to hold back a laugh, thinking about the two grumpy security guards from last weekend's party. Now the stanchions make sense, and I'm actually sort of grateful for them.

Turning toward the house, Kylian keeps hold of my hand for a few seconds, guiding me up the dock. By the time we step onto the beach, we're walking side by side.

I feel compelled to say something—to, I don't know, thank him for today? For his offer to help?

But when his gaze meets mine, I almost trip. His face sags, and his usually clear light blue eyes are slightly bloodshot behind his glasses. He looks utterly exhausted.

"I'll be in the Nest. Text me or just come up if you need anything."

I noticed his number in my phone this morning. All the guys' numbers were there.

"The Nest?" I question. I still don't know where his room is.

"There's a door at the end of the hall on the second floor. It has a set of stairs that'll take you up."

I follow him up the steps that lead to the house.

"I take it you don't like parties?" Come to think of it, I don't remember seeing him last weekend.

He shakes his head, checking his phone. Then he stashes it and turns back to me.

"Parties. People. Noise. Unpredictability." He runs a hand through his hair and sighs. He really does look tired. It makes sense—it was an intense game, and he was *on* the entire time. Even if he doesn't wear a uniform or play on the field, Kylian's role on the team is critical.

I have the sudden and inexplicable urge to hug him. Instead, I wrap my arms around myself and shift from one foot to the other.

"Okay. Well, good night, then, I guess."

I internally cringe at my awkwardness. What is wrong with me? The guy's nice to me for a few hours, and now I want nothing more than to follow him upstairs and cuddle with him in his bed. Cuddle or maybe—

"Joey!"

When I spin around, Hunter is tearing up the stairs toward me in a full sprint. I turn back just long enough to catch Kylian's gaze.

"Good night, Jo." And just like that, he's gone.

I don't have time to overthink our last interaction because Hunter practically tackles me in a bear hug. "We won!" she exclaims, jumping up and down. "We won, we won, we won!"

Her enthusiasm is contagious. The dozen or so people making their way up the stairs toward the house break out into a chant, hooting and hollering and carrying on with the same type of energy they had at the stadium.

If this is any indication, tonight's party is going to be wild.

"You weren't even at the game," I chide as she squeezes me tighter.

"I know," she whines. "I'm so mad I had to miss it. But I'll be at the next one. I promise. Now you need to promise me something."

She pulls back and searches my face, her expression suddenly serious, pointed, in complete juxtaposition to the joy and excitement radiating off her a moment ago.

"Don't go dark on me like that again, okay?"

I gulp past the prickle of shame. After my run-in with the guys at work on Thursday, I talked to Hunter. But then I landed in this weird twilight-zone existence, and I still haven't come up with a way to explain my new living arrangements. So yeah, I guess I did go dark on her. It was an extra shitty move on my part after what she shared with me last week. About how her mom ditched her without any real explanation or justification.

God. I'm an awful friend.

"Joey. Seriously." She cups the side of my face and pulls me close until our foreheads touch. "I was really worried. I got all worked up wondering if I upset you or wasn't as supportive as I should have been on Thursday when—"

"Hunter, no." I cut her off before she can blame herself for any of my behavior. "You didn't do anything wrong. Not at all."

Her expression softens in response, loosening the vise around my heart just a little.

I try my best to give her a reassuring smile. "I'm not used to anyone caring enough to check in or even notice if they don't hear from me for a few days."

The only adults who have ever cared about my whereabouts did not have my best intentions at heart.

"Okay. As long as you swear—"

"I swear," I tell her sincerely.

The moment is broken when a big, dumb-looking jock lumbers past us and shouts, "Hell yeah! Looks like we're gonna get to the girl-on-girl action early tonight!" Then he chants, "Kiss her! Kiss her! Kiss her!"

I hit him with my most bored expression, noting his Lake Chapel U football shirt and his still-wet, freshly showered hair. Figures this douche would be on the team. I make a mental note to ask Kylian for his name before planting both hands on my hips and giving him a long once-over.

"I assure you, if I wanted to kiss her, it would not be for the amusement of some second-string chump who gets off on the patriarchy-fueled self-insert fantasy of watching two women be intimate together."

Stunned silence follows as he slow-blinks at me, like he needs a minute to process my words. Before he can stammer a response, I grab Hunter's hand and drag her behind me toward the house.

"Joey!" She cackles, chasing after me as I scurry up the stairs. "That was epic. Winslow is still standing there with his mouth hanging open."

Winslow. Noted.

I smile over my shoulder at my friend. "What can I say? I took a gender studies class in high school. But just so we're clear, if I *was* attracted to women, you'd be my first pick."

Chapter 17

Josephine

It takes a significant amount of effort to not move through the house like I live here.

Which is crazy, considering I've been a resident of the Crusade Mansion for less than forty-eight hours, and I've spent the majority of that time in my room.

If only I could change my clothes or take a few minutes to freshen up, but Hunter has been glued to my side since we stepped foot on the marble floors tonight.

It's not that I don't trust her. Or that I don't want to tell her what's going on.

But I don't know how to explain my predicament without revealing the root cause of why I'm being kept here against my will.

"You don't want a real drink?" Hunter hollers, clinking the rim of her red cup with the top of the bottle of sparkling seltzer in my hand. We've been dancing for the better part of an hour—both sweaty and flushed from the sticky night air. Even without the body heat of a hundred plus people crammed into one room, the humidity would be off the charts.

"Too hot," I reply, practically yelling to be heard over the crowd. "I'm halfway dehydrated as it is. Thought I was going to melt at the game this afternoon."

"Fair point," she counters, the two words instantly reminding me of Kylian.

What's he doing up in the Nest right now? And what the hell is the Nest anyway?

"Want to get some air?" she asks, gathering her hair in one hand and piling it on her head to get it off her neck.

With an enthusiastic nod, I grab for Hunter's hand and weave through the crowd of gyrating, sweaty bodies, tugging her along behind me.

I have to maneuver around a couple practically dry-humping on the dance floor. I do a double take when I realize the guy in the pairing is none other than Kendrick. Damn. He's got moves. He doesn't see me, thank god. The last thing I need is for Kendrick Taylor to catch me ogling him.

We make a pit stop in the kitchen, each grabbing a chilled water bottle from the tub on the counter. Kylian and I were the last to leave for the stadium and the first back to the house, along with the first wave of guests, so there must be staff who come in to get things ready while the guys are at the game.

Just another thing to add to my list for Kylian. He offered to help—he can start by giving me more insight into the way things work around here.

Hunter heads back toward the living room, most likely to go out through the floor-to-ceiling sliding glass doors that lead out to the main deck. I assume it's crowded out there, so I redirect her toward a door off the kitchen.

A blast of humidity hits me as I slide the door open and step out onto the deck.

"Oh, I've never been out here," Hunter murmurs, shuffling to the ledge to look out over the lake. It's where I ate dinner with the guys last night. I didn't think a thing about it maybe being off limits until now. *Shit.*

"How'd you know this was out here?"

Before I have a chance to come up with a reply, a throat clears.

I startle and hold back a gasp, whipping my head around and peering through the dark.

"Josephine."

Of-fucking-course.

Decker is lounging on an L-shaped couch, legs spread wide, with his arms resting on the back of the cushions. He's surrounded by not one, not two, but three women—two of which are still wearing their Lake Chapel U cheerleading uniforms.

Go Crusaders.

"Cap," I reply curtly with a mock-salute. "Want to go down to the beach?" I ask Hunter, desperate to put some distance between myself and my captor.

Another voice slices through the thick night air with that sweet, familiar gravel.

"Joey. Can we talk?"

Locke is leaning against the far end of the deck. He has one forearm resting against the banister, and the thumb on his other hand traces his lip. He played well today. I won't deny that he looked good in that uniform either. And after his peace offering this morning, maybe I do owe him a conversation.

I don't have time to consider it for more than a second, though.

"Don't you think you've done enough, Lockewood? Rumor has it you had absolutely nothing to say on Thursday night." Hunter plants her hands on her hips as she comes to my defense. At least that's what she thinks she's doing.

Panic zings through my extremities when Decker sits up straighter in my periphery.

"Girl, it's fine." I place one hand on her arm, gently trying to talk her down. With more urgency, I give Locke a pointed look, then quickly turn to Decker.

Even through the darkness, the intensity of his glare is like zaps of electricity coursing between us.

I shake my head twice in a subtle movement, desperate to get through to him before he can make a scene or drag her into my mess.

Hunter's just being a good friend. I ranted to her about the strange reaction from Locke and Kendrick on my drive home on Thursday night. She has no idea what has transpired since then.

Tense seconds tick by as my heart rate skyrockets. Pulling in a breath through my nose and letting it out through my mouth, I try to steady my breathing, focusing all my energy on silently pleading with the guys to let it go. Decker eventually peers over at Locke, then looks back at me and tips his chin.

He sinks into the sectional again and pulls a cheerleader onto his lap, essentially dismissing me.

But before we can make our escape, he speaks again. "Your brother won his game."

I frown in confusion. Before I can question him, Hunter replies.

"He's my *step*brother," she corrects sharply. "And yeah. They won. 35-14."

Decker chuckles, a deep, melodious laugh that makes my belly clench.

"Tell him congrats. I'm looking forward to beating a worthy opponent this year." And with that, he adds, "You can go now."

I'd be pissed about being so blatantly disregarded if I wasn't grateful for the excuse to flee.

"Joey..." Locke tries again.

"Come on," I urge, pulling Hunter toward the stairs that lead to the lower deck and eventually the beach.

Peering over my shoulder, I find Locke's gaze still on me, so I mouth "later" as we retreat. I swear there's the tiniest glint in his eye—a flicker of hope that reminds me of just how into him I was only a few days ago. Our eye contact is abruptly cut off when a cheerleader cuts in front of him and runs her nails along the front of his T-shirt, pawing at his chest.

I resist rolling my eyes as I pick up the pace, Hunter hot on my heels.

The beach is much more crowded than I thought it would be. Not only that, but it seems like everyone's heading toward the dock. Almost as if the party is winding down already.

"What time is it?" I ask since Hunter already has her phone in hand.

"Few minutes 'til ten, but a big storm's about to hit." She turns her phone toward me so I can see the screen.

I shudder despite the humidity and survey the radar she has pulled up. The entire screen is green, punctuated with dots of yellow, orange, and red to indicate the storms.

"What time is it supposed to start?"

"Now."

As soon as she says the word, a raindrop hits the bridge of my nose and rolls down the slope. I brush it away in vain. A few seconds later, the rain picks up, and I'm peppered with sprinkles.

"A little rain and the party's over?"

"This'll be more than a little rain." She holds up her phone again. "When the storm gets closer, the ferries have to stop running. It's not exactly safe to be floating on a hunk of metal in an open body of water when lightning strikes."

Shit. I hadn't even considered that. Another chill runs through me.

I hate storms. And I hate how I react to storms even more. I have no intention of being anywhere near the water, let alone near a window, if and when lightning strikes.

"You ready?" Hunter asks, tucking her phone into her back pocket and linking her arm through mine. "You can come to my place if you want. Greedy is having people over, but it won't be anything like this scene." She twirls her hand through the air with a flourish.

"What position does your brother play?" I ask, recalling her exchange with Decker.

"*Step*brother," she corrects for the second time tonight.

Noted.

"He's quarterback for the South Chapel Sharks."

She cocks a brow when I tilt my head and look at her blankly.

"As in South Chapel University? Our school's biggest rival?"

I shrug apologetically, and Hunter laughs.

"Sometimes I forget just how new you are around here. The LCU and SCU football teams take their rivalry to the extreme. Shore Week is coming up, so you'll get to see it for yourself then."

I'm only half listening as Hunter goes on about a rivalry that, frankly, I don't give a shit about. My focus is glued to the stream of partygoers making their mass exodus toward the dock.

All four guys are upstairs, occupied. I saw it for myself.

There's hardly any time to think it through. But this feels like too big an opportunity to ignore. Is this my chance?

I assumed they wouldn't let me out of their sight tonight. I've run into them each a few times around the house over the last couple of hours, so I guess, in a way, they haven't.

But the huge number of people crowding the dock right now might give me the perfect opportunity to blend in and quietly disappear.

My phone is in my pocket, but the battery was hovering around 50 percent the last time I checked. I know I can't very well go back to my uncle's. That's the first place they'll look, assuming they'd come after me. But if the storm will prevent travel by boat tonight...

Fuck. I wish I'd had the idea sooner. I would have had time to make a legitimate plan.

I don't have my purse. My ID. A phone charger. My meds.

It could spell disaster. But I may not get another opportunity like this...

A boat horn blasts through the night, and as if on cue, the rain intensifies.

"Ah shit," Hunter mutters, her nose wrinkling as she tilts her chin and gazes up at the sky. "Hopefully, we can snag one of the covered seats."

Her concern is the rain. Getting wet. Ruining her hair.

What I wouldn't give to be plagued by worries so insignificant.

"Listen up!" a guy wearing a LCU hoodie hollers from the end of the dock. "The storm's eight miles away, so these are the last boats out until it passes. All ashore who's going ashore. Crusade's orders."

The noise picks up again as people board the two waiting vessels, calling out to each other and making plans for when they get back to the marina.

I chance a peek back at the mansion, noting the bodies scattered around the decks and the silhouettes of people still dancing in the living room. The scene is still pretty chaotic. I can only hope the guys are distracted enough to assume I'm somewhere in that crowd.

My phone dings in my back pocket as I keep pace with the people around me, shuffling slowly toward salvation.

Emo Boy: Where are you?

Shit on a crumbly cracker.

Is he checking up on me because he suspects I might make a break for it? Or is he just checking in with the hope of forcing the conversation I promised him?

The soles of my sneakers scuff against the wooden planks of the dock. We're close. So fucking close.

Ahead of us, people split between the docked vessels manned by guys wearing LCU apparel.

Decker didn't lay out rules for this party. But surely, he has some sort of failsafe in place to keep me here. I can't imagine he didn't think this through. Did he tell the boat boys who I am? Did he instruct them to not let me board or leave the isle? Kylian warned that security would be watching. Are there other security measures I don't even know about?

Then there's the scariest question of all: What will the consequences be if I try to escape and fail?

Panic makes my chest go tight as the crowd in front of us thins. There are a dozen or so people between me and the boats, but they're quickly climbing onto one or the other and taking their seats. Glancing behind me, I estimate there are maybe twenty people still waiting to get on.

There's more than enough room between the two ferries. Anyone who wants to leave the isle before the storm should be able to. Anyone, that is, except me.

My feet falter, causing Hunter to sort of rebound in place since we're still linked at the arm.

"You okay?" she asks, her eyes widening as she takes in what I assume is a mix of fear and indecision painted on my face.

I don't *want* to stay. But my gut instinct is screaming at me that I'd be stupid to try and leave.

"Joey. Let's go," Hunter urges.

Sticky air and cooling raindrops kiss the bare skin of my forearms while my head swims with indecision. Intoxicated excitement and drunken chaos surround me as the people aboard each boat continue their celebration. The guy behind us grumbles, then eventually steps around us, bypassing the middle of the dock where I'm frozen in place.

"*Joey*. Are you okay?"

Hunter's words are fuzzy around the edges as anxiety churns in my gut.

I slow blink, focusing on her gorgeous, worry-filled green eyes, willing the brain fog to clear and begging my feet to *move*.

Over her shoulder, lightning strikes.

I jolt, and Hunter's brow furrows deeper. Several seconds pass before the guaranteed boom of thunder grows into a steady rumble.

A boat horn blasts. Another streak of lightning splinters against the ominous night sky.

When Hunter pulls on my arm, no doubt prepared to drag me onto a ferry, I feel the tension in the crook of my elbow.

My body is resisting.

I can't make myself move.

In anguish, I close my eyes, shaking my head at my own mental blocks and ridiculous fears.

This could be my only chance—my best shot at escape.

Thunder booms again, far enough away that most of the partygoers don't even notice. But the disturbance seeps into the marrow of my bones. Water laps at the sides of the boats, adding to the kinetic unrest. Each drop of rain that lands on me is weighted, anchoring me in place.

"I—I think I'm going to stay."

Hunter tugs on my arm again, her face twisted in disbelief. "Stop joking around. We've gotta go." She drops my arm and steps forward.

I stay firmly planted in place with my jaw clenched to keep my teeth from chattering.

"Joey!" she yelps when she sees I'm not following.

"I'll text you," I promise, spinning on my heel and pushing past the last few stragglers on the dock. Somehow, I find all the forward momentum I couldn't muster just moments ago and hurry back toward the house, taking big strides that send an ache resonating up my shins each time I push off the wet planks.

Another boom of thunder sounds off in the distance as my feet hit the sand, and I break into a full sprint.

Chapter 18

Josephine

The Nest. He said he'd be in the Nest.

My heart hammers a frantic rhythm as I take the deck stairs two at a time.

I tear into the house, out of breath already. I still have so far to go.

Horns blast in the distance, drawing my attention, and I peek over my shoulder as the last ferry pulls away.

My eyes water and my mouth goes dry. The sinking sensation of hopelessness—the sadness of some sort of goodbye—slams into me with an intensity I don't have time to examine.

Lightning strikes. Thunder booms. The storm raging in my mind threatens to take me down if I don't get the fuck away from these floor-to-ceiling windows.

I push through the thinned-out crowd in the living room with the singular goal of getting to the staircase. I'm half jogging through the house, my hurried pace and frantic drive matching the energy of the room.

When I finally get to the stairs, I gasp.

The two henchmen Decker employs to keep everyone contained block my path.

"I—I need to get up there," I try, breathless.

Neither man moves. Neither so much as blinks. I open my mouth, ready to repeat myself, desperate to gain entry, when a hand brushes against my low back, making me practically jump out of my own skin.

"Locke!"

"Hey. I was looking for you. I was hoping—"

"I-I need to get upstairs," I stammer.

He assesses me for a beat before nodding slowly. "Are you okay?"

Thunder crashes so loudly the windows closest to us rattle.

"The storm. The Nest. Kylian said to come to the Nest."

"Joey—"

"Locke. Please," I beg, my voice trembling. I'm on the verge of losing my shit. "Can you make them let me up?"

He frowns, and concern swirls in his dark eyes. I'm getting pretty damn tired of people looking at me like that tonight.

"Let her up," he demands, looking from Thing One to Thing Two with a pointed stare.

Finally, the beefier of the two responds.

"Is she on the list?" he huffs, lifting an iPad.

"She is. Which you would know if you had been doing your job." Locke reaches past me and unclips one side of the stanchion.

"Go on," he whispers into my ear.

I swallow past the overwhelm clogging my throat and give him a terse nod. One foot in front of the other. One step after another.

Sucking in deep, ragged breaths, I focus on the stairs. My knees wobble, and my chest burns, but I don't stop. I finally glance up when I reach the top of the steps, only to be greeted by the judgmental gaze of a girl my age who's adjusting her dress in the hallway a few feet away from my room.

She watches me with raised eyebrows while I dip my chin to avoid her scrutiny.

I bypass my door. It's not really mine anyway, and I sure as hell don't want this stranger to see me ducking in there, or worse, following me. I brush past the rooms that belong to Locke and Kendrick. Kylian said it was at the end of the hall. I just have to figure out...

"*Wow*," she clips out dramatically. "He said he was going to bed. Tell him that next time, he should space out his sloppy seconds."

She quirks an eyebrow and hits me with her best mean-girl glare. She must have been coming from Kylian's room. The Nest.

And now I realize her comment was meant to insult me.

Frenetic energy and sheer exhaustion wage war in my mind, leaving me unable to muster a reply. Not that I'd be interested, regardless. The pressure behind my eyes that originally felt like tears is quickly morphing into the metronomic pounding of a migraine.

The signs are all there. I'm shutting down. I know what could happen next.

I have to find the Nest.

Seemingly of its own volition, my hand reaches out and turns a knob. I'm numb to the sensation of the handle in my grip. It takes an enormous amount of effort to open the door, then even more mental and physical strength to put one foot in front of the other and start yet another ascent.

The staircase is narrow: a sliver of space compared to the wide main stairway I just climbed. I'm grateful for the handrail I'm clinging to for dear life and the way it holds steady as I force out monumental effort to keep going.

There are no windows or other clues to the storm raging outside. Just the storm in here. I am the storm.

Up, up, up. I continue to climb.

I'm panting. From fear or exertion, I don't know.

So many fucking stairs.

Desperate for even the slightest hold on reality, I count each step. Each breath. Each moment that I'm still present and alive.

When I finally, mercifully, reach the top, I'm met with another door. Do I knock? Send a text? Am I even in the right place?

I'm hovering, hand on the knob, sucking in oxygen through a narrowed airway, seeking to calm the erratic pulse thrumming through me from head to toe.

The doorknob moves, slipping out of my hand. Pressing my forehead into the solid wood, I suck in another shuddered breath, desperate to get myself under control.

I am here. This is now.

Over and over, I repeat the mantra in my head. Until it stops feeling comforting. Then I repeat it out loud.

"I am here. This is now."

Squeezing my eyes closed, I focus on the smooth door handle again. Then suddenly, it twists, and the surface I'm leaning against disappears.

"Jo?"

My head snaps up, and I search his face, silently pleading for salvation.

"Jo? What's wrong?"

I use the last bits of strength I possess to heave my body forward, stumbling over the final stair and practically throwing myself at Kylian.

"Whoa—*whoa*."

He catches me, then extends his arms awkwardly, maintaining space between us.

"Are you okay?"

All I can do is shake my head. No words come out as I open my mouth in a pathetic attempt to make him understand.

"Come sit."

He uses his grip on my shoulders to guide me toward the edge of the bed. Once seated, I take in what I can see of the small, dark space. There are no windows. No natural light. Red, blue, and purple LED track lights line the walls, emitting a colorful glow.

I take a deep breath—the deepest I've accomplished in several minutes—and relish in the hint of calm that flows through me with the oxygen. Eventually, I look up and meet his gaze.

As soon as we lock eyes, a boom of thunder shakes the damn house. I yelp and jump to my feet.

"Fuck. Sorry, sorry," I mumble, trying to catch my erratic breath as I pace in front of his bed.

"I'm texting Locke—"

"No!"

The thought of him—or anyone else—seeing me like this is too much to handle. With Kylian, though, I feel safe. I don't know why it doesn't bother me to be in the midst of a panic attack in front of him, but I get the sense that he won't judge me. Like I might be okay.

"Please. No." The request is weaker the second time, but it's enough to make him stash his phone in his pocket.

"I hate storms," I confess, wrapping my arms around my front as if that will protect me from the next rumble of thunder.

It's not until I'm hugging myself that I realize I'm shaking. Frustratingly, the awareness of my own trembling only makes it worse.

I'm so wrapped up in my own head that I don't realize Kylian's come closer until his fingers find my chin and lift it. The contact startles me so badly I let out a pathetic whimper.

"Here," he says, a breath away. He removes something from his ears—earplugs, perhaps? And slowly lifts his hands so I can follow his movement as he inches even closer and gently pushes against each of my ears.

The sounds around me muffle in an instant. I hiccup a breath as I search his face. The sharp angle of his jaw and the rims of his glasses glow red from the LEDs.

"Sensory earplugs," he explains, his voice faraway and dreamlike, even though he's just inches from my face.

"Lie down," he encourages, nodding toward his bed.

My heart rate ratchets up again, and my lungs threaten to close off. But Kylian holds both hands up and takes a step back.

"Jo... you're safe. Please lie down."

Safe.

Safe, and so fucking tired.

I don't give myself time to overthink. I just do as he says.

As soon as I'm flat on my back, he drapes something warm and heavy over my body. The weight of it presses into all my limbs and eases the tightness in my chest, stripping away a layer of anxiety.

Fuck. Okay. I'm all right.

I am here. This is now.

I am here. I'm safe.

Though I can feel the intensity of Kylian's focus on me, I don't dare look at him. I focus on the ceiling instead—on the track lighting—on the individual points of light that connect and blur together when I squint.

The windowless space is small and perfectly square. It's just big enough for the bed, a desk with multiple computer monitors set up against one wall, and several bookshelves opposite that.

In the middle of the ceiling is a square that's lighter than the surface around it. It isn't a light, but rather a translucent patch that illuminates each time lightning strikes. Watching the storm through that square is like looking at a picture through a filter. It's softer around the edges... subdued, somehow.

A few more minutes pass before my breathing is completely under control. I really do feel safe, even if I'm lying in bed beside a man I barely know.

Eventually, I turn my head and pop out one of the earplugs.

"I'm sorry, Kylian. But thank you."

"You don't have to apologize," he murmurs, lifting a hand as if he's going to touch me.

I follow the movement with my eyes, and he freezes. Changing course, he runs the hand through his hair, mussing it up and making it stand on end.

"You're scared of storms," he states matter-of-factly.

"Fucking terrified," I admit, just above a whisper.

Nodding, he pulls out his phone again.

"Damn. This one's just getting started."

He flashes the screen toward me. The sight of all the green and orange sends my anxiety through the roof again, so I hold one hand in front of my face, shielding my eyes from the weather radar.

Kylian lowers the phone immediately, understanding my silent signal.

I peek over and search his face. Gulping past the fear of rejection, I ask, "Can I stay here with you tonight?"

His eyes narrow behind the lenses of his glasses. He inspects me for several seconds, then takes in the room.

Sighing, he nods. "Yeah, Jo. You can stay up here with me. Will you be able to sleep?"

"I think so."

He stands and locks the bedroom door, then takes off his glasses and sets them on the nightstand. He shakes some pills out of a bottle, pops them into his mouth, and swallows them dry. Then, wordlessly, he pulls off his shirt with one hand, tosses it across the room, and lies flat on his back beside me.

I put the loose earplug back in place, instantly soothed by the way it dulls the ambient sound of the room and the near-constant rumble of thunder. Gravity and the weighted blanket press me into the mattress, settling me further. Pulling in a breath far more easily than I have since that first drop of rain, I turn on my back so Kylian doesn't think I'm some sort of creeper staring at him in the dark.

Exhaustion overwhelms me. Sleep threatens to consume me. I take in another long, calming breath and blow it out over several seconds as my body finally gives up the fight.

"Thank you," I whisper to the LED lights overhead as I fall asleep.

Chapter 19

Josephine

The soft kiss of sunshine warms my upturned cheek, rousing me from sleep. I yawn and force my eyes open, disoriented by the heat and stickiness of my other cheek.

A prism of color dances in my vision—reds, purples, and blues. Warmth and coolness. A dichotomy of hues.

I cast my gaze to the ceiling, searching for the source of the jewel-toned rainbow. Above me, an ornate, square-shaped box nearly blinds me. It's transparent, like a four-sided window, made up of vibrant panels of stained-glass on each side.

The colors. The light. The warmth of the sun.

I blink a few times before I remember where I am and why.

The Nest.

I fled up here last night. That's the only way to describe my desperate, pitiful attempt at escaping the storm. It's not exactly possible to flee from weather, a reality I've had to face time and time again over the last several years. The saddest part? It's the storm inside my mind that ultimately wrecks me every time.

My cheek sort of sticks to the surface it's resting on. So with a sigh, I lift my head, only then understanding that I'm peeling my face off a warm, bare chest.

Shit.

I swallow my startled gasp and peer up to confirm that Kylian's still asleep.

I move slowly, removing my arm from around his tapered waist and shifting away so I'm no longer draped over his torso like a koala.

Once I've put some space between our bodies, I rearrange myself into a more innocent position. Thankfully, he doesn't stir.

With my head propped in my hand, I admire his sleeping form. It barely registered last night when he got into bed beside me that he was shirtless. But it's damn well registering now.

His body is ridiculous: hard muscles and lean, sinewy lines. Even in sleep, his abs are defined, taut muscle sculpted all the way down until they taper into the hem of his sweatpants.

Good grief.

The other guys are all beefed up and muscly from football, but I clearly underestimated Kylian. I don't know what he does to stay in shape, but it's really working for him. And for me, too. What a delicious surprise.

I could look at his body all damn day. But it's his face that's the most disarming.

Without his glasses, he looks softer. Younger. Almost boyish. Kylian is usually so angular and sharp—quick-witted and high-energy. He's all numbers and facts. Details and stats.

In this moment, he's different. Peaceful. He looks like a different person—like the man who gently eased me out of my panic spiral and took care of me last night.

I gulp past the gratitude that surges at the memory. I push down the embarrassment, too. If I was going to break down like that in front of any of them, it was probably safest to do so in front of Kylian. Sure, he'll probably tell Decker. But he's the kind of guy who sticks to the facts. So hopefully he'll spare me the embarrassment of divulging the intimate, pathetic details of my almost-panic attack.

The panic that almost consumed me isn't novel, especially during a storm. But having someone hold my hand as I toed the edge of the cliff is new.

Kylian saved me from spiraling. On occasion, I've hyperventilated and even passed out during a storm. I almost always succumb to nightmares afterward, too, like I'm stuck in a hazy anxiety hangover. But none of that happened with him by my side.

There was undeniable concern in the way he looked at me. Concern, and maybe even care. But no pity, and definitely no judgment.

And now I'm all but resigned to being stuck at the Crusade Mansion. My inability to get on a damn ferry last night is proof of my own self-imposed limits. The impending storm was a factor, but still. I couldn't have made my feet move if I tried.

Mostly because it wasn't worth the effort—or potential consequences—of leaving and being dragged back to this place. What would I even say if I found someone willing to listen to my story? Some rich, hot guys are making me live with them against my will? They've given me my own room and want me to eat dinner with them on Friday nights and they require that I attend all their games? So far, they haven't actually threatened me or harmed me in any way.

Maybe that's why Decker didn't bother laying out more rules. No one was even keeping close tabs on me last night. He knows I won't leave. He knows I can't. The fear of an unknown consequence is worse than anything he could threaten me with.

From here, though, I'll need to figure out what to tell people—especially the few people I care about, like Hunter and my uncle.

Sighing again, I glance back at Kylian.

"Holy shit!"

His eyes are wide open now, and he's watching me.

"How long have you been awake?" I demand, lifting my hand to my chest to steady myself. My heart rate is through the roof.

"Two hours and twenty-eight minutes," he offers, pushing up onto his elbows as he reaches for his glasses. His abs flex with each movement, like he's taunting me in a way. The boy is *cut*.

"Jo," he says quietly, amused. My eyes flit to his face, and my cheeks flush with embarrassment.

Busted.

"Do you want to get up?" he asks. "Or do you want to stay up here and ogle me a while longer?"

So busted.

I burrow under the sheets and pull the weighted blanket over my head. Which is a huge mistake, because now I'm surrounded by the citrusy, eucalyptus smell of him. I allow myself one big inhale—holding back a groan when the fresh scent fills my lungs—then sheepishly peek up at him.

"Thank you for last night," I offer, holding the blanket firmly against the bottom half of my face.

"I promised I'd help."

He did. Which is what gives me the courage to make my next request.

"Do you think you could take me to my uncle's place today so I can get my stuff?"

Chapter 20

Josephine

I follow Kylian down the stairs, feeling lighter than I've felt in days. The promise of getting off the isle temporarily is doing all sorts of things to lift my spirits.

"Hope you're hungry," he murmurs over his shoulder as he bounds down the last few stairs and heads toward the kitchen. "We go all-out after home games."

I don't know what I was expecting to find the morning after a raging party, but it wasn't the sight in front of me.

The kitchen is spotless, aside from the enormous spread of breakfast items setup on the island. There's no evidence of the party anywhere, and every surface is gleaming. It's hard to imagine this space was filled with coeds last night.

"Good morning, Mrs. Lansbury."

An older woman turns from the open dishwasher and smiles warmly at us.

"There you are," she singsongs in a distinguished accent. "You're never last to the table, Kylian. Are you well?"

"I'm fine. Just needed a bit of extra rest this morning," he assures her as he grabs two plates and hands one to me. "This is Jo, by the way."

Her eyes meet mine, and her smile widens, deepening the wrinkles around her eyes.

"Ah, yes. Miss Meyer. Decker informed me of your arrival. It's a pleasure. If there's anything you need at all, dear, don't hesitate to ask."

I nod mindlessly, unsure of what I could possibly need beyond the massive buffet spread laid out in front of us.

Beside me, Kylian piles his plate with bacon, sausage, two bagels, four waffles, and a huge serving of crispy hash browns.

"How do you take your coffee, Miss Meyer?" Mrs. Lansbury's accent is enchanting—Scottish? Or maybe British? I could listen to her talk all day.

"Um, you can call me Joey. Cream and sugar is fine. Usually I use way too much flavored creamer, but—"

"What flavors do you prefer?" she demands.

Kylian meets my eyes and quirks a brow.

"Vanilla is fine. But I'm not picky. I like sweet cream or hazelnut, too."

"I'll get a few of each," she insists, lifting a tablet off the counter and tapping away.

I open my mouth to protest, but Kylian cuts me off.

"Fill your plate. We're late."

Late?

I comply as Mrs. Lansbury busies herself at the sink. By the time I've made up a plate, Kylian has filled up a second one.

"Where are you going to put all that?" I tease. I'm hungry, too, but damn.

He shoots me a confused look. "I'm not putting it anywhere. I'm going to eat it."

Um. Okay.

"Syrup, ketchup, and condiments will be on the table. Follow me."

He leads the way, pushing through a door I haven't explored past and into what I now realize is a dining room.

All talking ceases when we enter. Four sets of eyes land on me, only three of which I recognize.

"Kylian. Good of you to finally join us. Although you probably could have left your groupie upstairs."

My cheeks flush as I eye the woman at the head of the table. She's older than us by about ten years, sharply dressed in a crisp white sleeveless dress, and her hair slicked back in a tight bun.

"Misty, this is Josephine Meyer. Josephine, this is Misty, our PR rep."

Misty lets out a *hmph* and plants her hands on the tabletop like she's ready to stand. "Do we need to take this elsewhere, then?" Her question is aimed at Decker.

He meets her gaze head-on. "No. Proceed. Josephine will be staying here for a while and will be attending NIL appearances for the foreseeable future."

What? That's news to me.

Obviously to Misty, too.

"Decker," she purrs, her tone soft and placating in a way that tells me it usually gets her what she wants. "I doubt I can get her clearance for half the events on—"

"You're the best in the business, Misty," he interrupts, crossing his arms over his chest and sitting straighter in his seat. "I know you'll make it work." His declaration leaves no room for argument.

She looks me up and down, like she's sizing me up. My neck goes hot at the inspection. Primarily because I'm wearing Kylian's basketball shorts rolled several times with a pair of knee-high socks and the same LCU crewneck I've been rocking all weekend. I'll be so damn happy to have my own clothes later today.

Misty passes folders to Decker and Kendrick, then opens one of her own and takes out a stack of documents. Kylian and I take our seats on the side of the table where Locke is stationed.

"Good morning," he whispers, shifting in his seat so he's facing me a bit more and knocking his knee against mine. His plate is still piled high, filled with mostly fruit and protein. He must have gotten in here just a few minutes before us. "You doing okay today?"

I stuff a piece of bacon in my mouth to give myself a moment to eye him warily before I respond.

The incident at the base of the stairway comes back to me as he studies me with a soft expression on his face. Honestly, I probably wouldn't have made it past the security bros had it not been for him. And if that had been the case, I likely would have passed out right there in front of half of LCU.

Despite how angry I've been with him, I have a decision to make. Do I want to spend the next few months salty as fuck and trying to punish Locke? Or should I apply the logic I'm using with Kylian and use our shaky bond and his inherent kindness to make this whole ordeal more tolerable?

Decidedly, I nod.

"I'm okay. Thanks for helping me last night."

His face lights up in one of those dazzlingly disarming smiles I found so damn sexy a few days ago.

Ugh. Who am I kidding? It still makes me swoon. It's just a more guarded, cautious swoon now, because swooning sucked me in, chewed me up, and spit me out last week.

A throat clears at the head of the table, garnering my attention.

Misty packs up files, sticks them in an expensive-looking briefcase, and rests her hand on Decker's forearm in a familiar, almost intimate touch.

Decker's answering smile is civil. Professional. A practiced response that tells me this isn't the first time he's had to play nice to get his way.

Misty bends forward, flashing us all a glance down her dress, and whispers something to Decker. Then she turns on her heel and shows herself out.

I'm still looking toward the head of the table when Decker turns and sets his sights on me—onyx irises boring into me with calculated focus. The shift is disarming, sending a shiver quaking through my body before I can stop it. His eyes narrow when I refuse to look away, despite the visceral reaction he commands.

Not three seconds pass before Kendrick shoves up from his place at the table. The scraping of the chair snaps me out of whatever the hell kind of connection had my attention locked solely on my captor. I finally blink, and Decker looks away.

"Hold up, K," he calls after Kendrick. Then he peers back down the table in our direction. "Locke. Are you coming with us to the Boatyard this afternoon?"

Locke's gaze shifts to me for just a flash before he turns back to his fearless leader.

"Wasn't planning to, but I can." His response is drawn out, his tone softer than normal, less playful. I barely know the guy, but if I had to guess, something isn't right.

Decker's brows come together. "Shit. Sorry, man. How are you feeling this morning? I should have led with that."

Locke flexes one hand on the tabletop. His movements are slow and methodical. When his hand clenches into a fist, he winces, shaking his head and puffing his cheeks out with a heavy sigh.

"My knees are screaming. Hands and wrists, too. I've got three spoons to my name today, tops."

"What do you need?" Decker's demand is laced with sympathy. He sounds so docile and caring, I almost laugh. Is this a joke? How can someone be so infuriatingly bossy and cold, yet so genuinely kind where his friends are concerned?

"Rest. Ice bath. Maybe a massage. I thought I'd head to the field house later if I feel up to it."

Decker's shaking his head before Locke even finishes. "I'll get a trainer to come to the house. Finish eating, rest, and take care of yourself. If you can make it to the Boatyard, that'd be best." His eyes flick to me, and although they don't linger for more than a moment, I'm still hit with the daggers behind his glare. "That way Josephine has someone besides Kylian to keep her company."

A scoff escapes me. I'm right here. Right fucking here. And still, he's talking about me like I'm a child who supposedly needs not one, but *two* babysitters?

"And you?" Decker asks, turning his attention to Kendrick, who's standing behind the chair he vacated and gripping the top rung with both hands like he can't wait to escape the room.

"All good, Cap. My utensil drawer's overflowing."

Decker smirks. "Love to hear it. But if you start—"

"I will," Kendrick interrupts, seemingly anticipating the lecture Crusade was about to launch into. And with that, he strides to the door.

Decker rises from his chair as well, the movement making my panic flare. Because Kylian hasn't said a word to him about our plans.

Should I bring it up now and risk Crusade's intervention? He implied that we're all leaving the house today, but when?

I'm desperate for my own things. A lifeline. A reminder of who I am. Why I'm here.

If I don't get off this damn isle and make it back to my uncle's today...

I swallow past the nerves and shoot my shot before the guys can leave the dining room.

I jump up quickly, and the legs of the chair grate against the floor so loudly there's no way they didn't leave a mark. I wince but steel my spine.

"Kylian agreed to take me back to Sam's so I can get my stuff today."

The room goes silent as chaotic energy crawls up my throat. A blush creeps up my chest along with it, but I don't care. I need my shit. I needed it, like, yesterday. And I freaking deserve to have the comforts of home here. My own clothes, my schoolbooks and my laptop, my makeup, the jewelry from Alice, and the few other possessions to my name.

Decker's eyes rake over my body. Despite wearing Kylian's shorts and an oversized sweatshirt, the heat of his stare bores into my skin. I inhale to stop myself from shuddering *again*.

It's like he has X-Ray vision. His glare is as strong as the force of the goddamn sun.

I'm going to need a lot more willpower and at least 100 SPF to protect myself from the intensity of Decker fucking Crusade.

Cocking one brow, he smirks.

"Did he?"

Beside me, Kylian hasn't said a word. Not that I need him to, I guess. But a little backup would be nice.

I look between the two men, watching as Decker's cocky expression turns into a quizzical frown.

Kylian, on the other hand, just keeps shoveling food into his mouth.

For several seconds, Decker scrutinizes me silently, forcing me to fight the urge to fidget. The guys, though, are unaffected. Locke is ignoring us, and Kendrick is slouched against the doorframe, looking borderline amused.

Finally, *finally*, Decker tilts his chin. "Be back in two hours."

Two hours? Indignation swirls up into a storm of outrage. "It takes forty-five minutes to get off this goddamn isl—"

Decker holds up a hand.

My traitorous mouth snaps closed in obedience.

"And take Kendrick with you."

"Seriously?" Kendrick grunts, pushing off the wall and pulling his hoodie up over his head.

I try to hide my smirk. Now I'm not the only one protesting.

"We had a game yesterday," Decker offers, leveling Kendrick with a pointed look. "He's only got a few spoons." He points to Locke, who looks more beaten down and weary the longer I look at him. "And something tells me Kylian didn't get a full night's sleep last night thanks to an unexpected guest."

An indignant huff escapes me. How the hell does he know that? I wait a breath for Kylian to deny what Decker is implying, but he remains silent.

I glance over to where Kylian still sits beside me. He's been solely focused on his breakfast throughout the entire exchange. His placid expression proves that we aren't anywhere near on the same page. We may not even be in the same character series or fictional universe. It's as if he doesn't notice any of the tension swirling around us.

"I can be ready to go in twenty," he finally says. But his words aren't aimed at me. They're for Kendrick.

With a pissed-off grunt and an even deeper scowl, Kendrick storms out of the room.

These men and their mood swings. But at least I'm getting off the isle.

Chapter 21

Josephine

Kendrick's driving. Kylian's riding shotgun. And I'm sitting in the back of a spacious Suburban, begrudgingly appreciating the soft leather while trying to peer out the windows that are tinted so dark they have to be illegal.

I guess illegal window tint isn't a big deal to the guy whose dad is the sheriff.

"Are you purposely taking the scenic route?" I snap.

It feels like we've been driving forever. Between this and the leisurely boat ride to the marina, we've eaten up an hour of our alleged two hours.

I'm not driving, so theoretically, I can't take the heat if we're late according to Decker's arbitrary time limit. Although I'm sure he'd spin it and assign the blame to me anyway.

Kendrick's eyes flit to the rearview mirror and meet mine.

"It's Sunday morning in Lake Chapel, North Carolina. That mean anything to you, Ohio?"

I shrug, clueless.

"Jesus doesn't care about your agenda on Sundays in the south. I've had to avoid seven churches, and we've been rerouted twice since your uncle's junkyard isn't exactly on the same side of the lake. I'm doing my best to get you where you need to go."

Oh.

Shit.

So he has been taking the scenic route, but in an attempt to get us there faster.

Still.

I doubt Crusade will make religious exemptions for lateness.

As we pull into the gravel driveway and dust clouds my view, a thought occurs to me.

"What, exactly, am I supposed to tell my uncle about where I've been when he gets back?" I've resigned myself to my new living arrangement, but that doesn't mean the way it came to be doesn't still boil my blood.

I lock away my rage for later. It'll keep. I just hope I have the opportunity to make use of it if and when the time comes to put Decker Crusade in his place.

Kylian twists around in his seat. "I can make arrangements to keep him away longer if needed."

I blink once. Then again.

That's it?

After everything that went down between us yesterday—the game and boat rides, his offer and the storm—I expected more. Our connection amplified in the last twenty-four hours. At least it did for me.

Fisting my hands and glaring at the back of his head, I try to make it make sense. "What's that supposed to mean, Kylian?"

The accusation hits as intended, and he spins in his seat to face me.

"I wouldn't hurt him," he insists, his eyes softening a touch. I think. I swear I can't get a read on this guy to save my life.

"I know enough about his business dealings to keep him occupied for a few weeks. Maybe even a month," he adds. "That would buy you time to figure out what—"

He stops short when the car jolts to a halt.

"Jesus!" Kendrick shouts.

Kylian turns to his friend. "He's really messing with your vibe this morning, huh?"

Kendrick cranes forward, peering over the hood of the SUV. "What the hell was that? A radioactive junkyard rat? It was huge!"

Scout.

"Did you hit her?" I cry, craning my neck and searching. Except I can't see shit out of these ridiculously dark windows.

"Her? No, I didn't hit *her*." I swear Kendrick shudders before turning to me. "Get out and get your shit, Ohio. I'm not risking another run-in with that oversized rodent."

Turning around again, he throws the SUV into park and scowls at me through the mirror. I ignore him, unbuckling and hustling out of the back seat. I don't have a minute to waste, considering it took us exactly one hour to get here.

By that logic, I have zero minutes to collect my things.

"Want help?"

Kylian is already closing the passenger door carefully and squinting behind his square frames.

He looks hilariously out of place. Hills of discarded car parts and scrap metal create a bizarre backdrop for this conversation.

I'd love nothing more than to call Kylian out on his bullshit. He's practically ignored me all morning, erasing almost all the trust and connection I thought was growing between us.

But I don't have time to figure him out right now. And I really could use his help.

"Let's go." I head toward the back door, scanning the lot to confirm that Jeannie's car isn't here. Thankfully, the few spaces in front of the building by the office door are vacant.

Dust kicks up as I hurry inside. Once the door is shut behind us, I stride through the living area. My room looks impossibly small.

Forgettable. Was it really just three nights ago when I was trying to sleep and was unceremoniously snatched from this place?

Planting my hands on my hips, I sigh.

"What can I do for you?"

Tell me why you're acting so different this morning.

Distract Kendrick so I can make a run for it.

Make it make sense.

I don't say any of that, though.

"There are two plastic totes under the bed. Pull those out and start filling them."

"What do you want to take?" Kylian asks, squatting to pull out the storage containers I unpacked less than a month ago.

"All of it."

He snaps his head up and gives me a questioning look, brows furrowed and a slight frown marring his face.

But I hold his eyes, then shrug. "I've only been here for a few weeks. Everything I own fits in those totes."

Defeated, I pick up my shower caddy and head to the bathroom to collect my makeup and toiletries. A hand on my elbow stops me.

"Hey."

I freeze and pull in a slow breath, then turn to face the guy who's been so damn hot and cold with me over the last twenty-four hours.

"What?" I snap.

"Something's wrong," Kylian surmises, his hand lingering on my arm, cupping my elbow and caressing the skin on the underside.

"Ya think?" I move to pull away from his hold. But he grips my elbow tighter.

"Jo."

My ire builds at the way he says it. At the nickname he's created for me. He's not solely responsible for this situation, but he's here. And he's been frustratingly cool toward me today. As if he didn't help me through a near-panic attack last night. And like I didn't wake up practically straddling him this morning.

"I need you to spell it out for me. What's bothering you?" Kylian presses.

My instinct is to snap again, to hit him with the sass, because there's obviously a myriad of reasons for my irritation. Because none of this is okay. It would be easier to answer what *isn't* wrong. Frustration rages inside me, growing until it's almost as consuming as my anger.

But his gaze—so even and searching—promises that he really does care. And maybe he really does need me to spell it out for him.

Boys.

So hot. So dumb.

"This is all a lot." I drop my chin and study the empty plastic bin he's holding, starting with the obvious. "I'm overwhelmed, honestly. Then there's you. It's like we've gone... backward, since yesterday, somehow."

"Backward?"

He really is going to make me spell it out.

"Yes, Kylian. Backward. You and me? I thought we were... I don't know. We connected yesterday. At least I thought so. And last night. And this morning..." I trail off, refusing to dwell on the memory of the comfort and safety I felt when I woke up in his arms. "It's stupid. I just thought I had a friend in all this."

His brows draw together, and his eyes swim with confusion—the first real reaction he's given me—but he holds my gaze. Is he being purposefully obtuse? Is he making fun of me? Or maybe playing some sort of mind game to fuck with me more than the four of them already have?

When he remains quiet, I can't help but ramble on. "You practically ignored me at breakfast, Kylian. You were silent on the drive here. I guess I'm just trying to figure out why you're so hot and cold, especially in front of—"

My words are cut off by the sound of the bin he was holding clattering to the floor. Then he's stepping forward and crowding my space. He grips my chin with his thumb and two fingers, tilting my head to meet his gaze.

"Hot or cold?" he murmurs. "Those are the options?"

I swallow my anger and inhale sharply as he lowers his lips until they're a breath away from brushing mine.

"I don't do in between well, Jo. And I don't always notice subtlety. So if you need me to pick when it comes to you..."

Behind the lenses of his glasses, his eyes are practically ablaze. This close, the little gold flecks sprinkled in the blue irises look almost like paint splatters.

My heart rate picks up as he angles so close the heat of his breath tickles my lips. I try to swallow, but my mouth's gone dry.

This is what's been driving me insane. This palpable tension between us. There's no way it's one-sided; he *has* to feel this, too. It's like I'm his sole focus when we're alone—a single star pinpricking the midnight sky.

It's when we're with the other guys—burning in the glow of Decker's impossible sun, fighting the gravitational pull of Locke and Kendrick—that I'm invisible.

"Hot." He captures my mouth, pressing a searing kiss to my lips. Then he pulls back for one second, adding, "So fucking hot," and claims my mouth again while his fingers caress up my arm and tangle in my hair.

He pulls me closer, wrapping me up in a tight embrace and lifting me off the floor.

I'm completely suspended as Kylian hauls me against the wall and presses his body against mine from knee to clavicle. He trails hot kisses along my jaw, sending shivers coursing through me, then licks a path up my neck.

"Fuck, baby. You taste just as good as you look." His words are muffled as he continues to lick and nip the delicate skin along my neck. "There's no fucking question about how I feel about you, Jo. Hot. Hot. Hot." He peppers kisses all over as he makes his declaration, then sucks the delicate flesh of my neck into his mouth.

My hands find purchase against his stomach, fingertips trailing against the taut muscles beneath his T-shirt.

"But this morning—" I protest.

He pulls back then, peering at me through his glasses.

"Last night you came to me in a panic, did you not?"

My face flushes with the call-out, and I drop my gaze to avoid his scrutiny.

"Hey..." He tilts my chin up, then cups one cheek with the same hand. "I'm not judging you. I'm fucking glad you came to me rather than unravel at the party. But last night, you weren't okay. And I wasn't sure how you'd feel in the morning. I wasn't about to be the asshole rubbing my dick on you while you were in a vulnerable position."

My chest squeezes at that admission. Now that he puts it like that...

"But at breakfast..."

Kylian watches me for a moment, frowning, as if he's trying to make sense of the implication. I can practically see the wheels turning in his head.

Eventually, he shakes his head. "I don't remember saying or doing anything at breakfast."

"Exactly!" I cry, dropping my head back against the wall.

He's still hovering close, scanning my face like I'm a puzzle he's desperate to solve.

"Black and white, Jo. Explain it to me from your perspective."

I peer up at him, trying not to focus on the way his Adam's apple dips with each swallow or how my hands sink into his stomach with each inhalation.

"You barely acknowledged me during breakfast. Decker pulled his typical big dick energy act, and you just... you didn't..."

I trail off, annoyed with myself for my inability to articulate my frustration. Dropping my shoulders, I glance at the door, then over at my bed. My former bed, I guess. Shit. What am I going to tell Sam when he gets home and finds that I've effectively moved out? I don't want to hurt him—I can't. Maybe he'll believe me if I say I got a place closer to campus. At least he'll get his bed back.

"Jo." Kylian raises his other hand to cup my face, gently turning my head until I'm looking at him again."Decker is who he is. There's nothing I can do or say to change that. And maybe I misread you, but you don't seem like the type who wants to be saved."

I swallow thickly. Dammit, he's not wrong.

"Here's what I was focused on when we sat down for breakfast: First, I was worried about how the guys would react. Because I'm never late. You needed sleep, though," he says, sincerity coating his every word, "so I made a choice, and I was prepared to deal with the consequences."

He places a soft kiss on my lips.

"Then I was focused on Misty's updates. I was also anxious to go over the changes based on week-one stats and rankings with the guys. We usually spend a few hours debriefing on Sunday mornings, and my mind can't help but run the numbers on a loop until I share them with the guys. Once Nicky admitted he was in rough shape, though, my focus was on him. He needs rest to stay well, but I knew he'd try and power through and play down the pain if we started to talk football."

Locke. He really did look worse for wear this morning. I hope he's resting and taking care of himself.

"I went into that breakfast thinking you and I were in sync. I had already agreed to help you. In my mind, that was settled. I didn't even think to mention it to anyone until you brought it up to Decker. Which wasn't necessary, by the way. We don't need his permission."

I quirk one brow haughtily. "Don't we?"

He presses his forehead into mine and shakes his head. "Not for this," he murmurs, his lips close enough to tease me into pushing up on tiptoes.

"This..."

A thrill races up my spine, leaving goose bumps in its wake. I desperately want him to kiss me again now that I'm more confident that I'm not just a pawn in some game.

Running my hands up his chest, I relish the heat of his skin pulled taut over the lean muscles under the cotton of his shirt. Craning back to meet his gaze, I link my arms around his neck.

"What is this?" I whisper.

Kylian squeezes my side, then rests both hands on my low back, pulling me closer.

"This is us. Whatever you want us to be."

He doesn't give me a chance to answer before he's taking me with another all-consuming kiss. I let out a ridiculously girlish sound—something between a sigh in a whimper—as he dominates the moment and takes charge.

His tongue teases against my lips, and I willingly open to him. The first brush into my mouth is tentative, testing. My knees wobble at the second dip inside, making me grateful to be leaning against a wall.

Moaning, I meet his tongue stroke for stroke, loving the way he takes control, then backs off and lets me respond.

His kiss is both frantic and unhurried. Passionate yet methodical. It's intense and unquestionable: black and white, just like him. I moan again, then startle on the next breath when a car horn blasts in the distance.

"Fuck. We gotta go."

And just like that, the fire is out, and it's back to business.

Dumbfounded, I stand there for a moment, watching as a switch inside Kylian flips, and he resumes filling the plastic tote on the bed. Like we weren't just getting hot and heavy against the wall.

I believe what he said, though. He's given me no reason *not* to trust him, and his explanation makes sense.

He's a bundle of contradictions in a lot of ways. Hot and cold. Black and white. Clearly brilliant, if not a little socially inept.

So I'll take him at his word and put my trust in him. It's not like I have much of a choice anyway.

Resigned, I spin on my heel and take off toward the bathroom as the car horn blasts again, this time for longer.

"I'll get this one loaded and tell him we need five more minutes," Kylian says as he follows me out of the bedroom but turns left and heads toward the back door.

"And Jo?"

I pause outside the bathroom door and pivot to face him in the hall.

"Your ass looks so damn hot in my shorts."

He winks, then he's gone.

I'm as flattered as I am blindsided.

Chapter 22

Josephine

We made it back to the mansion with a few minutes to spare. There was far less traffic on the return trip, and Kylian drove the boat this time, so the trip across the lake was much quicker, proving that Kendrick purposely took his time on our way to town. Jackass.

Kylian and I hauled everything to my room. I confirmed how much time we had before we had to leave for the Boatyard, and what, exactly, the dress code was for the event, before taking a quick shower.

I assumed he'd head to the Nest to get ready himself, but I can still hear him in my room as I turn off the hair dryer.

Glancing at my reflection in the mirror, I try to force a smile.

My dark, cinnamon-brown hair is blown out and smooth, curling in soft layers that frame my face. Several new freckles have appeared since I arrived in North Carolina a few weeks ago. I'm grateful to have access to my skin care products and sunscreen again.

After I swipe on a coat of mascara, I pinch my cheeks for color, then add a layer of sheer lip gloss.

I adjust my black tank top and smooth my hands down the front of my raw-hemmed white denim shorts.

One more fake smile, and I almost convince myself that this is all okay.

Almost.

I decide I look good enough. Especially considering I don't know what's expected of me today.

I asked for details in the car, but Kendrick just mumbled something about a work commitment. Kylian met my eyes in the mirror and gave me a reassuring smile. I hope he'll fill me in sooner rather than later.

Exiting the bathroom, I'm surprised to find Kylian bustling around. He's got an armful of my clothes in one hand, and he's headed for the closet.

He's so focused on his task he doesn't notice I've emerged.

"Uh, thanks, but I can do that," I insist from across the room.

He pauses and smiles at me over his shoulder, then continues forward. "It's not a problem, Jo."

I follow him into the closet and watch, shifting from hip to hip and feeling all sorts of awkward. He methodically catalogs the items in his grasp—a jean jacket and two sun dresses—then puts them on hangers and hangs them on the rod that spans one side of the space.

"I've got almost everything put away. You can rearrange it how you want it later, but at least it's all sorted," he murmurs as he hangs the last dress and assesses his work.

Nodding once, he turns back toward me.

"Damn," he rasps, dragging his gaze up and down my body. "You look gorgeous."

"You're just full of compliments today, huh?" I keep my tone light so he can't see how his words make me feel all girly on the inside.

"I'm a quick learner," he quips. "You said you weren't sure where things stand between us, so now I'll make it abundantly clear as often as possible."

He holds my gaze for several seconds, the heat in his expression making it *abundantly clear* that he likes what he sees. I'd be lying to myself if I said I didn't love the way he inspects me from head to toe. When Kylian focuses on something, he *really* focuses.

The spell is broken when he clears his throat.

"There are only a few things left to put away." He nods toward a random assortment of objects spread out on the bed.

Once we've emerged from the walk-in, I gather my curling rod and a reusable gel eye mask to stash in the bathroom. When I walk back into the bedroom, Kylian holds out a sage green case.

"Sunglasses?" he guesses, moving around the bed and holding it out for me.

"Uh, not exactly." I bite back a smirk and snatch the case out of his hand.

Except he's too quick. Mentally. And physically.

Tightening his grasp, he regards me with a quizzical smirk. I try—and fail—to pull the case out of his hand.

"What is it, then?" He tilts his head to the side, his expression earnest. There's no way he's prepared for the answer to that question.

Biting back a laugh, I tug on the case again. "This would be my vibrator."

Kylian's mouth falls open, but he doesn't loosen his grip.

"This? *How*?"

The shock in his widened eyes is almost comical. It's also distracting enough that I let him pull the case right out of my hand.

"Seriously. *How*? I thought vibrators were like, twelve inches long? And usually purple or pink?"

Rolling my eyes, I hold out my hand again. "Give it here. We've gotta go." We had less than twenty minutes when I got out of the shower, so we're pushing it now. I'm not interested in giving Decker an excuse to harp on me today.

"Hell no. I've got questions." He turns the case over in his hands, examining it the way one would admire a precious jewel or a rare artifact.

"Kylian," I urge.

"Jo," he counters playfully, his eyes gleaming with mischief. "I need details. What's it called? How does it work?"

"You're shameless," I accuse, eyes wide.

"I'm curious," he corrects. "And now that we both know where things stand between us," he hits me with a serious, heated stare, "I want to learn all I can about you."

"Including how I like to get off?" I quip, planting my hands on my hips.

"*Especially* how you like to get off."

I gulp past the insecurity tapping me on the shoulder. Instead, I opt for the overconfident sass I rely on when I'm uncomfortable.

"It's called the Thumper. It has three modes. I like the air pulse setting best."

Kylian's expression morphs from curiosity to fascination as my face heats in embarrassment.

"Satisfied?" I mumble, walking past him toward the door.

If we don't get going, someone's going to come looking for us.

"Not in the least," he replies without missing a beat, striding toward me. At least he's following me to the door.

"The Thumper. The Thumper... Hold up. It has *five* intensity settings for each of the three modes?"

I whip my head around and suck in a breath.

He's still holding my vibrator in one hand while scrolling on his phone with the other. "Wait." He lifts his head and meets my gaze. "This doesn't look like the one online."

Slapping a hand over my eyes, I groan. "Kylian... that's just the case."

I peek between my fingers and hold back a laugh as his eyes double in size.

"Can I open it?"

With any of the other guys in the house, I'd be mortified. But Kylian has been my safe place for the last twenty-four hours. And he looks nothing but earnest, albeit a little too eager.

"I guess?" I can't help but laugh at the absurdity of this situation.

If I said no, I have no doubt he'd honor my decision, but I can't deny him when he looks this excited.

He opens the case and plucks the toy out of the shell, the opposite of shy about holding it and turning it over as he analyzes it from all angles. I'm meticulous about toy hygiene, so the vibrator's clean. I'll just sanitize it before I use it next time.

"It's shaped like a comma," he mutters reverently. "And these little buttons turn it on?" He glances up at me to confirm.

Biting down on my bottom lip, I nod. There's no way he's actually going to—

The toy buzzes to life as he clicks on the thump function.

"Wow. That's intense."

I giggle. Freaking *giggle*. What is wrong with me right now?

Kylian pops his head up at the sound. His pupils are totally blown out as he peers at me through the lenses of his glasses.

"This is what you like?" he murmurs, stalking closer as the toy pulsates in his grip.

I bite down on my lower lip and shake my head. I like the air pulse better than the thump feature.

His eyes narrow on me as he saunters closer. And with the slightest quirk of one brow behind his glasses, he clicks another button.

"*This* is what you like?" he surmises as the second feature whirs to life.

Pursing my lips, I fight back a coquettish grin as I nod. My gut is filled with fizzy bubbles: freshly poured champagne, a jacuzzi on the highest setting. I'm nothing but air and anticipation.

"There's one more," he murmurs as he stops in front of me, his body so close our chests brush on my next inhale.

He clicks the third button, and the vibrator buzzes louder.

Thumping. Pulsing. Vibrating.

He's holding the sex toy trifecta in his hand. Emanating a heavy, hazy lust, his aura pulls me deeper under his spell with every passing second.

"This is really something." Kylian smirks, raising the toy to eye level as he inspects it more meticulously. "There's no way you could possibly need all three settings on at once though, right?"

He hums, the breathy contemplation barely audible over the steady buzz. He surveys me again, and I swear my thighs clench involuntarily.

"Unless..." His mouth quirks into a teasing smile as he watches me through hooded eyes.

I'm hanging on his every word, and he damn well knows it.

With the buzzing sound echoing between us, he draws the moment out, ratcheting up the tension until I finally find the wherewithal to swallow past the lump in my throat.

"Unless?" I ask in a needy voice I don't recognize.

His smile widens, and a barely there dimple on just one cheek appears.

"Unless the Thumper is intended for more than one person to use simultaneously."

Another cock of an eyebrow.

A heavy, heated pause.

And then— "Should we try it?"

I'm nodding before I fully process the question. Leaning back on the bedroom door, parting my legs slightly, *aching* for him to try.

Desire zings through me as he maintains eye contact, clicks the button to increase the intensity, and lowers his hand.

I don't dare look. Don't allow myself to overthink.

I just squeeze my eyes shut as he presses the vibrator between the apex of my thighs, lining it up with my zipper and sending a jolt of electricity through my entire being.

He places it perfectly, lining up the thumping side with my clit, then pinning the vibrator between us with his hips.

"Holy shit," he murmurs, raising his arms to brace himself against the door on either side of my head.

"Holy. Shit," he hisses when he rocks his hips forward and presses into me harder.

My thoughts exactly.

The thrum of the toy is intense and relentless—a constant pounding that's almost too much, even through the thick denim of my shorts and my underwear.

But the vibrations are only partially responsible for the sensations rolling through me.

Kylian's maintained eye contact, making this almost comical situation anything but, sends sparks of electricity through my extremities. Staring into his eyes feels intensely intimate. We're chasing mutual pleasure from two sides of the same toy.

I close my eyes and shudder as warmth pools in my core.

Kylian hums softly. Then he brushes his hand against my cheek and gently grips my chin.

"Open," he murmurs. "I want to see you, baby."

My eyes fly open, and my lips part, too. A second later, Kylian's thumb is in my mouth. I close my lips on instinct, then swirl my tongue around it.

He growls in approval. "That's it. Suck it. Suck it like the needy girl you are and let me see you."

I'm nodding again, feeling like an incoherent bobblehead, unable to muster any more control over myself.

He slowly draws out of my mouth, and I nip at the pad of his thumb. Groaning, he pushes back in, this time pistoning his hips in rhythm with his hand.

I moan, my breath coming fast and hard as the telltale tingle of release builds inside me. Sparks ignite from my toes to the crown of my head, signaling my impending unraveling.

"Kylian." His name is a plea as I can't help but thrust my hips forward and feverishly suck on the digit in my mouth.

"Fuck. I'm right there, too. Let go for me, Jo. Show me how good I make you feel. Show me how good you can be for me."

Desire squeezes every muscle in my body as a mindless haze consumes me. I can't think. I can't see. I can't hear. I just feel.

The thumping intensifies, either because Kylian clicked the button again or because my orgasm is still building. Because somehow my body's *still* climbing.

Climbing, climbing, climbing. Scaling so high I'm almost fearful of the intensity of the fall.

I whimper and meet his eyes. The desire in his gaze matches the unrelenting undulations rendering me senseless.

He nods encouragingly, and I hit my peak. Time stands still as the first clench of my inner walls tears through me and steals my breath. I gasp, then cry out.

In an instant, Kylian covers my mouth to muffle the sound. All as my pussy pulsates and arousal soaks my panties.

The climax is so intense I lose my grasp on time and space. There's nothing but this moment, Kylian's eyes, and the toy he's still pressing against my body, using it to draw out an orgasm that just won't quit.

A pounding on the surface behind me, sharp enough to rattle my head, jolts me back to the moment.

"Josephine!" Decker's voice booms through the thick door. "We have to go. Have you seen Kylian?"

My eyes shoot open, and I squeak behind Kylian's hand. He stays laser-focused on me, his mouth parting ever so slightly as his hips slow, and he grunts.

"Fuck, Jo," he grits out between clenched teeth, thrusting the toy between us one last time.

"Josephine!" Decker booms.

"We're coming!" Kylian calls back.

My eyes practically bug out of my head as I burst into a fit of giggles.

Kylian smirks, caging me in with both arms and resting his forehead against mine as we pant in unison, working to catch our breath and come back down to earth.

"Naughty girl," he murmurs against my lips. "You did so good for me, baby."

And then he catches them in a searing kiss, sending my thoughts spinning once again.

He pulls away a moment later, adjusting himself and giving me a slow, satisfied appraisal.

"Go get cleaned up," he says, tilting his head toward the bathroom.

I start toward the en suite without a second thought. Bizarrely, his dominance doesn't grate on my nerves the way Decker's does. Maybe because I never expected him to be so bossy—or *vocal*—in the bedroom, or in this case, against the door.

Bottom lip pulled between my teeth, I offer him a coquettish smirk over my shoulder. *Did we really just do that?*

"Jo," he scolds, running one hand through his hair and tugging on the ends. "Don't look at me like that." He puffs out his cheeks and blows out a long breath, pulling out his phone from his back pocket to check the time. "We really do have to go."

"Take this," he tells me, holding out the vibrator. "I've got to go change my pants."

A surprised huff escapes me as my focus drops to his crotch.

Holy shit. Yep, he does. I didn't realize he'd come, too. But there it is. Literally.

"Be downstairs in two minutes," he instructs, lunging forward. He kisses me once more before unlocking the door and taking off toward the staircase at the end of the hall.

Chapter 23

Kylian

My dad always made pancakes on Sunday mornings.

Fluffy monstrosities with crisped edges, smeared with butter and doused in syrup.

I'd sit at the kitchen table and watch the way he warmed the skillet, waiting until the butter was sizzling to spoon out the batter.

He was a patient man every day of the week, but he was different on the weekends. Relaxed. More playful.

Easy like Sunday morning, he'd say.

Mom would sleep in, eventually joining us when the smells from the kitchen overwhelmed the house. Sometimes it was a good smell. Sometimes it wasn't. Dad usually burned at least one batch of pancakes.

I guess not everything was easy on Sunday morning.

She'd shuffle into the kitchen, wrapped in her robe, and tousle my hair before she sauntered toward my father.

He'd wrap her in his arms, and they'd stand in front of the stove, rocking back and forth in an awkward dance as Dad sang a song from the 1980s under his breath.

The references to sorcery were off-putting enough. But then there were the words.

I'd pull up the lyrics on my tablet, repulsed by the glaringly bad grammatical error in the middle of the chorus.

Clocking in at 161 beats per minute, the time signature was expectantly peppy. It wasn't a bad song, per se. Fine, even. But the words.

References to magic and arousal. Seductive lyrics paired with a seemingly innocent beat. I didn't get it. I didn't like it. I didn't understand any of it: the lyrics of a love song, or the impractical, sickly sweet Sunday morning ritual between my parents.

As a child, I watched my parents often. Observing them, studying how they interacted. Pondering what, exactly, was so appealing about cohabitation, compromise, and all the other complications that came along with a relationship.

None of it made sense back then. It wasn't black and white.

I would scowl at those song lyrics, desperate to derive meaning from the words my dad recited to my mom every weekend like a solemn vow.

I didn't understand any of it until this moment. Until *her*.

Over the top rim of my glasses, I catch sight of Jo just as she stretches her arms overhead, inadvertently pushing against the stretchy black fabric of her tank top.

Fuck. She has great tits. I didn't get to spend nearly enough time savoring her this afternoon.

Shaking my head, I tear my attention away and scan the boat, stopping on Decker, who's watching me from the bench seat opposite mine.

Although *watching* is too mild a term for the way my best friend's glowering right now.

He works his jaw back and forth. It's one of his tics. One I've seen many times when he's facing an adversary or opponent.

Pretty sure that look has never been directed toward me.

"You good?" he grits out, averting his eyes to glance over at Kendrick as he slows the boat.

The dock is already packed, PWCs and boats of all sizes lined up at attention. We don't have any trouble tying up, though. They always reserve a spot for the guests of honor.

Today's commitment is two hours, but if the quantity of vessels is any indication, we're in for a long afternoon.

"All good," I reply, hopping to my feet to help Kendrick on the dock.

"Sorry you're stuck babysitting," Decker tries, rising to his feet and squeezing my shoulder as we climb out.

He's digging. Just changing his approach. Maybe he thinks I won't catch the subtle questions or prompts. Sure, I'm not usually good with people—they don't always make sense like numbers and stats—but I am good with *my* people.

Decker wears his emotions on his sleeve. He's passion and fire, joy and pain. Quick to anger. Fast to forgive. He thinks he hides it well, but even I can read him easily. He only knows how to feel deeply. He approaches everything with intensity, full stop.

He'd make a shit poker player.

But he's an excellent friend.

I turn to him and hold his gaze, cocking one brow and calling him out without actually saying a word.

"I just want to make sure..." He trails off.

And that's it. He won't push it. At least not now. Not right before an event.

He won't say it, but we both know what he's thinking.

He doesn't have a read on her. Or on me and her together. I've never shown any sort of lasting interest in someone like this. He's not in control, and he's worried.

And rightfully so.

I know Decker better than almost anyone. But he knows me, too.

He sees the way I look at her. Notices how I'm trying harder and putting in the effort when she's near.

And he's worried that I'm spiraling.

Not in the traditional sense—I don't unravel and topple completely out of control.

When I spiral, it's with internal momentum. It's an interest that builds and grows. I'm a thread on an infinite spool, winding tighter and tighter, spinning faster and faster.

He's worried I'll get all wrapped up in this girl. This girl he brought into our home. This girl he refuses to let go.

But there's no need for his concern.

Because he doesn't know what I know. What I found.

Jo's no threat to us. If anything, she's battling deeper-rooted demons than all four of us combined.

But her story's not mine to tell. And *she* may never tell it, either, if the only way she can move forward is to leave what happened in the past.

So I'll stay quiet. Keep the secrets I shouldn't have uncovered in the first place. Reserve judgment for how she manages, for how she's survived.

She's not a threat. At least not in the way Decker is concerned about. He's only looking out for me—ever the protector, even when it's unnecessary—but there's no point in him getting worked up about an impending hyper-fixation.

I'm already fucking in it.

Chapter 24

Josephine

Kendrick sits at the front of the room, behind a table situated on a platform. He's sitting next to Decker, posing for a picture with two preteen boys. The two football players look like royalty. Kings holding court. Big-headed egos yukking it up, shaking hands, smiling for the camera, and signing footballs and posters and athletic shoes.

Kendrick's gleaming white teeth almost make him look kind.

"I didn't realize he knew how to smile."

Locke chuckles beside me, lifting his glass of ice water to his lips. He takes a slow, measured sip, then gently sets the cup back down on the table.

He hisses and blows out a long breath, then he flexes the hand that was just holding the ice water, grimacing.

"You okay?" I ask, gently brushing my knee against his under the picnic table, going for nonchalant.

"No." He presses his lips together in a tight line. "But I'm used to it."

I don't know what to make of that. Or where things stand between the two of us. So I'm not sure how to navigate this.

We went from hot and heavy to pissed off and resentful in a matter of days (at least from my end). But this morning felt okay. Like maybe we could make amends. Even if we don't end up where we were headed, I could certainly use another friend in the house. I have a feeling I'll need all the help I can get in order to survive the insufferable grinning bastards at the front of the room over the next several weeks.

Now's not the time to delve into any of that, though. For starters, we have an audience.

I'm sandwiched between Locke and Kylian. Kylian, who had me pressed up against my bedroom door and served up a delicious, toy-assisted orgasm just a few hours ago. Kylian, who has grazed his hand over my low back and teased his fingertips along the raw hem of my shorts more than once since we've been here.

We're also surrounded by hundreds—yes, hundreds—of people, all waiting for their turn to speak to and take pictures with Decker and Kendrick.

The Boatyard is a massive venue. With indoor and outdoor seating and at least three separate bars, it's a wonder we found a table.

Although as I take in our surroundings, I realize no one has tried to sit down across from us, or on either side of the guys.

With a quiet huff, it clicks. Obviously, they've got some sort of reserved seating arrangement worked out. Just like how there was a prime docking spot open when we got here.

"I'm going to order food," Kylian announces, rising up from the picnic bench seat. He turns back and regards me.

When I tip my head back, I'm met with a heavy dose of liquid heat radiating from his gaze.

"Will you be okay here?"

His concern is sweet but unwarranted.

"I'm good," I assure him, clearing my throat when my voice comes out shakier than intended.

With that, he walks away, lithely moving through the crowd.

"So that's a thing now?" Locke murmurs, tracing the condensation gathered on the outside of his glass.

My hackles raise at the callout. "It wouldn't be any of your business if it was."

He licks his bottom lip and bites down, holding the plush flesh between his teeth for a few breaths. Then he offers me one of his brilliant smiles.

"Something you should know now, Hot Girl."

I grind my molars at the use of the endearment. Things are less volatile between us today, but that doesn't mean we're back to flirting and pet names.

"If something concerns one of us," he juts his chin toward Decker and Kendrick, "it most certainly concerns all of us."

I assumed as much. Based on everything I've observed since moving into the Crusade mansion, it's clear that the guys are close. I'm at a major disadvantage, and I'd do well not to forget it. Locke's words are a good reminder that, regardless of his kindness, and regardless of the attraction between Kylian and me, I'm still their captive. Anything I tell them or participate in is fair game.

I gulp past the anxiety that threatens to take over. I'm okay. I'm not in control… but I'm not out of control, either. I am here. This is now.

Desperate to change the subject, I steel my spine and sit up straighter.

"Can I ask you something?"

Locke regards me, giving me a slow, deliberate nod. "You can."

"Why aren't you up there with them?"

The subtle clench of his teeth tells me I hit a nerve.

"You play football, too. Are you not good enough?" I push.

This time, the dig has the opposite effect.

Locke smirks, and in a fluid movement that's faster than any motion he's made all afternoon, he swings one leg over the bench so he's straddling our shared seat. Scooting close enough that his knees bump my outer thigh, he tilts forward.

"Joey, Joey, Joey," he murmurs in my ear. Goose bumps erupt from the crown of my head and skate down my chest. "You know firsthand just how good I am."

He licks the pulse point of my neck, then catches my earlobe between his teeth in the quickest of nips.

Sharply inhaling, I squeeze my legs together, fighting the surge of desire he just jettisoned through my body.

I shift slightly, desperate to put a sliver of space between us. Because if I don't, I can't be held accountable for what I'll do next.

My body reacts to him with total disregard for anything my brain has to say on the matter. What's even worse? My cheeks are flaming, and the glint in Locke's smile tells me the reaction is outwardly noticeable, too.

Thankfully, Kylian pops back into existence in that moment and sets a full tray of food on the table before lowering himself back into his seat on my other side.

"All good?" He takes a massive bite out of a soft pretzel stick, then offers the basket to me.

I'm still full from breakfast, but I gladly accept one and take a bite that rivals his. Anything to avoid responding to Locke.

"Joey was just asking about Decker and Kendrick's NIL deals," Locke says, cocking his head to the side and making absolutely no effort to hide his flirtatious grin.

I almost choke on my pretzel as I stammer to clarify. "No, I wasn't."

The last thing I need is for Kylian—or worse, Decker and Kendrick—to think I'm trying to get all up in their business.

Kylian glances from me to Locke, then back to me again.

"You two are being weird."

"Says the neurodivergent nerd who spent all of seventh grade wearing a tail," Locke quips without missing a beat.

Neurodivergent? Frowning, I dart a look at Kylian, but rather than glowering like I expect, he's grinning as he swallows and points past me toward his friend.

"Hey. At least I was wrapping the extra appendage around my waist instead of stuffing it down the front of my pants."

"Low blow!" Locke throws his head back and laughs. "I can't help it if I'm a grower, not a shower!" He reaches past me and playfully shoves Kylian's side.

Breathing out a sigh of relief, I let my shoulders drop. They're teasing each other, and they both seem to be in on the joke.

"How long have you two known each other?" I ask, swiping another pretzel stick from Kylian's tray.

He pushes the platter of food my way so it's centered between us. "Try this with it." He holds out a condiment cup of dipping sauce.

Locke groans. "Fuck. What I would give for a whole tray of pretzel sticks and a cold beer." He puffs out his cheeks, exasperated.

"Do you want one?" I ask through a mouthful of food.

"Nicky follows a strict diet during football season," Kylian cuts in before Locke can even open his mouth to answer me.

Nicky. I seriously love that.

"It helps temper the pain from my rheumatoid arthritis," Locke mutters. His expression is far less playful now. Instead, there's a weariness in his eyes, and his shoulders are hunched.

"Pretzel sticks covered in salt and dripping in spicy mustard don't quite make the cut in terms of anti-inflammatory foods," Kylian adds before taking a savage bite from the snack in question and chewing it almost obnoxiously while smirking at Locke.

"How did you two meet?" I ask again.

Both men go quiet for a moment, watching each other. Finally, Kylian inclines his head toward his friend.

"My foster parents lived next door to Kylian's family. I was in the system by age six, and I bounced around for a while. But I moved in with Gary and Brenda when I was ten, and it stuck."

Taking in a slow, steady breath, I work to keep myself from reacting outwardly. I know enough about the foster system—mostly because I spent half my childhood trying to avoid it—to respect that he's shared an exceptionally vulnerable part of his past with me. I refuse to pry or make a big deal about how he grew up. Just like I won't harp on the mention of Kylian being neurodivergent.

Kylian adds playfully, "It stuck because my mom wouldn't let you go."

Locke ducks his head subtly at the callout. "True. Not my fault I was willing to hang out with her kid, who clearly preferred computers to people for the first two years of our friendship."

"Not just computers," Kylian defends. "I was obsessed with my iPod, too."

"*Dude*. Remember that Christmas you got an iPod? The one with the little screen?"

A grin takes over Kylian's face. "We hid under the covers and watched four seasons of *Lost* on that two-inch screen over winter break."

"It took us the entire break, too, because someone had to keep pausing the show to look up fan theories."

"Yeah, Okay," Kylian admits with a grin. "Or maybe it took so long because *someone* was scared of the island monster?"

"Low blow!" Locke exclaims, pounding his fist into the picnic table playfully. The second he makes contact, he winces and lets out a curse. With a shaky breath, he closes his eyes and drops his head back.

I spin on the bench, looking to Kylian and noting the concern etched on his face. He's watching Locke with his brows pulled together.

"Nicky..." he hedges. Whether in warning or in comfort is anyone's guess.

Eventually, Locke opens his eyes and rights himself. He offers me a hollow smile that's probably meant to be reassuring, then looks past me to his friend.

"How much time do we have left?"

Kylian pulls out his phone and examines the activity at the front table. "Forty minutes on the clock, but you know Misty'll push to extend it if the line's still out the door."

"And Decker will gladly comply," Locke mutters.

"Catch me up to speed," I insist. "I still don't know what we're actually doing here."

Kylian answers this time. "This is one of Decker and Kendrick's many, many NIL obligations this season."

"NIL?"

"Name, image, and likeness," he clarifies. "Appearances. Sponsorships. Endorsements. Meet and greets. You name it, they do it." He adjusts his glasses. "Nicky has a few obligations this year, too, but not until later in the season."

I scoff. Why does none of this surprise me?

At the front of the room, Decker and Kendrick are still cheesing it up for the camera and putting on what I now realize is a very convincing act. "So people pay just to meet them or get their autographs?"

Kylian shakes his head. "Not people. Companies. Brands. The Boatyard, for example." He waves his hand. "A few thousand people will come through here today because of the guys, and the beer sales alone make it worth it for the owners."

As if Decker Crusade needs another reason to pump up his almighty ego.

"All this just because they're good at football?" I quip.

Locke scoffs and rests his forearms on the table. Kylian cocks an eyebrow. They're both silent for several seconds as my flippant remark just sort of hangs between us.

Finally, Kylian replies. "Decker and Kendrick aren't just good at football, Jo. They're literally the best of the best. Without a shadow of a doubt, they'll be among the first picks in the draft next spring. If Decker follows in his dad's footsteps—"

"Oh yeah. My uncle mentioned this. Decker's dad plays football, too, right?"

Locke barks out a laugh.

"Seriously?" Kylian regards me. "I don't always register sarcasm. Are you joking right now?"

My blank stare answers that question.

"Decker is the son of Thomas Crusade. QB1 for the Carolina Cougars? The GOAT of quarterbacks with seven rings to his name?"

I blink once. Then twice. It sounds impressive, but it doesn't mean much to me.

"You really don't know what you've gotten yourself into with us, do you, Hot Girl?"

Locke's comment eats at me the rest of the night.

Because I really don't.

Chapter 25

Josephine

I stayed up until two in the morning Googling.

Internet creeping makes me nauseous. I know firsthand just how misrepresentative and twisted that shit can be, but after the revelations at The Boatyard, I felt way too out of my depth to walk around this mansion completely unaware any longer.

I need to know what I'm dealing with. And *who* I'm living with.

There wasn't a ton of information about Kylian or Locke. Scholarships and academic achievements in the local paper for Kylian. A few pictures from high school featuring Locke on the football field.

Kendrick's search results were more fruitful. I found football news. Blog posts. National media coverage. Promotions for a ton of sports brands and athletic companies he's done endorsements for or been tagged in.

His reaction when I caught them at the med spa makes a lot more sense now, given his notoriety.

And then there's Decker.

Prodigy. Golden boy. Legend in the making. The number of articles I combed through regaling his ability and raw talent started to go to *my* head. It's no wonder the guy walks around thinking he's god's gift to football.

And then there's his dad. Everything Kylian said was true. And now that I really think about it, the name Thomas Crusade is familiar. I've never followed sports—I was literally banned from attending extracurricular functions at my own high school after my junior year—but I have enough common sense to recognize that the man is a big deal.

Once in a generation. And also the father of the next prodigal son.

The most recent articles talk about Thomas and Decker as a unit: father and son. A story of hope birthed from tragedy. I was already wondering about his mom when I stumbled upon the first clip.

Because that's what it was. A video clip. A grainy shot on an outdated cell phone with hundreds of thousands of views.

A young Decker at his mother's funeral. Little Decker next to her casket at the gravesite.

I stopped watching as soon as I realized what it was. That a person would take a video like that and upload it is sickening. And the sheer number of views makes my stomach roil in disgust. Nothing irks me more than nonconsensual filming or photography.

He was a child. A heartbroken, grieving child. And this is a blatant invasion of privacy. There were tons of pictures, too.

The whole thing makes my heart ache for the devastated little boy in the photos. His expression in some of them? *Fuck.* How could anyone think it's okay to exploit him like that?

My sympathy toward Decker Crusade is short-lived though, because a few days later, I'm reminded that he's not the heartbroken little boy anymore. No, he's an icy, domineering asshole who's on a mission to make me as miserable as possible.

Locke and I are in the kitchen on Wednesday night, prepping veggies for dinner and cooking up a stir-fry to share. Kylian is up in the Nest, I think, and Kendrick and Decker are holed up in the media room, watching game footage.

"Are mushrooms okay?" I ask over my shoulder. It's not just pretzel sticks and beer that flare up his arthritis. We're using brown rice instead of white, and something called coconut aminos instead of soy sauce. Peppers are a no-go, as are all other veggies in the nightshade family.

"Mushrooms are fine," he confirms from where he's rinsing rice at the sink. "Smells awesome," he comments as he saunters up behind me.

Leaning toward the stove, he ghosts his chin against my collarbone. That's the extent of the contact. If I had to guess, he's making a concerted effort not to touch me anywhere else. But his heat soaks through the thin material of my shirt, and the sheer presence of him engulfs me as he peeks over my shoulder.

The tension is as delicious as it is torturous.

We've settled into a purgatory. One where he doesn't push, and I don't take. One that's undefined, because we keep putting off the conversation I know he's itching to have. But the sexual strain is there—a connection humming between us when we're in the same room.

He's waiting for me to make the first move. Although I guess it's not really the first move. Just the next move?

I'm paralyzed with indecision.

The unfettered attraction that hit me when I met Locke hasn't dissipated. If anything, it's grown. That's more than apparent by the way my nipples pebble under my tank top, pressing against the thin lace of my bralette and making me so damn glad I'm facing the stove.

But I'm still holding a grudge of sorts. I'm salty that, despite what I thought was an instant and mutual bond between us, Locke didn't—or couldn't—reason with Decker. Maybe he tried. But I don't know, because we haven't talked about it.

We've danced around the issue, letting the anticipation build as we spend more time together and sink into a rhythm I've never experienced with another person.

Life is easy with Locke. He makes things fun. I'm okay staying in purgatory for now. I fear that if I push, I'll be faced with the possibility that what he did or didn't do is unforgivable.

I need more time to sort through my feelings. Or maybe I need proof that if I give him another chance, he'll have my back when I go toe to toe with Decker.

With my lip pressed between my teeth, I shift ever so slightly from hip to hip. My ass brushes against him—I knew it would—and Locke holds back what I swear is a groan.

"Do you want to take over so I can start the rice?" I hold out the spoon, peering over my shoulder through my lashes.

He zeros in on my mouth. It's then I remember that my lip is still trapped between my teeth. Sucking in a quick breath, I release it and shimmy away from the stove without letting my body come into contact with him again.

"What are you doing to me, Hot Girl?" The words are almost inaudible since he's speaking directly into the pan.

"I'm making you dinner," I quip, measuring out the water for the rice.

His focus is fixed on me as I return to the stove and turn on a second burner, but I busy myself with the pot, stifling a smile.

"Smells good in here."

I glance over my shoulder and catch sight of Kendrick just as he halts when he spots me.

"We made plenty," Locke offers, either not noticing or choosing to ignore the glare that fixed itself on Kendrick's face the second he realized I was in the kitchen, too. "You're welcome to join us if you're hungry."

Kendrick doesn't have time to reply before Decker storms into the kitchen.

"Good. You're all here."

Except we're not. Kylian is probably still in his room.

"We need to talk about travel and sleeping arrangements for the game."

I bite down hard on the inside of my cheek.

Hunter asked me in class today if I was going to the game this weekend. It's an away game, but a lot of students are planning to carpool and tailgate beforehand since it's only a few hours from here.

I intended to ask Kylian about it tonight. Mainly, I wanted to figure out whether staying behind was a possibility. I'm pretty sure that's not going to be an option based on the way both Decker and Kendrick are glowering at me.

"Obviously, Josephine will be traveling with us."

I snort. It wasn't obvious to me.

Decker raises one brow, his onyx eyes piercing me as he continues. "I'm not comfortable with her staying in her own hotel room, given the circumstances. She'll be with Kylian at the game, but for the rest of the time—"

"I don't need a babysitter," I huff, crossing my arms over my chest as I return Decker's hard stare.

He doesn't reply—doesn't even react—before clearing his throat and continuing.

"She needs to be with one of us at all times." He looks from Locke to Kendrick, then back to me. "We leave Friday afternoon. We'll stay at the team hotel overnight, then head home after the game on Saturday, understood?"

Understood. As if it's a question of comprehension. This asshole.

Emboldened, I plant my hands on my hips. "I'll room with Kylian," I declare.

The corner of Decker's mouth curls up.

"No, you won't. Kyl needs to keep his head in the game. We need him focused and rested on Saturday."

I don't dignify that implication—that Kylian wouldn't be "rested" if he shared a room with me—with a response. Kylian and I have already shared a room *and* a bed. He slept just fine that night, but Decker doesn't get to know that.

Shrugging as if it doesn't matter, I provide an alternative. "I'll stay with Locke, then."

Locke flicks a glance at me and sticks his tongue in his cheek. "Works for me."

"No," Decker barks.

I swear steam billows from my ears at his response.

No?

My focus shifts to Locke once more. I get that Decker is the quarterback. That this is his team. His house. His boys. His captive. But this shouldn't be his call.

"Nicky needs rest before the game. It's hard enough on him to be in a different bed on the road. He doesn't need a roommate to add to his plate."

I watch, horrified, as Decker's words register with Locke. His face drops, first in disappointment, then with acceptance. He sighs—a long, drawn-out sound of defeat. When he finally meets my gaze, all the playfulness from earlier has been sapped. He looks a little pissed, but mostly just resigned.

"Sorry, Joey. Decker's right."

So much for hoping Locke would find it within himself to side with me for once. This can't be happening. I'm not allowed to room with Kylian, and now Locke isn't an option. That means...

"You wanna win on Saturday?" Kendrick's words are cool and measured. His tone is surprisingly even given the way his hands are digging into the edge of the kitchen island. With his head bowed, he turns to face Decker, waiting him out.

I hold my breath as tension thrums between them. Finally, Decker takes the bait.

"What kind of question is that? You know I want to win."

"Then keep her the fuck away from me."

Kendrick pushes off the island and storms out of the kitchen, pounding up the stairs without a backward glance.

I close my eyes and pull in a long, shuddering breath.

Shit on a crumbly cracker.

Decker Crusade's ability to morph a decent day into the stuff of nightmares takes true talent. If this whole quarterback thing doesn't work out, he could very well have a future in dashing dreams and ruining lives.

"What's going on?"

When I open my eyes, Kylian's entered the kitchen, his focus shifting from Decker to Locke to me, then repeating, as if he's an oscillating fan.

"Just getting things squared away for this weekend," Decker offers coolly.

"I take it that's the reason I passed a raging bull on the stairs just now?"

I can't help but roll my eyes. Kendrick made his point—rudely, I might add. His feelings about me are abundantly clear. I doubt even Decker would push him on this. There's no need for him to storm out of the room, huffing and puffing.

"Josephine will be rooming with me on Friday night. Can you make sure we've got enough key cards at check-in, Kyl?"

Pressure builds behind my eyes, so I focus on the gleaming quartz countertop, refusing to blink in case tears try to spill over.

I've always been an angry crier. People often view it as a weakness. I refuse to let Decker Crusade see me that way.

By the time I trust myself to glance up, Decker is striding out of the room. Like he didn't just ruin my whole fucking day and set me up for what's bound to be an exceptionally awkward weekend.

"Thanks for your help," I bite out in Locke's direction, then take off toward the stairs.

"Jo... wait!"

Kylian catches up to me just as my foot hits the second step. His fingers encircle my wrist and squeeze just hard enough to stop me in my tracks.

"What happened?" he implores.

"Decker happened." I pull my arm out of his grasp.

That doesn't deter him. He launches himself up the stairs in front of me, his long legs taking them two at a time until he's a few steps above me, hovering.

"You can ride with me to the hotel on Friday afternoon. And we'll be together at the game. Decker's not completely unreasonable. Maybe if we try talking to him—"

I scoff at the very notion of Decker being anything close to reasonable where I'm concerned.

"Save your breath, Kylian. I'm on my own here. Just like I've been from day one."

Chapter 26

Josephine

We arrive at the hotel several hours after the team. When Kylian said we didn't have to leave until evening, I thought that was a great idea. But now that I'm faced with settling in after Decker and the guys have been here for hours, I'm doubting that line of thinking.

I raise my keycard up to the door, then pause. Should I knock? Can I assume Kylian texted him when we arrived?

Whatever.

The smell of generic cleaner hits me when I step inside the room, followed by a scent that's warm, sensual, and heady. *Decker*. He may be an infuriating, broody asshole, but damn, he smells divine.

I creep through the doorway and scan the space. The room is nothing special—dimly lit and an average size. Just a standard room in a chain hotel.

I catalog the TV mounted on the beige wall and the small table and café chairs set off in the corner. An abstract industrial print is the only décor. That, and the two silver and white sconces that frame the headboard of the bed.

The *one single* king-size bed.

Panic radiates through every limb as I survey the singular sleeping surface.

There's only one bed.

Why the hell is there only one bed?

And not only that. There's no couch. No cot or rollaway. Not even a cushioned chair.

This is not going to work. Sharing a room is one thing, but I can't sleep on the floor. I'll be better off sneaking into Kylian's room, or even Locke's, and dealing with the consequences. What could Decker even do? Scold me? Ground me? Spank me? Carry me caveman-style back to his room and tie me to the bed?

A throat clears behind me, from near the doorway I just walked through.

"Josephine."

The broody bastard himself leans out of what appears to be the bathroom, arms braced on the doorframe. He's shirtless, because of course he is. Decker fucking Crusade. Freshly showered and still dripping wet. I allow myself two seconds of ogling, sweeping my gaze over the hard muscles of his chest and the dip of his slender hips, before I take a measured step backward, deeper into the room.

"You made it." His tone is conversational. As if he's Mister Nice Guy all of a sudden. He runs one of his huge hands through his still-wet hair, then offers me the smallest hint of a smile.

He's acting *different*. Softer. Maybe even cordial? But the shift in behavior doesn't have time to fully register. I've got a one-track mind, and I can't help but blurt out the obvious.

"There's only one bed," I accuse.

A grimace colors his expression.

"Yeah. About that... The hotel is fully booked because of the game. The team always requests king-size beds, and by the time I thought to call..." His arms flex as he grips the doorframe and drops his attention to his bare feet.

He's wearing athletic shorts, at least. Solid black—like his soul. The band of his Calvins peeks out of the top, taunting me. But I don't have the luxury of being distracted by Decker Crusade's underwear right now. We have to figure this out so I can ease the unbridled fear threatening to consume me.

"You expect me to believe the almighty Decker Crusade couldn't get a room change request?"

Dark eyes dancing with playfulness meet mine as he pushes his tongue into his cheek and smirks. "Almighty, huh?"

I don't have it in me to respond to his flirtatious jab. My brain is already seizing up, and the first licks of panic are caressing my insides. Every nerve in my body is on high alert. Every muscle is locked up tight.

Decker lowers his arms and takes a tentative step toward me.

I immediately take two steps back.

"We're not in Lake Chapel, Josephine," he murmurs, brows dipping low as he watches me. "I don't have any pull in this town or with these people. The bed situation is what it is."

I huff out a breath, shooting for annoyance rather than trepidation. "The other guys have kings, too?"

Maybe we could switch rooms. Hell, I'd be willing to subject myself to Kendrick's wrath if it meant I didn't have to sleep on the floor.

Decker grits his teeth. "They do. But we've already been over this. Even if they didn't, that's not an option. I need them focused and ready for tomorrow. There's no alternative to this arrangement."

This arrangement. This shit-tastic situation in which he'll insist on taking the bed and I'll be stuck on the floor.

I've done more than my fair share of sleeping rough. Though not every one of those situations has been terrible. I've slept on friends' couches. I've crashed in the back seat of cars. But I fell asleep leaning up against the front door more times than I can count when my mom forgot that she had a child and was supposed to be responsible for another human life.

On those nights, Mrs. Rubin would inevitably find me outside. She'd shake me gently and wordlessly indicate that I should follow. She'd let me sleep on the pull-out couch in her trailer, then make a huge breakfast in the morning and insist she made much more than she could possibly eat on her own.

So yeah, I've spent plenty of nights sleeping rough. But not since *that* night.

I need pillows. Sheets. A comforter to cocoon myself in so that the moment I come to, I have a grip on reality. I need the comfort of a bed to convince myself of what's real—of where I am, and more importantly, of *where I'm not.*

Sleeping on the floor—on any floor, or on the ground, in any situation—has the power to send me catapulting into an episode.

Decker's making me room with him because he thinks I'm going to run? *This*. This is what'll make me run. This'll send me over the edge.

I know how my body and brain will react if I try to sleep on the floor. Being that exposed and vulnerable is not an option.

And I refuse to let Decker Crusade see me like that. I won't throw away everything I've worked for over the last few years, including my solid grasp on reality, to bend to his will and appease this man.

But how the fuck am I supposed to explain conversion disorder to this heartless bastard?

"Josephine."

Trying to calm my breathing and keep my cool, I reluctantly meet his gaze.

His eyes widen in surprise, but to his credit, he doesn't look away. I'm sure he wasn't expecting me to react this way. I wasn't fucking expecting it, either.

"You're freaking out right now. Talk to me."

It's not a request.

And yet... my mouth opens and closes twice in an attempt to reply. But no words come out. I gulp, then try in earnest to slow my racing thoughts.

If I don't calm down, I'll end up having an attack right now, triggered by the prospect of having an attack later. Anxiety. It's the shittiest shit.

I mumble something that I hope sounds like "just give me a second" and close my eyes, resorting to a mindfulness exercise.

I inhale through my nose and hold it for four counts. Opening my eyes, I scan the room for something I can see: a pillow. I see a pillow. I exhale, blowing out for four counts.

With another long, deep breath, I focus on what I smell. Decker's body wash. Sea salt and amber. Ocean air and summer nights. I smell Decker's body wash.

Exhaling, I close my eyes and strain to hear something—anything—over the sound of my accelerated heartbeat whooshing in my ears. Music. Something low and melodic, folksy and soulful. Decker is playing music in the bathroom. The strum of a guitar and a male voice. I hear music.

There it is.

Calm washes over me. I'm okay.

Embarrassed by my reaction but decidedly more centered, I meet his gaze again.

"I can't do it," I say with as much steel in my voice as I can muster.

"Can't do what?" he asks, running his thumb along his bottom lip, examining me.

Unable to maintain eye contact any longer, I hang my head. I'm about to reveal a vulnerability I don't like sharing with the people I'm closest to, let alone a man who could damn well turn around and use it against me in harrowing, damaging ways.

I focus on the bed as I answer his question.

"I can't sleep on the floor. I'm not trying to be difficult or dramatic. But I physically *can't*. Something... something happened to me years ago. Now I have conversion disorder, which causes paralyzing panic attacks. If I panic for too long, I'm afraid I'll slip away again. Please. Don't ask me about it. I just need you to believe me. I'm... I'm begging you, Decker."

After several seconds of silence, I peek up at him through my lashes, finding his onyx eyes locked on me with so much intensity it hits me like a physical blow, and I flinch.

"Please don't make me sleep on the floor."

I hate being at anyone's mercy, but unless I'm honest with him, there's no way I'll get through this night.

Decker frowns at me, but for once, his dark eyes aren't hard. Instead, his expression is stoic and thoughtful. I wish I could get a read on him. Though the disdain has dissipated, his eyes bore into me until I swear I can feel him under my skin. Whether he's trying to intimidate or just figure out if I'm lying, it's working. I'm totally and completely exposed in this moment.

Flustered, I look away first. What's the point of staring him down? He knows the power he holds over me right now. There's no sense in pretending otherwise.

When the silence continues to stretch, making my stomach sink with dread, I steal a glance in his direction. But he's not there. He moved—and he's coming right at me.

I stiffen when his fingers find my chin. Then I sink into the feel of his hand on my face when the tenderness of the gesture registers. His touch is gentle in the most unexpected way.

"Josephine," he murmurs.

My eyes shutter closed from the gentleness in his voice. He's said my name dozens of times in the last week. But never like this.

"You're okay. You're safe. You don't have to sleep on the floor. No fucking way."

I release a breath and will myself not to cry. I hate when people are nice to me. Kind. Compassionate. Because it never lasts.

"You're okay," he repeats as his fingers brush against my skin and the edge of his thumbnail traces my lower lip.

I quickly catch my lip between my teeth to stop it from trembling. His kindness is disarming. I never imagined that he'd offer to take the floor, especially considering he has a game tomorrow. But maybe he's one of those guys who can sleep anywhere.

"Thank you," I murmur, racking my brain for a way to verbally express the extent of my gratitude.

"You're welcome."

It's a straightforward exchange. The kind of pleasantries typically offered up without thinking. But the simplicity of the words adds to the authenticity of the moment and the tether between us.

He's still holding my face, caressing my lower lip as he homes in on my mouth. I let my lip slide out from between my teeth, and something hot and fiery flares behind his eyes with the motion. Gulping, I clear my throat, then shift back on my heels slightly.

Just enough to break the spell we're both under.

And with that, Decker blinks back to the moment, too. He cracks his neck, then nods to himself once.

"Pick which side you want. I'll see if there are extra pillows in the closet."

Oh.

Shit.

Chapter 27

Josephine

I've replayed his words over and over in my head, searching for a way to pin this predicament on him. I keep coming up short.

Decker wasn't deceptive. His words weren't unclear. He said I didn't have to sleep on the floor. *He never offered to give up the bed.*

My body thrums with anxiety as I lie only inches from Decker Crusade. Sure, there's a pillow dam between us, and the bed is technically big enough for two people.

But still.

It doesn't matter that I can't see him. I can feel him. Smell him. He's surrounding me. I swear in the five minutes he was nice to me, he burrowed under my skin and took up residence.

Then there's the not-so-minor issue of his sleep attire.

Or should I call it a lack of attire?

He's shirtless. And pantless. The man sleeps in his boxer briefs. Not just any boxer briefs, though. He's wearing white Calvin Kleins. They're fitted and made of silky, lightweight fabric that leaves absolutely nothing to the imagination.

Fucking imagination.

Because now I'm lying here, restless and, okay, maybe a little horny, trying to squash all fantasies of what it would feel like to have Decker Crusade inside me.

Arrogant. Egotistical. Bossy. I list his lesser qualities and cycle through them in my head, determined to replace my attraction with loathing. I have to hold on tight to my hatred. It's the only shield I have left tonight.

Reminding myself of my intense dislike of the man lying practically naked mere inches from me, I stretch my legs straight and squeeze my eyes shut, replaying the *I Hate Decker Greatest Hits* playlist over and over in my mind.

He practically *kidnapped* me. He's holding me captive. He dragged me across state lines for his stupid game this weekend. I'm forced to share a bed with him because of his controlling, distrusting attitude.

His heavy sigh hangs between us in warning.

I bristle, knowing damn well he's about to speak. It doesn't even matter what he has to say. I'm so keyed up right now, he's undoubtedly about to set me off.

Too bad he's not interested in getting me off.

Fuck. No. *Bad* Joey. Bad girl. Those are not acceptable thoughts.

"I thought the whole point of you sleeping in bed was to prevent you from freaking out," he growls quietly in the dark.

I don't dare peek over the pillows piled between us.

"I'm not freaking out," I squeak.

He scoffs.

And there it is.

His dismissiveness tears through me like a grenade, and I detonate.

"I didn't tell you any of that so you could use it against me, *Cap*. I shared something personal, and you're already throwing it back in my face. For fuck's sake! Do you have no shame? Are you even human?" I sneer.

"And for the record, this isn't me freaking out. Believe me. If I was spiraling, you'd fucking know. You'd be calling 9-1-1, or we'd be heading to the hospital. Excuse me if I'm having trouble getting comfortable in a strange place lying next to a man I hardly know but most definitely despise."

I punctuate my monologue with a huff. My heart's hammering against my ribcage, and I'm breathing so hard my breasts are straining against the fabric of my T-shirt with each inhale. I have to force myself to loosen my grip on the sheets.

Silence fills the room, followed by the rustling of sheets.

Oh shit.

His silhouette looms over me, and there's no doubt he's got those damn onyx eyes locked on me again. But I don't dare turn my head to face him. I study the ceiling and resist meeting his gaze for as long as I can, but he doesn't back down. When I finally glance over, he's propped up on one elbow, eyebrows quirked.

"Are you done?"

I glower at him, all hot and agitated, both mentally and physically.

"Roll over," he says.

My heart drops to my stomach, and my cunt tingles traitorously. But I make no move to follow his command.

He blows out an exasperated breath and squints at me through the dark. "I'm not going to hurt you. Just do as I say, Josephine. Roll over and lay flat on your stomach."

My heartbeat thunders with the urge to resist. I should argue, but I'm too flustered to form words.

Except I'm not actually scared of Decker *or* worried he'll try to hurt me. He's had ample opportunity to take advantage of me or put me in a compromising position, but so far, that hasn't been his MO.

Defeated, and honestly a little curious, I roll over, being sure to keep the covers pulled up to my shoulders.

I jolt when his hand cuffs the back of my neck.

"Shh," he soothes. "You're okay."

He massages the base of my skull, his strong, capable fingers digging into muscles I didn't even know were tense. My body relaxes as all conscious thought focuses on what he's doing.

Each squeeze of my neck cuts through another layer of tension. The warmth and power behind his ministrations have me sinking into the sheets as my body winds down little by little.

"That feels really good," I admit into the pillow. I swear I hear him chuckle, but I'm too comfortable here to look over and confirm my suspicions.

I'm almost embarrassed by how easy it is for him to help me settle, but soon enough, my pulse evens out and my breathing slows. Even as I visibly relax, Decker doesn't let up. His fingers are magic. Every knead smooths away another knot of the tension wound tight in my neck and shoulders.

The contact is almost too good. As I settle, my mind wanders, and I can't help but consider what his hands could do to other parts of my body.

The urge to squeeze my thighs together and squirm again prickles in the back of my mind.

The whole point of this was to relax me, but now that I'm putty in his hands, hints of desire tingle up my spine. If I'm not careful, I'll get all the way worked up again.

"Um, I think I'm good. You can stop now," I mumble.

He squeezes my neck in response. "Can you just let someone do something nice for you for once?" he grits out. "You need sleep. *I* need sleep. I'm not stopping until you're out."

Of course he's not. Decker Crusade requires control of all things. So I have no choice but to let him use his magic hands to massage me into a trance. I squirm as I think about the power in his fingers, how it would feel if he dug them into my thighs or kneaded the fleshy part of my ass as he—

"Settle," he growls, clearly aware of my heightened state.

I inhale slowly, clearing my mind and willing myself to sleep. It takes concerted effort, but the haze of unconsciousness eventually washes over me.

I'm close to unconsciousness when he whispers, so quietly I almost don't make out the words, "You're okay, Josephine. You can go back to hating me in the morning, but tonight, I've got you."

Chapter 28

Decker

I call on every ounce of self-control I possess to force slow, even breaths.

Breath in. Breath out.

Power in. Control out.

Desire in. Restraint out.

But I can't fucking focus on the rise and fall of my chest, because it's not just my torso that moves with each breath.

It's her.

Josephine is draped over me. Her arms are wrapped around my stomach and her face is smashed against my chest like I'm her favorite fucking teddy bear.

How did I not sense her shifting in the night? At the very least, I should have felt her touch. But my body betrayed me. Now I'm trapped under the supple curves of a woman who wants absolutely nothing to do with me.

The blame doesn't solely lie with her, either.

We're smack-dab in the middle of the bed. Cuddling at the fifty-yard line.

Fuck.

What happened? And how did I *let* it happen?

After she fell asleep, I put as much distance between us as possible, got myself comfortable, and passed out. There was even a pillow barricade, I swear.

She smells good. Really fucking good. And the way her body is molded over mine? She's a perfect fit.

Though every inch of her body is pressed up against me, I keep my hands to myself. That is, until my phone buzzes on the nightstand. Then I have to softly cup the back of her head so I don't completely dislodge her as I reach for my device.

Kylian: How'd it go last night?

Kylian: Is she still sleeping?

Kylian: She hasn't answered my texts.

Fuck. I blow out a slow, quiet breath to rein in my reaction. He's got it so bad. Kylian's already fixated. This situation has disaster written all over it.

My phone vibrates again, this time with a question mark. Gotta hand it to him; he's relentless to a fault.

The irony isn't lost on me. I insisted on this sleeping arrangement to help him focus. To keep her from distracting him last night. There's something going on there—whether it's an infatuation or a one-time kind of thing remains to be seen.

Either way, it's clear my meddling was in vain. She doesn't have to be in the same room to dominate his every thought. Shit. Maybe he would have slept *better* if they'd roomed together. Not that I'll admit that to either of them.

Anger flashes through me when I consider how Josephine could hurt him. *Use* him. Chew him up and spit him out. Does she know the power she possesses?

Kylian's a big boy, but he doesn't always grasp the finer nuances of interpersonal relationships. If Josephine realizes the hold she has on him and decides to use that somehow...

Another vibration. But this one's not from Kylian.

Locke: Is Joey up? I'll take her down to breakfast so you can get on with your routine

My whole body tenses when I read his attempt at casual. Kylian's clearly not the only one entranced by this girl. I'm trying to muster up the cold distrust I'm used to associating with women. But then Josephine shifts on top of me. *Fuck*. She's so soft and malleable when she's asleep. Her softness presses into my chest, and it's all I can do to not hold her tighter.

Before I can lose myself down that rabbit hole, I drag my attention back to the screen. At least Locke has the decency to try and downplay his interest. Although I'm not sure if he's doing it for my benefit or hers. Or, hell, maybe even his own? He hooked up with her first, according to what Kendrick saw in the butler's pantry during our first party of the season.

Though Josephine pins at least some of the blame for her predicament on Nicky. He was with Kendrick when she spotted them at the spa. According to her, he's the reason she ran after them in the first place. As far as I know, things have cooled off between them considerably since then. I haven't found the gumption to ask him point-blank where they stand, though.

And then there's K. I hadn't even considered how having her at the house might affect him. He's such a softie when he's not on the field. I figured he'd be the easiest-going of the bunch when our house guest moved in. It's turned out to be worst-case scenario there. He can hardly stand to be in the same room as her. And every time I've tried to ask him about it, he blows me off.

That's not him. That's not *us*. We've been playing together for a decade; living together for years. I know him as well as I know myself. Hell, I know all of them to that extent. Their hopes. Dreams. Fears.

Frustrations. There's a bond between the four of us that's always been unshakable.

Until now.

Until *her*.

The wail of my alarm ricochets through the room, eliminating every other thought from my mind. I can't dwell on what's happening or what might be, on what she's doing to us or how this whole arrangement could backfire in epically awful ways. I can only control the here and now. I owe it to my boys—to my team—to show up ready to win.

Chapter 29

Josephine

I startle awake at the sound of a shrill phone alarm blaring at full volume.

I'm warm. Maybe even a little overheated. The humidity in the south is relentless. I swear I can feel it seeping through the walls and thickening the atmosphere even when the air conditioning runs all night.

Yawning, I gasp when my cheek slides against something sticky. I blink my eyes open, only then realizing that my face is pressed against soft, supple skin.

Not just any skin. The tanned, taut, hot skin of my captor.

Awareness prickles down my spine as I do a full inventory of my body. My cheek against his chest isn't the only point of contact between Decker Crusade and me. Not by a long shot.

My face is practically smashed into his pec.

My arm is draped over his waist.

And yep. Fuck. I do, in fact, have my leg hitched up over his upper thigh. As if I'm about to mount him like a pony.

In a painfully slow retreat (literally, because my cheek is partially glued to his skin from a combination of his sweat and drool), I peel my face off him and extricate my limbs as best I can. I hold my breath as I roll to my back, but the pile of pillows behind me makes it almost impossible to put distance between us. So much for Decker's carefully crafted pillow dam.

An exhale laced with shock and relief presses out of my lungs, though the sound is masked by the still blaring ringer of the alarm.

I'm no longer touching him when he begins to stir.

Thank fuck.

I would have died had he woken up and found me in his arms.

Despite the way I like to ogle him when he's not barking orders out of his bossy facehole, I don't need an awkward cuddle session to contend with today.

"Time to get up," he murmurs. He sits up with ease—and the way his abs ripple with the movement is immediately imprinted on my brain—then runs a hand through his rumpled hair.

I give him a quick assessment, because, yeah, I'm only human. And yum. It's hard to fathom that he *is* human with a body like that. My cheeks blaze at the sight of the red marks I left on his trunk.

"I have a meeting this morning. Plans with Kendrick. Pregame rituals." He's speaking to me, obviously, considering I'm the only one in the room. But he hasn't even glanced my way. No, his eyes are still fixed on the ceiling.

"You can go hang out with Locke now," he adds, jutting his chin to the door connecting this room to the next. "His room is next door."

I say nothing at first. Only hit him with a well-deserved scowl. That's it? After the way he eased my concerns and helped me fall asleep last night, he doesn't have anything else to say?

Apparently, Decker Crusade is back to his broody self in the light of day.

Sliding off the bed, I give him the same cool, unaffected treatment he's offering me. Without a backward glance I say, "Sure thing, Cap. Let me change and freshen up, then I'll be out of your hair."

I scurry toward the bathroom. Once I'm safely inside, I close and lock the door, grateful he won't have access to the mirror in here to inspect the marks on his body before they have a chance to fade.

With my toiletry bag open on the counter in front of me, I go through my morning routine quickly. I apply SPF and keep my makeup light then don my favorite pair of white cut-off shorts.

When I'm nearly ready, I dig through my overnight bag and pull out my surprise.

I can't help but grin as I hold the jersey out and inspect it. Hunter helped me get it right. She insisted on picking it up for me, too, and won't tell me how much it was so I can pay her back.

She had questions, and I gave her enough answers to appease her curiosity for now. I'm not ready for her to know that I technically live at the Crusade Mansion. Or that I've hooked up with two of the guys. Because I'm not sure I can explain how things have evolved without revealing too much.

I pull on the bright red and white jersey and assess my reflection with a wide smile. Flipping my head, I pull my hair into a high ponytail as planned. I don't want anyone to miss the name on the back.

"Are we meeting up with everyone for breakfast before your *pregame rituals*?" I call from the bathroom.

To my surprise, it's not Decker who responds.

"We're all here so we can head down together. Ready when you are, Jo."

Kylian.

My grin grows so wide my cheeks hurt. I take two quick mirror selfies—one of my fit from the front and one of the back—and shoot them off to Hunter, then unlock the bathroom door and sashay into the main room.

Four sets of eyes bore into me.

They each look like they could eat me alive, albeit with very different intentions.

Dominance. Heat. Anger. Desire.

"Hot Girl," Locke groans reverently.

I cock one hip and strike a pose, standing before them in my white shorts and custom Crusaders jersey.

"You like?" I tease with a cheeky smile before I turn around and offer them my back.

I don't dare peek over my shoulder as their reactions hit my ears.

Confidently, I grab my crossbody bag and make my way to the door.

"Come on, boys. We're burning daylight," I call back.

Kendrick's grumbling is the loudest. Something about it not being a *real* team jersey.

I was prepared for this. So prepared, in fact, that I've been holding my breath, waiting to quip what I say next.

Tamping down my glee, I hurry down the hall and stab the elevator button, looking from Kendrick to Decker, then Locke and Kylian.

"That's funny," I muse, running my thumb and forefinger over my chin. "Last I heard, Kylian *is* the fucking team."

Locking eyes with Decker as the elevator doors slide open, I deadpan, "Go Crusaders."

Chapter 30

Josephine

Blinking behind my sunglasses, I crane my neck and scan the stands for Hunter. She swears she's standing up and waving, and I think I'm looking in the right section, but I still haven't spotted her. I already explained to her that I'm one of the team photographers, so I'd be on the field for most of the game.

There's so much commotion surrounding our spot on the bench I don't notice the people approaching until they're within earshot.

"Sweetheart!"

The speaker isn't just calling out to me; she's reaching out, arms fully extended, with a grin plastered to her face. Caught off guard and more than a little confused, I take a step back. It's not until she's within arm's reach that I realize her sights aren't set on me. No, she's going right for Kylian.

He lets out a quiet, rumbling "hi" as he returns her affection with a one-armed squeeze. Hilariously, he hasn't taken his eyes off the field.

Swiping quickly through screens on one of his devices, he asks, "How did you guys get down here?"

"Decker surprised us!" the other woman in the group squeals, her hands clasped in front of her chest. "Misty texted and said to meet her at will call, then handed us field passes for today."

"We never get these at away games," one of the men marvels, holding out the pass attached to the red and white Crusaders lanyard hanging around his neck.

The hug. The intimate familiarity. If I didn't know any better, I would suspect...

"Jo, these are my parents, Charlie and Claudia Walsh. And those are Locke's parents, Brenda and Gary Marshall." When I turn to him, wide-eyed, he's already looking up from the screen and scanning my face.

"I was planning to meet up with them after the game," he offers, holding my gaze for two more beats before focusing on setup again.

Kylian wasn't expecting them down here. Decker surprised them with passes...

And here I am, mouth agape, rocking my short shorts, with Kylian's name embossed on the back of my jersey.

Touché, Crusade. Tou-fucking-ché.

"I didn't catch your name, dear," Brenda says to me.

I never asked Locke if he kept in touch with his foster parents. Seeing them here, at his game, inspires an ache in the hollow of my chest.

"I'm Joey," I offer, hand outstretched. "I know Locke from school," I offer weakly, sparing these people insight into just how intertwined my life has become with their son's.

Brenda takes my hand but quickly pulls me into one of the warmest, longest hugs I think I've ever received. I'm thoroughly embarrassed by the time I try and wiggle free. "Any friend of Locke's is a friend of ours," she tells me.

When I finally start to pull away, a gasp sounds behind me.

"Heavens! Where did you get that?"

My cheeks heat, likely flushing to a shade that matches the Crusaders jersey I'm wearing as I slowly turn to face Claudia. I look to Kylian for help, but he's focused on his tablet. I've never once begrudged him his intense commitment to his role on the team, but I have to fight back the urge to kick him in the shin and get his attention. I could use an assist right about now.

Shifting from hip to hip, I bite down on my lower lip and laugh uncomfortably.

"Um, well, I had it custom made, actually, because Kylian's my favorite player." The shtick seems far less funny now that I have to explain it to his parents. Fucking Decker...

"What's the number on the back? Is that supposed to be an *o*?" Claudia presses.

"Sigma, Mom. It's a Greek letter used to symbolize standard deviation," Kylian interjects.

Finally. I try to catch his eye, but he's already turned back to the field.

"Because Kylian does the stats..." I reason.

"Wonderful. And so clever!" Charlie chimes in, clasping his hands. "You said you had it made? So we could order them, too?"

Pursing my lips to hold back a laugh, I nod. This is absurd. I had no idea they would be here. Or that this would become a thing...

Claudia digs a pen out of her purse and writes her number on a torn piece of paper, along with her shirt size, and Charlie's, too. She's going on and on about how she'll pay for the jerseys, and how maybe she should order one to wear, plus one extra to display.

It takes several more minutes before the parents say their goodbyes and head back to their seats. I'm all sorts of frazzled by the time they leave, so I sit on the bench and blow out a breath, trying to get my bearings.

Kylian takes a seat beside me, legs spread wide, a device balanced on each thigh. All signs that the coin toss is imminent. His headset is in place, and a few of the coaches come over to speak to him. He's locked in, focused, with his head in the game.

Watching him work is like watching an artist paint or a sculptor sculpt. His fingers fly over the screen, his eyes moving frantically as he assesses the numbers in front of him. When he speaks, he's eerily calm, calling plays and making suggestions into a headset that I now know is linked to Decker, the head coach, and their offensive coordinator.

"Sorry about that," Kylian murmurs, still not looking up. "I'll help you get back at him for pulling that stunt."

Kylian doesn't exist in any shade of gray. He's right and wrong. Black and white. He knows Decker upset me, and he's agreeing to back me up on this.

Thoughtful, but not necessary. I have more than a few ideas for retribution after this unexpected parental meet and greet.

"They liked you," he adds as an afterthought. Or maybe a reassurance.

They don't know me. But it's still kind of Kylian to say that.

"You didn't have to say what you said about the jersey."

I still. There's a hollow sort of doubt in his words that I can't ignore.

Sure, my comment about the jersey was playful and a bit cheeky. But it was still very much the truth.

"Do you really not understand that I'm wearing this for you?"

He blinks, his focus shifting so he's side-eyeing me before his attention snaps back to the action on the field.

"I did not. I assumed the jersey was just a way to piss off Decker."

"Fringe benefit," I admit with a shrug. "But I thought you'd be into this. After everything that's happened this week..." I trail off and drop my chin, suddenly filled with doubt.

"You're serious? This isn't about him?" In my periphery, he's watching me, searching my profile. This time, I'm the one focused on the field, embarrassingly avoiding his gaze.

Finally, I shift on the bench and face him. "No Cap," I assure him with a smirk.

Literally. Figuratively. In all the ways.

His grin is so wide, it lifts his glasses, and that single dimple appears.

The refs and players circle up for the coin toss.

"No Cap," Kylian repeats, tongue in cheek, his attention laser-focused on what's happening on the field once more.

I'm so caught up in watching him watch the start of the game that I jump when his arm circles my low back. But I don't fight him when he pulls me as close as possible to him without disturbing his setup. I startle again when he brushes his fingertips along my leg, leaving goose bumps on my skin despite the heat of the sun radiating down on us.

"You look really fucking hot in my jersey," he murmurs with a quick squeeze of my thigh.

The Crusaders win the coin toss. And the game begins.

Chapter 31

Josephine

Professor Hinkley has been droning on for so long it's possible that at any moment, he'll pass out from not taking a breath. I chose this course because it fulfills my gen ed requirement for math, and Logic 200 sounded more appealing than pre-calc. Based on the makeup of the class, I wasn't alone in that thought.

Hunter is dutifully taking notes since the class counts toward her prelaw major. I catch her eye as Professor Hinkley turns from the whiteboard and regales us with the story of how he won *Wheel of Fortune* in the early '90s.

She hides her smirk behind her hand, then shields her face from view completely when I give her a look.

We aren't the only two not paying attention.

"She's Crusade's girl. Swear it. I saw her get out of his G in the parking lot this morning."

I stiffen and side-eye Hunter. The scowl on her face tells me she heard them, too.

"Nah, I heard she's dating the nerd. What's his name? Kevin?"

I whip my head around and shoot daggers at the two asshats running their faceholes. Jocks, from the look of it, but obviously not football players. Because they wouldn't dare.

"Really?" I deadpan.

The guy with the shaved head nudges his buddy while smirking and maintaining eye contact with me. "I heard she's hooking up with all of them."

"Oh, hell no..." Hunter hisses, spinning around in her seat.

She scoffs when she sees who's behind us.

"Figures," she whispers dismissively. "You two just love to run your mouths, don't you?"

I glance over at my friend while trying to make it look like I'm still listening to Hinkley as he writes out the *Wheel of Fortune* categories with a streaky, dried-out marker.

"You know them?" I ask under my breath.

"Unfortunately," Hunter quips, not so quietly.

"Brody and Warren," she tells me, throwing another glare over her shoulder at the meatheads. "Club rugby players. Because they didn't make the LCU football team." She bares her teeth and offers them a saccharine smile.

"You're lucky we know better than to mess with Greedy's sister," the other guy growls.

Hunter rolls her eyes. "He's not my brother. And even if he was, do you really think he's the one you should be concerned with? You're sitting back there talking shit about my friend who got a ride to campus with Crusade. Wake up, ding-dong, or Decker and his boys will catch you by surprise."

"Excuse me!"

My attention snaps to the front of the room again, where Professor Hinkley is scowling, his hands turned up in outrage. Or at least as much outrage as a professor in his midfifties can muster while talking about a game show. "Do you four have more important things to do than earn credit for today's class?"

I press my lips together and shake my head. Hunter doesn't make a peep, either. One of the dummies behind us says something under his breath about game shows, but I doubt it reaches the front of the room.

"As I was saying..." Hinkley turns back around, focused on the course material again as he writes out definitions for sentential and predicate logic.

Two minutes pass, then Hunter is sliding a folded-up piece of paper across my desk.

I bite back a smile. She could have easily texted me. Or waited four more minutes for class to end.

I unfold the grid paper and scan her note.

Okay... but seriously. Select all that apply.

Check boxes are drawn out below her pretty handwriting, with names next to each box.

Locke

Kylian

Kendrick

Decker

I examine the paper, then peek over at my friend. She's watching me out of the corner of her eye and biting on the end of her pen.

Glancing back to ensure the rugby players are focused elsewhere, I fill in the note.

A question mark for Locke. A checkmark for Kylian. An *X* for Kendrick. And several deep, dark lines striking out Crusade's name. I refold the note, pass it back, and watch her face as she opens it.

With her tongue in her cheek, she quirks one eyebrow at me.

"*Never* Crusade," I mouth, inspiring a silent snort that she covers with her hand.

A minute later, we're all packing up. I hold back, not interested in bumping into the rugby players in the hall and having to continue that conversation.

"Let's get going before one of your *boyfriends* catches us," Hunter teases as she scoots to the end of the aisle. "We have places to be and cereal to buy."

I shush her as she practically skips down the wide steps of the lecture hall.

Chapter 32

Josephine

Of all the ideas I came up with to get back at Decker for the parent stunt, this one was the cheapest and easiest to execute.

Hunter and I were in and out of the grocery store so fast I wasn't even late to meet up with Kylian in the parking lot of the marina. And just like I suspected, he didn't ask what was in the extra bags I was hauling.

I'm in the lake now—actually in the water for the first time after weeks of being surrounded by it—floating on my back with my limbs stretched out as far as they can reach.

"Josephine!"

I grin so wide my eyes water at the way he bellows my name.

My ears are submerged, but even with the water muffling the sound, I'm certain he's still up toward the house, most likely on the upper deck. From that angle, he can very clearly see me where I'm floating. It's only a matter of time...

The only flaw in my plan was that I wasn't in the room to see his reaction when he realized that I'd replaced all his beloved almonds with sugary cereal.

And not just any cereal.

Cap'n Crunch.

The water ripples around me as he stomps down the dock. A larger-than-life shadow casts my world into darkness as he looms over the edge of the lake, blocking out the late afternoon sun.

Peeking one eye open, I keep my face placid as I catch my first glimpse of a furious Decker Crusade.

His deep scowl leaves him almost unrecognizable. He looks... villainous. It's kind of hot, actually, the way the sun is projecting a halo of hazy light around him as he fumes so intensely I half expect smoke to billow out of his ears.

After several seconds of silence, he finally speaks.

"Josephine. Where are my nuts?"

Done. Gone. There's no hope for me now.

I burst out laughing. The hilarity of his words juxtaposed against the seriousness of his tone sends me into a fit of giggles that threatens to pull me under. Literally. I have to fight to stay above water.

"You think you're funny?" he demands, pacing the edge of the dock as he fists the ends of his hair.

I can't. I just can't. I right myself and tread, because if I keep trying to float while laughing this hard, I'll surely drown. I had a whole sassy remark locked and loaded about him being an almond daddy, but I thought I'd have to poke and prod to get a reaction out of him.

I never expected him to go *this* ballistic when I replaced all his almonds and trail mix with Cap'n Crunch.

I'm laughing so hard my stomach's starting to cramp when I look over and find him staring at me, standing stock still.

His jaw ticks incessantly, his fury so intense I swear he's vibrating with rage. The sight of him sends me into another fit of giggles.

I've officially lost it. I don't have a care in the whole damn world. After weeks of upheaval because of this man, I finally feel vindicated. And all it took was twenty dollars' worth of cereal and a stupid prank to level the playing field.

I swipe the tears out of my eyes, then drop back and starfish my arms and legs, floating on my back as I smile up into the sun.

"You can swim?"

Caught off guard by the question, I find my composure and turn toward him, then propel my body backward on instinct when a roguish glint twinkles in his eyes.

He doesn't bother waiting for an answer. Nor does he repeat himself. Instead, he lowers onto the end of the dock and slowly, methodically, unlaces his shoes.

His socks go next. Then he stands and does that ridiculous thing guys do where he grips the back of his T-shirt at the neck and whips it off in one fluid motion.

I'm transfixed. By the way his hands make quick work of folding his T-shirt. How his arm flexes when he fishes his cell phone out of his pocket and places it in his shoe.

Then his eyes find mine. Bottomless onyx lagoons. Infinite black holes with the power to consume entire galaxies.

He straightens and smirks. Finally, he lifts his hands over his head and dives in.

I was so distracted watching him I don't have time to swim away.

He breaches the surface inches in front of me, his bare chest so close it brushes against my breasts with each inhale.

I hold my breath, expecting him to pull back the second he realizes that we're practically sharing oxygen.

But instead of pulling away, he reaches out under the water and drags me *closer*.

An ironclad grip encases my hips, squeezing so hard it's almost painful. The crackle of a firework zaps through me, each one of his fingertips a sparkler ablaze.

If I wasn't submerged in water, I swear this man would be burning me up from the inside.

I want to burn with him.

The thought doesn't even fully register before he's lowering his face toward mine, droplets of water cascading off his hair and sprinkling my face.

A single drop lands on my lower lip.

Without my permission, my tongue darts out to sweep it away.

His eyes track the movement, going molten.

And in that moment, I know I'm not the only one under a spell.

I bite my bottom lip, and he growls in warning.

One hand leaves my waist, and the next thing I know, he's gripping my chin and plucking my lip free from between my teeth.

We're both treading. Panting. Our bodies boldly brushing against each other again as he watches me with a fire that tells me he wants to set me ablaze as badly as I want to burn for him.

Shaking his head and thumbing my bottom lip, he positions himself close enough to whisper in my ear. It takes every ounce of restraint I possess not to wrap my legs around him.

"You. Are. Infuriating," he snarls. "Everything you do is designed specifically to piss me off. I do not have the strength to fight you day in and day out. Stop *testing* me, Josephine."

Arching out of his grasp, I narrow my eyes and defiantly bite my lip again.

"And if I don't? What then, Cap? You'll lock me up and never let me go?"

Strong hands find my bare stomach and grip me tighter. He pulls me so close I can't tread water.

So I stop trying.

I let go.

I wind my arms around his neck as he wraps his around my low back.

Our bodies dance together in the water, slick and wet, warm and fluid. His grip is tight and unyielding. I wouldn't want it any other way.

Between strong legs, his rigid length taunts me. Unmistakable evidence that though he may hate me, he most certainly wants me.

More than once, his erection presses into the apex of my thighs—a blissful tease that's there one second, then gone the next. I roll my hips, chasing the pressure. Searching for it again. Needing more of him.

We're a jumble of limbs, two halves coming together, clinging so tightly that if either of us stops moving, we'll both go under.

Blinking away the water accumulating on the ends of my eyelashes, I scrutinize Decker. His face is backlit by the setting sun. I loathe to admit it, but he's beautiful. Sharp angles. Masculine features. Eyes so dark it's hard to distinguish between the pupil and the iris.

Between the ego and the man, he's an anomaly.

Stereotypical in so many ways. The alpha male. QB1. Leader of the pack. Envy of his peers.

But then he has these moments...

When he's deferring to Kylian, trusting him to take the lead.

When he's checking in with Kendrick and Locke, asking about their pain levels.

When he's sharing his bed and rubbing my neck, soothing me to sleep.

And now. Holding me so close I swear he might not ever let me go. Peering into my eyes with an unmistakable heat he doesn't bother to hide.

Until he catches himself, that is.

"Fuck," he groans. He puffs out his cheeks and shakes his head, releasing us both from the reverie of this uncharacteristically intimate moment. Once more, he squeezes—his grip so tight on my ass I'm certain I'll have bruises tomorrow—then he pushes away from me in a jerky movement that partially pulls me under.

Resurfacing, I sputter to clear the water from my throat, disoriented and confused. His arms rise out of the lake in broad strokes as he swims toward the dock.

I watch him push up and out of the water but look away before he can turn around and catch me staring.

Toweling off his face with his shirt, he calls out to me in his typical bossy tone.

"Family dinner's in less than an hour. You better get washed up."

And then he takes off toward the house, more tension radiating off him than there is water rolling off his back.

I tread, dumbfounded, and watch him retreat back into himself and the enormous fortress he calls home.

I make a mad dash into the house and back to my room. Mostly because I don't want to run into Decker. But also because I don't want to be the last one to the table for family dinner.

I almost slip on the polished wood floors as I circle the island in the kitchen. Mrs. Lansbury is digging through the fridge, and Locke has his back to me, stirring something in a pot on the stove. I almost make it past them unseen.

Almost.

"Hot Girl. Come try this." He holds up a wooden spoon with what looks like a cream sauce clinging to it. The kitchen smells divine. I honestly would stop and be his taste tester if I had more time. Instead, I shoot him an apologetic look and continue my mission.

"Sorry, Emo Boy. I've got to shower before dinner. It smells great, though!"

I take the stairs two at a time, droplets of water cascading down my body and leaving a trail in my wake. I'm moving so fast I don't see Kylian until his arms dart out to steady me.

"Jo. Whoa. You're all wet."

"I know. Gotta shower," I pant.

"Are you okay? I heard Decker shouting." He skims my bare arms with both hands and cups my face like I'm the most precious thing in the world.

My heart skips a beat at his concern.

"All good," I assure him, slipping out of his grasp and hauling ass up the last few stairs to the second-floor landing. Over my shoulder, I grin. "Save me a seat at dinner."

Kylian smiles, a soft, easy grin that has no right to inspire butterflies in the pit of my stomach the way it does. I've noticed he doesn't smile often, or at anyone else. It's like he's saving them all for me.

I'm in such a rush, high on Kylian's affection and still perplexed by Decker's behavior, that I'm not paying attention to where I'm going. It's not until I smack into a warm, wet, shirtless, scowling mass of muscle that I see him.

Kendrick.

Chapter 33

Kendrick

Whack.

I barely have time to put my hands up and brace myself before her wet, supple body slaps into mine.

This girl.

Not a girl. Fuck. Not by a long shot.

I wrap my hands around her upper arms and peel her off me.

"Ohio," I hiss through clenched teeth.

She's got me twisted in goddamned knots. She's changed the energy in the house, and she's sunk her tenterhooks into each of my brothers in different ways. Worst of all? Every time she's near, my dick jumps to attention and stands at half-mast, ready to fucking go.

Not. Happening.

"Shit. Fuck. Sorry," she stammers, raising a hand to her chest in surprise. As if I ran into her.

She's in my head.

She's in my way.

Despite myself, I track the movement of her hand. I'm momentarily mesmerized by the rise and fall of her tits in that tiny pink bikini.

The gall of this girl. Skipping up the steps without watching where she's going. Smacking into a 230-pound running back like she could bowl me over. She could have gotten hurt.

She's bad news. I've been telling Decker since day one.

She's weaseled her way in, and she's gotten far too comfortable in the house and with the guys. They don't see the calculations behind her eyes. They don't see her as the distraction she is, running around half-naked in the halls, making herself right at fucking home as she wraps each and every one of them around her finger.

I huff in frustration when she makes no move to get out of my way.

Extending my arms to put more space between us, I go right, and she follows, unintentionally stepping in my path. I shift to move around her, and her body mirrors mine. So fucking responsive.

"Shit, sorry, sorry..." she mumbles again, like she's agitated with herself for being in the way. Or at least putting on a decent enough show to make me *think* that's what she's doing.

Finally, I spin, moving around her, and make my way down the hall. "Dinner's in half an hour," I remind her as I jog down the first few stairs. "We have guests tonight. Put some goddamn clothes on."

I don't wait around for the indignant sass she fires back at me.

Football.

Family.

My girls.

The guys.

My priorities have always been straight.

Take care of my health. Focus on the game. Take care of my people.

There's no room in my life for anything else.

Especially not some manipulative hustler from out of state whose story is as murky as her intentions.

Not today, Ohio.

Not fucking ever.

Chapter 34

Josephine

After my literal run-in with Kendrick in the hall, I was tempted to show up to family dinner in a bathing suit. Or maybe my birthday suit.

The *gall* of that man.

But now that I see the guests, I'm glad my rational side took over, and I pulled on a pair of leggings and a LCU T-shirt instead.

I slipped into my seat just as Locke and Decker brought the food out onto the deck. I'm sitting between Kylian and Locke tonight, with Decker positioned at the head of the table. Kendrick is directly across from me, and on either side of him are the two guests I wouldn't have expected in a million years.

Emilia and Jade.

Emilia and Jade *Taylor*.

Kendrick's little sisters.

"She has more meatballs than me," the one on the right—Jade, I think—announces. She's eight, maybe nine years old, and I'm almost certain they're twins. They're dressed in matching skirts and polos, obviously a school uniform of some sort. Glittery purple beads adorn the end of Jade's braids. Emilia is rocking Crusaders red and white.

"Hush. I gave you both three meatballs. Eat those, and you can have more," Kendrick tells her.

He plated their food with ease and wordlessly moved Emilia's cup to the middle of the table when she almost tipped it over. It's clear he's used to caring for them.

I had no idea Kendrick could be anything but gruff and rude. But he's smiled more in the last ten minutes than in all the time I've spent with him over the last few weeks combined. It's mindboggling that I didn't even know these girls existed until tonight.

That's not the only thing that has me twisted. Despite my speed shower and the distance between us at the table, I swear Decker's hands must have left permanent imprints on me. I'm too in my own head to make eye contact with him, although I can feel his onyx gaze flit to me every now and then.

I'm still reeling from my run-in with Kendrick. There's no way I'll push my luck by asking questions or engaging with his sisters right now.

I sit quietly and eat my pasta, focused on twirling the long noodles and dragging them through the sauce on my plate.

"This is really good," I murmur to Locke, who acknowledges my comment with a smile.

"So, is anyone going to tell us why there's a *girl* here?"

I lift my head, surprised, and meet Emilia's assessing gaze.

"Yeah," Jade chimes in. "Uncle Ducky always says no girls allowed except us!"

Uncle. Ducky.

When I tear my attention from her and home in on Decker, he's already glaring. "Don't," he bites out, pointing his fork at me.

Uncle. Ducky!

I bite my tongue and stow the nickname away for future use, curious as to who'll answer the question and how they'll explain my presence. Especially since there's a no-girls-allowed rule that I wasn't privy to. Satisfaction sparks inside me at the idea that Decker broke his own rules for me. I guess even almond daddies have to make exceptions from time to time.

"That's Josephine," Decker says. "She's a friend of Kylian's. And Locke's."

He cocks one eyebrow at me, hinting at the nature of my relationship with each of the guys. I return the look head-on. I won't engage him. Not like this.

I haven't talked to Kylian about Locke, or vice versa. Until I figure out where things stand with Locke, it's unnecessary. I also refuse to participate in any sort of manipulation when it comes to sex. I'm not in a committed relationship with either of them, nor do I have anything to be ashamed of. Decker has no right implying otherwise.

Emilia accepts Decker's response, then turns to her brother.

"Why isn't she *your* friend, K?" She's laser-focused on him, with one elbow on the table and her chin propped up on her fist. This girl's too smart for her own good.

I fight back a grin, but as silent seconds tick by, I'm more and more compelled to speak up and answer the question Kendrick is ignoring.

"We're all friends here," I offer, smiling across the table in a way that I hope smooths things over. "And you can call me Joey," I add.

Jade beams back at me, but Emilia's assessment is less friendly. Her lips are pursed, and she's squinting as she takes me in.

"You can't *all* be friends," she counters. "Uncle Ducky only has five friends."

Locke snorts.

Kendrick mutters "just eat" under his breath.

But Emilia's not backing down.

"What?" she snaps at her brother. "That's what he always says! You, Nicky, Kylian, me, and Jade. Uncle Ducky's fab five."

I can't hold back my laughter. This is really not Decker's day.

An awkward silence falls over the table, once again encouraging me to speak up. Maybe I'm trying to overcompensate for the face-off with Decker in the lake, or maybe I'm anxious to make nice with Kendrick. Either way, I push past the trepidation and go for it.

"I guess I've always thought of friends like sprinkles."

"Sprinkles?" Kendrick challenges. His eyes meet mine, then he quickly looks away. Almost as if he let the question slip. Like he's embarrassed to have spoken to me at all.

"Yep." I pop the *P* and don a bright smile, silently daring him to shut me down in front of his sisters. "Have you ever had a cupcake or an ice cream sundae and thought 'oh, that's just too many sprinkles'?"

"Never," Jade replies emphatically.

"Exactly."

"I love sprinkles," Locke adds, side-eyeing me as he runs the tines of his fork against his bottom lip.

"You never order sprinkles," Kylian argues.

I press my lips together to stifle a smirk, but Locke reaches behind me and smacks his friend in the head.

"Trust me, bro. Me and sprinkles get along just fine."

"Oh. *Oh*. You're not talking about sugar confections, are you?"

"Anyway," I interject before Kylian can connect the dots in front of Kendrick's sisters, "what's everyone up to tonight?"

The guys all mutter some version of the same: staying in, going to bed early to rest up for tomorrow. When I ask the girls if they're going to the game, they wear matching smiles and explain that their aunt is taking them.

Jade, the little sweetheart, asks me about my evening plans, too. Unsure about how much detail to provide, I keep it simple. They don't need to know that in addition to crashing their family dinner, I'm also one of their brother's roommates. His unwilling, captive roommate.

"I thought I'd paint my nails. Maybe watch a movie and go to bed early, too."

It's Emilia who perks up this time. "You know how to do nails?"

"I do," I answer cautiously, certain I know where her line of questioning will lead. "Before I came to Lake Chapel, I worked at a salon. I went to cosmetology school when I lived in Ohio," I explain.

"I didn't know that," Locke murmurs, angling toward me, purposefully brushing my arm with his.

"I did," Kylian declares.

Cocking my head, I turn back to him, but he's focused on his phone, squinting at a jumble of numbers on the screen. I don't remember ever telling him about my previous job.

"If you're going to do your nails anyway, you could always paint ours, too." Emilia's delivery is cool and even. There isn't an ounce of hopefulness to her suggestion. God, that prickly exterior is so much like Kendrick's.

"I'd be happy to paint your nails. If you have time. And if it's okay with your brother, of course."

In a move I'm sure they've perfected over the years, both girls turn on Kendrick with wide eyes. A cacophony of *pleases* and *Can we? Can we?* tumble out of their mouths.

Kendrick looks like he's going to blow a gasket. The vein that runs along his temple is throbbing to its own rhythm, and his jaw is set in a way that has me concerned he'll crack a tooth. For the girls' sake, I hope he doesn't make this into a big deal. Eventually, he lifts a finger to his lips, hushing his sisters.

"I can bring my stuff downstairs and set up in the kitchen," I offer. I highly doubt he wants to leave the girls alone with me. Or be forced to hang out in my room.

He inspects me, his rich brown eyes assessing so long that I'm sure he's formulating a way to reject the idea.

But finally, he glances away and nods.

The girls erupt into cheers, then gush about what colors they want and can they have an accent nail and do I have any glitter polish. They clear the table without complaint, talking a mile a minute while I excuse myself to grab my manicure supplies.

"I'll be back in five minutes," I assure them as I head for the stairs.

"Okay, Jojo!" Jade enthusiastically calls back.

Gah. She's so sweet. I don't think I've ever been on the receiving end of such innocent, unabashed affection before.

I turn back to give her a smile, but she's already rinsing her plate at the sink. Beside her, Kendrick is supervising. His smile is soft—so different from any expression I've ever seen on his face. The tenderness radiating off him is beyond unexpected.

My heart catches in my throat as I secretly watch him watch them. Every child deserves to be looked at with that much love and adoration.

He may hate me for reasons unknown. He may relish the role of the moody bad guy in this house. But Kendrick Taylor can't fool anyone when these girls are in his orbit.

He turns, his focus shifting my way, so I scurry up the stairs before we can make eye contact. Before he realizes I see his true colors, and I know his secret: Kendrick may have a hard exterior, but he is more than capable of being soft and sweet when he wants to be.

Chapter 35
Josephine

I don't know that I'll ever get used to the magnitude of college football in the South. It's a home game this week, and the stadium is practically pulsing with energy at the start of the second half.

Lake Chapel is up, 24 to 7, and we start the third quarter with possession of the ball.

After meeting up with Hunter for halftime, I settle in next to Kylian on the bench. I'm not sure if the other guys know that I spend most of the game coming and going as I please. Kylian and I have an understanding, even if we haven't clearly defined it. Sort of like our relationship.

"Brought you a water," I offer, holding out the cold bottle I already cracked open for him. He accepts it without a word, never taking his eyes off the screens on his lap.

I love watching him work. There's a calmness that settles around him when he's in the zone during a game. He's so focused and intense.

I'm wearing my custom Walsh Crusaders jersey again today, but this time with my hair down. Thank god, too. Kylian's parents are here again, along with Locke's. Kendrick's sisters are also in the stands, sitting with their aunt.

At last week's game, Locke's foster mom asked if I'd share action shots I capture of him on the field. I spent an hour fiddling with the settings and watching YouTube tutorials this morning so I could figure out how to work the expensive camera I wear along with the media pass around my neck.

The camera is nice, and seriously expensive if my online investigation is accurate. I've got it set to sports mode for now. Eventually, I'll try to figure out the manual settings. But even with the most basic settings, the zoom is incredible.

The game is more vivid through the lens of the camera. Slower, somehow. The tension coiled in Kendrick's muscles as he gets in position is more obvious, and the confident set of Locke's jaw as he prepares to protect his QB is more crisp.

Then there's the man himself.

Decker radiates control, his poise and collectiveness evident even from the sidelines. His physical skills are impressive, but it's the way he commands the team that makes me lightheaded when I watch him for too long.

The tip of his chin. Directions spouted off in two- or three-word bursts.

I'm zooming in on his face when he falls back into position, baring his teeth as he bites down hard on his mouth guard.

Ouch. Apparently, I'm biting my own lip. And holding my breath. There's an intensity to witnessing the scene so closely. The Crusaders aren't playing like they're already up by two touchdowns. They're playing like a team that doesn't consider losing an option.

As the ball is snapped, I click the shutter, then try my best to track Decker's movements on the field. I catch a great shot of him with the football near his face, ready to launch. I focus on every shift and pivot, determined to capture the moment he sends the ball flying.

Everything happens at warp-speed when I zoom in.

The ball doesn't leave Decker's hand as he drops to the field. I follow with my lens, unsure of what's happening as he gets tackled to the ground.

The guy on the next bench over—an assistant coach's intern, maybe?—flies off the bench and screams something about a horse collar.

I watch, horrified, as Decker's body slams into the ground and bounces.

My focus remains locked on the zoomed-in lens, but in my periphery, Kylian's head snaps up. He observes the action on the field for all of two seconds before returning to his tablets.

"He was still in the pocket. They won't call it," he responds so quietly I doubt the intern hears him.

I don't look away from Decker, and he doesn't move for a beat, then another.

Locke jogs up and offers him a hand, so I start clicking away again. I bet Brenda would love a few shots of the guys together on the field.

But as I shoot, I notice the hesitancy in Decker's reaction. He's slow to rise, then loose-limbed and floppy when Locke pulls him to his feet.

Zooming in farther, I gasp but still take the shot.

"What is it?" Kylian murmurs without looking up.

I don't respond right away, because I'm not completely confident in what I think I saw.

Peering down at the camera, I pull up the preview of the picture on the tiny screen.

Shit.

Decker's eyes were unfocused and pointed in different directions when he finally got to his feet.

"It's Decker," I finally tell Kylian. "He looked funny when he got up. I think he might be hurt."

Kylian searches the field, homing in on Decker and rising to his feet. He stands there, watching, but there's nothing to see anymore. Both teams are already lining up for the next play. It's like nothing happened, and yet...

"You're sure?"

"Positive. Here. I can show you..." I stand up and lift the camera, but Kylian just shakes his head.

"I believe you."

He speaks quietly into his headset, then a whistle blows on the field.

"Did you just—"

"Time-out!"

The players jog off the field, and Decker doesn't look any worse for wear. Sweaty and breathless, yes, but his eyes are fine now, and he's keeping up with the other players.

Maybe I overreacted?

Locke and Kendrick make their way over to us while one of the coaches pulls Decker aside.

Kylian hands Kendrick one of his devices, and Kendrick immediately starts scrolling.

Locke squirts water into his mouth, jutting his chin in acknowledgment toward Kylian. "Cap said you told coach to call it. What's up?"

"Jo thought she saw something happen when Decker got sacked."

"The fuck?" Kendrick's head snaps up, his hard gaze darting first to Kylian, then over to glare at me. "We stopped the drive because Ohio thinks she knows the first fucking thing about football now that she's been to three games?"

"When Decker got hit—"

I swallow my words mid-sentence and jump as Kendrick lunges forward and gets in my face.

"You don't know shit," he spits out. "First my family. Now football? You keep digging your manipulative claws into my world, and you and I are going to have a real fucking problem, Jojo."

He snarls, sweat dripping down his face as he fists his helmet. And with a shove of the iPad in Kylian's direction, he storms off.

I close my eyes in disbelief.

"Shit. Joey..."

"It's fine," I insist. When I open my eyes, both Locke and Kylian are staring at me wide-eyed, so I drop my chin, avoiding their scrutiny.

Maybe I should have showed Kendrick the pictures. I know what I saw, even if it isn't as bad as I originally thought. But clearly, there's no such thing as "better safe than sorry" when it comes to Kendrick's attitude and this team.

"He's intense during games. He's just—"

Before Locke can continue, I hold up my hands. I won't fall apart because of some hotheaded egomaniac. I've dealt with far worse than the likes of Kendrick Taylor.

"It's *fine.* I'm not just saying that. I'm good. Focus on the game. But please keep an eye on Decker. He really didn't look okay for a few seconds there."

Locke nods, and the refs alert the team that play needs to resume.

Kylian and I sit back on the bench. I don't pick up the camera again.

Chapter 36

Josephine

The party is in full force by the time we get back to the house.

The Crusaders won, securing their record of 3-0 for the season.

Kylian grasps the handle of the sliding glass door but pauses to look back at me before opening it.

I'm learning his quirks and picking up on his tells. He is so focused and on-point during football games. Then afterward, he crashes. Hard.

Right now, his jaw is set, and his eyes are a little glassy. He does an excellent job of keeping it together until we get home. To most, he probably just looks tired. But I see the way he reacts slower and really has to process each word spoken to him in this state. Almost as if he has to work to remember how to carry on a conversation before he can engage.

He's looking me in the eye, but his expression is blank. I can't get a read on him for the life of me. It's nothing personal. This is just how he gets. He needs rest. Quiet. Solitude. The exact opposite of what happens every week after a home game.

"Why does Decker insist on hosting a party every damn weekend when you're clearly exhausted after the games?" I blurt out.

His brows furrow as he considers my question. A few beats pass, then his eyes narrow like he's trying to work something out.

Great. Now I'm the asshole for forcing a conversation that's obviously requiring a concerted amount of effort on his part.

"Forget it," I huff, blowing out a long breath.

Kylian catches my hand in his, tracing my knuckles with the pad of his thumb. "You worried about me, Jo?"

I am. And I'm annoyed that Decker and Kendrick need to surround themselves with superfans and cheerleaders to boost their egos after a game at the expense of their friend.

Without waiting for a response, he tugs me a little closer. "I live in a literal mansion. I have a private room that my best friend paid to have soundproofed. He went as far as to install a floating floor in the Nest. I'm an integral part of a championship team. I already have job offers from four different professional clubs. Believe me when I say that I'm good. I have everything I need right here." He squeezes my hand in a way that makes me wonder if he considers me as one of those things. "Including my brothers," he adds.

Yep. I'm definitely an asshole. I hadn't considered that Decker or any of the guys went to such great lengths to accommodate Kylian. Silly, really, because it's on-brand for the broody asshole to go out of his way to take care of his friends.

"Are you coming up tonight?" Kylian asks.

Part of me wants to. Really, really wants to. But his eyes are weary and bloodshot. And I know him well enough now to know he won't truly let himself rest if I'm in his space.

Shaking my head, I give him a soft smile. "Not tonight. You're exhausted. Go rest. I'll see you at breakfast?"

He nods and leans in to kiss me quickly, murmuring "good night," against my lips. Then he heads inside and takes off like a shot toward the stairs.

I don't bother trying to keep up. He's desperate to wind down, and I want him to have that tonight.

Slowly, I close the sliding glass door, then take in the scene in the living room, scanning each face, many of which I recognize. Football players. Superfans. Even Dr. Hinkley's TA on the dance floor. *Yikes*.

I'm halfway to the kitchen before I admit to myself that I'm looking for Decker.

Part of me wants to see if Kendrick already got to him. Does Decker know what happened? Does he share Kendrick's outrage over my interference?

More importantly, though, I need to make sure he's really okay.

I stick my head out the door and peek around the upper deck where we had dinner last night. This is where I found him holding court at the last party.

A quick scan confirms Decker's not out here. But his groupies are.

Three girls—a blonde, a redhead, and a brunette—perch on the sides of one of the cushioned love seats, waiting for their king to take his throne. I snort at the absurdity of it and turn on my heel, ready to retreat to the kitchen, but freeze at the shrill voice cutting through the humid air.

"Excuse me. Miss? Miss?"

I pop back outside and lock eyes with a cheerleader sitting snugly in Kendrick's lap.

Ugh. I didn't even notice him out here a moment ago.

"Oh good. Hi," she singsongs, examining me from head to toe and squirming on the big guy's thigh. "Can you bring me another vodka seltzer? Peach, if you've got it." She holds up the empty can in her hand and shakes it.

Kendrick chuckles, the rumble in his chest deep and cruel, as he smooths a hand over her thigh.

I wait a beat, then another. Until it's obvious he's not going to correct his little girlfriend.

"I'm not a server," I snap, cocking one hip and scowling.

"Oh. Huh. I thought I saw you here before..."

I open my mouth to tell her exactly why she's seen me around the mansion before, but before I can, Kendrick jumps to his feet, cutting me off. Hmm. He must not want his superfan to know that he and I are actually roomies.

"Come on, baby girl. Let's go see if the hot tub's occupied."

I jump out of the way so they can pass. I didn't even know this place had a hot tub.

"Um, excuse me?" The redhead still stationed on the love seat has the audacity to jump in next.

"Get your own drinks," I snark, moving a step closer and crossing my arms under my breasts. I'm over this mean-girl shit.

She picks at her nail polish and has the decency to look bashful. "No, no. That's not what I was going to say. Ignore Angelica. I know you're not a server. But I have seen you here before, haven't I? With the guys?"

I stare at her, deadpan, scrambling to get ahead of whatever trap she's setting.

"Your point?" I ask to buy myself some time.

"Um, well..."

Seriously. What's this girl's problem?

"I was just wondering if you've seen Decker." She looks up at me with wide puppy dog eyes and bats her lashes. Her uncertainty finally makes sense. She's wondering where her boy toy's gotten off to, and she's also trying to figure out if I'm a threat.

Noted.

"I haven't," I answer honestly, dread churning faster in my gut at the reminder. "Sorry."

With that, I head back into the house and continue my quest to track down Decker Crusade.

"Hot Girl!" Locke comes at me from behind, wrapping me in a bear hug and lifting me off my feet. "We won!"

His scent envelops me—sugar cane and mint; sweet, fresh, and perfectly him—delivering a heady rush that inspires tingles through my whole body.

"You always win," I laugh, swatting at his arms until he sets me down. Every eye in the kitchen is on us. I can only imagine the questions. None of which I want to address tonight.

Locke obviously doesn't share my sentiment.

Ducking to lower his lips to my ear, he winds one big hand into the hair at the back of my head.

"Maybe we should celebrate," he whispers with a smile against the crook of my neck. "I bet the pantry's available."

He nips at my earlobe, and I shiver, despite the arousal stoking warmth in my belly. I lean back against his broad chest, glancing up to follow the lines of his neck piece.

I love the way he purrs and holds me tighter when I run my nails down his forearms. And after all the highs and lows of this week, plus that run-in with Kendrick on the sidelines? I could use a little stress relief in the form of Emo Boy–delivered orgasms.

But then one of the many team cheers is chanted by the crowd throughout the house. And my thoughts ping back to Decker.

Pushing up on tiptoes so my lips graze his jaw, I murmur "raincheck?" then swivel my hips against him in a tantalizing promise. "Maybe we could hang out and watch a movie this week?"

"Hell yeah. You're serious?" he asks, his eyes bright.

"Yeah, I want to hang out," I answer with a smile, "but I need to take care of something right now."

Reluctantly, I spin out of his arms, giving him a quick glance over my shoulder as I retreat from the kitchen.

At the bottom of the stairs, I pass the sentries standing guard on either side of their ridiculous velvet rope. The one on the right—Corbin, I think—offers a nod of recognition. At least I won't have to fight my way up to my own room tonight.

I bypass the living room, where the same DJ who's here every week has the whole place bumping and grinding. There are so many bodies smashed together on the makeshift dance floor, it's impossible to figure out who's dancing with whom.

I don't think I've ever seen Decker dancing at one of these parties, so I give the crowd a cursory once-over.

The media room and the gym are unoccupied. I call out in the garage, but it's empty aside from jet skis and sports equipment. I double check the pantry just to be sure—although wouldn't that be the irony of all ironies if I found him in there? Finally, I come to the only place on the main level I haven't checked: the master suite.

I knock quietly, unsure of what I'm doing or why. Decker finished the game. The Crusaders won. And not a soul has mentioned any cause for concern.

But I know what I saw. And there's this nagging in my gut that insists I check up on him.

There's a special flavor of dread to being sure but having absolutely no way to prove or disprove the notion. It's the antithesis of belief.

To believe someone or something makes it so. On the contrary, disbelief has the power to dispel people, places, or things from existence. Authority, influence, and control all exist in the realm of belief—of power. It's the elusiveness of instinct that makes it so disconcerting.

If instinct nudges a disbelieving person toward the truth, the reaction is one of regret. If instinct misdirects, there's a sense of betrayal.

Right or wrong. Truth or fiction. Instinct is rarely a welcome reflex.

Unless it's a game of Clue, exclaiming "I knew it!" doesn't do anyone any good, because confirmation doesn't come until it's too late.

A sense of urgency washes over me when I knock again and get no answer.

Pushing into the room, I call out his name. "Hey, Decker? Are you in here? It's Josephine."

I'm greeted by darkness. Darkness and silence.

Defeated, I turn on my heel and pull the door shut.

But then I hear it. A guttural, painful groan.

Chapter 37

Josephine

"I'm fine," he insists again, head still hanging in the toilet.

"You're very clearly not," I whisper.

He winces at the sound anyway.

"I'm sorry," I say, softer still. "But I really think—"

"Shh," he hushes me, whether because his head is pounding or because he doesn't want to hear it, I'm not sure.

"Decker. Please. You need help."

"No."

"Decker..." I don't know why I'm pleading with him, or why I even care. Maybe I feel a strange sort of responsibility, considering I'm the only person who knows what's going on.

But I won't be the only one for long if he keeps this up. I'm not above texting Locke or even Kendrick to come help me, and I know they'll insist we take him to a hospital.

I've been huddled near the toilet in Decker's palatial black and gold bathroom for almost an hour. My legs are tingly from the loss of circulation, but I'm not concerned about anything but the man beside me right now. I have no idea how long he was in here before I showed up.

From what I've gotten out of him so far, he felt off after the hit (his word choice) but recovered quickly and was fine after the time-out.

The nausea hit on the boat ride home. Sensitivity to light and sound followed.

I know firsthand the unnerving agitation that accompanies a concussion, even a minor one. The battle of wills between us would be daunting without the crankiness brought on by the injury. But with it? I feel like I'm wading through a master class in patience as I try to convince an agitated, restless, uncoordinated Decker Crusade to seek medical attention.

"Fuck." And with that, another wave of vomit hits the toilet bowl. He groans again, likely because of the way the action makes his head pound.

I'm desperate for a way to comfort him and to force him to face the reality of the situation. Because regardless of his stubbornness, he needs medical attention.

"You're okay," I murmur, cuffing the back of his neck with my hand.

He startles on contact but relaxes when I rub back and forth.

Back and forth. Over and over. As if my desire to ease his pain could have any real effect on his symptoms. Desperation is setting in now, and I'm toeing the line between respecting his wishes and doing what's best for *him*, regardless of the resentment he'll hit me with for undermining his authority and autonomy.

I have to get through to him. I will him to hear the sincerity in my words; to be soothed by my touch.

"You're okay. It's going to be okay."

Changing tactics, I continue massaging his head and ask, "What would have to happen for you to go to the hospital and get checked out?"

When he doesn't immediately lash out at the question, I push further.

"You've puked three times so far. You're dizzy and you feel weak, right?"

"I'm always exhausted after a game," he interjects, then grimaces as if just stringing words into a coherent sentence caused him physical pain.

"Do you think this might be a little more than exhaustion?"

He's quiet. So quiet for so long that I wonder if he dozed off.

"No one can know. *Fuck*. No one can know, Josephine."

Thank god.

"I understand," I assure him.

"You don't," he argues, his voice distant and tinny because his head's still half inside the toilet bowl. "We can't go to any of the hospitals in North Carolina. Or South Carolina, for that matter. We'll have to go out of state. Knoxville would be safe. Or Bristol."

"We can do that," I agree, even if I'm unsure of who he wants included in the *we* or why we need to travel out of state. I'm so relieved he's willing to get help, I'd probably agree to anything he says right now.

I sit up straighter, then pull out my phone to text the guys. "I think Locke's been drinking, but I can text Kendrick? Or I can go up to the Nest and get Kylian."

His hand shoots out and latches around my wrist.

"What part of *no one can know* don't you understand, Josephine?"

Wide-eyed, I jerk my arm out of his hold.

"I—I didn't think you meant the guys," I stammer. "Don't you trust them?"

He huffs in frustration, closing his eyes and wincing. "Of course I trust them. But we've got a house full of people, all with cameras in their pockets. There's no way to get to them without risking someone overhearing or getting a peek at a text message."

Pressing the heels of his palms into his eyes, he rises to his knees but keeps his head bowed.

I'm so out of my depth here. He needs help, yet he doesn't want me to get anyone to help him. He's willing to get checked out, but only at an out-of-state hospital. I'm at a loss about how to proceed, so I go back to rubbing his neck.

After a few minutes, I push my luck, hopeful he'll let me find Kendrick.

"Any chance you're being a little paranoid, Cap? Or could this be the potential concussion talking?"

Decker turns his head to look me in the eye. His pupils are so dilated it's comical.

"You don't understand. You have no fucking idea." He groans, then locks his jaw and inhales deeply through his nose, either fighting back another wave of nausea or catching his breath.

Before I can press him to explain, he continues.

"They're everywhere. All the time. They're always watching me. Waiting. They don't give a shit about privacy. Only looking to make a quick buck. I've lived this life for too long to luxuriate in the hope that I could go to a local hospital or send a text to my coaches without having to read stories about myself online tomorrow."

Well, shit. I'd love to brush off his concern and attribute his paranoia to his ego, but the defeat in his voice and the exhaustion in his eyes affirm the truth. Plus, I've seen the evidence firsthand in my own Internet searches.

"Did it hurt your brain just now to use 'luxuriate' in a sentence?" I jibe.

He attempts a smile, shifting closer to me as I continue to rub his neck.

"That feels good," he admits with a sigh.

Decidedly, I suggest a new plan. "What if we sneak out your patio door and stay close to the house until we get to the dock? I could text the ferry guys from your phone and tell them to clear the beach for half an hour. Then we'll have one of them take us over to the marina."

He nods, ever so slowly, as the muscles in his neck strain against my palm.

"That could work. You'll have to drive my G," he hedges.

Shrugging, I hop to my feet and hold out a hand. "Meh. It's probably not as smooth as my Civic, but I'll manage."

Decker snorts. I would be pleased with myself for making him laugh if his reaction wasn't immediately followed by a sharp wince. He accepts my hand and rises slowly to his feet.

"I want to grab a hat. Sunglasses, too. I need a few minutes to get cash out of my safe."

He peers down at me wearing a slight frown. It would be warranted for him to question why I'm so eager to help him. Honestly, I'm wondering the same damn thing.

"What do you need to do before we go?"

It feels like time is of the essence, and we're already wasting hours by driving out of state. If I venture all the way up to my room and back, there's no telling who'll see me or hold me up.

"If I can borrow a hoodie and use your bathroom, I can be ready in five minutes."

A flash of relief passes over Decker's expression. But then his Adam's apple bobs, and an awkwardness settles around us as the reality of the situation sinks in.

I'm offering to help Decker.

He's accepting that help.

Although he hasn't come out and said it, the trust he's putting in me in this moment is uncharacteristic and alarming.

Maybe it's the concussion.

Or maybe it's something more.

He squeezes my hand once, and I quickly pull away in surprise. I hadn't even realized we were still holding hands.

"Five minutes," he reminds me as he slinks out of the bathroom and pulls the door closed behind him.

Chapter 38

Josephine

When Decker checked in at the emergency room desk, he gave them a fake name: Nicholas Meyer. Maybe because he thinks he's funny, or maybe he just couldn't come up with anything more creative on the fly. He went on to claim that he had no health insurance but offered to pay the estimated cost of care up front, in cash.

I hovered by his side when we arrived, then settled into one of the plastic shell waiting room chairs when they took him back for a CT scan.

According to the Internet, CT brain scans take thirty to sixty minutes. Then there's waiting for the results and talking to the doctor. It's highly unlikely that they'll admit him, but Decker will be unavailable for at least a few hours.

The possibilities are endless.

I'm alone. Hours away from Lake Chapel. With access to a car and a pocketful of cash, since he left his keys, wallet, and Crusaders hat with me.

If there was ever a time to make a break for it, this is it.

My heart hammers in my chest as my brain buzzes with indecision. I've pulled up a dozen browser windows on my phone, ready to look up... well, everything. Where I could go. Places I could stay. The fuel efficiency of a G-Wagon. But I'm so flustered by this unexpected opportunity, I don't know where to focus.

What I do know is that this is my shot.

I could start over. *Again.*

I'm under no delusion that they couldn't find me. But it's possible that if I slip away quickly and quietly, Decker will decide I'm not worth chasing.

The risk might be worth it to get out from under his thumb. I could go deeper south. Or maybe toward the coast. I've never actually seen the ocean. There's at least two grand in cash still in Decker's wallet. The other guys don't even know we're gone.

The other guys.

That thought is what gives me pause. The men who might be hurt by my actions if I up and disappear without a trace.

They're like magnets, each holding me in place with a force I can't see or name.

Locke. He was so damn hopeful when he wrapped his arms around me earlier. And practically giddy when we made plans for later this week. Over the last few days, I've become more and more willing to let go of the grudge I've been holding. I just haven't had the chance to talk to him yet.

Then there's Kylian. I know he'll miss me if I'm not at breakfast in the morning. Will he come looking for me when I don't show up? Or will Decker tell him what happened first?

There would be no love lost from Kendrick. Hell, he'd probably help me get out and stay away if given the chance. The way he got up in my face during the game tonight... I physically shudder at the memory of his wrath.

Finally, the man himself. Decker Fucking Crusade. Thorn in my side. Dominating control freak. Captor extraordinaire. A week ago, I would have been chomping at the bit to get away from the almighty asshole.

Now? I don't know what's happening between us or how I'm supposed to feel.

He doesn't treat me like I'm the bane of his existence anymore. On the contrary. More than once in the last several days, the tension between us has sparked, trapping us in genuinely puzzling moments together.

Like tonight.

He let me help him. He let me *see* him. He trusted me to get him here, and he's trusting me to keep his secret safe.

Not that he had much choice in the matter.

But this experience—just like last weekend at the hotel or yesterday in the lake—is more significant than either of us expected it to be. We keep crashing together, the two of us. Finding ourselves in these intense, intimate micro moments. What should be blips in time. Except when I consider them together, they add up to so much more.

I don't know what's going on between Decker and me.

Just like I don't know how to classify my feelings for Locke or Kylian.

I'm playing a game I've never played before. If they ask me to choose, I don't know what'll become of me. I'm too attached. Too into both Kylian and Locke. Hell, maybe all three of them. And now, instead of the desperate nagging sensation urging me to get as far away from them all as possible, I'm worried *they* might leave *me*.

So many unknowns. More questions than answers.

What I do know is I won't get another opportunity like this. This is my chance to run. A narrow window that's been left open long enough for me to potentially make a clean break.

And yet I don't feel compelled to do it. I should run. But I don't want to. I should seize this moment. But I can't.

All I want is to make sure Decker is okay. That he gets home safe. That he gets the rest and care he needs so he can recover and get back on the field with his team.

So here I'll sit. Waiting for him. Worrying about him. Inhaling the heady combination of amber and sea salt that clings to the hoodie he let me borrow. Ready to help in any way I can once we know what we're dealing with.

When it's all said and done, I will get behind the wheel of his G-Wagon and drive the three hours back to Lake Chapel, get him tucked in, and wake up tomorrow in the Crusade Mansion.

Chapter 39

Decker

She didn't run.

Josephine didn't argue or make things harder than necessary when I explained all the extra hoops we had to jump through to get to a hospital where I wouldn't be recognized.

She was poise and grace. She knew just what to do, what to say, how to act.

She's been my rock for hours. Calm and steady. Comforting and kind.

Fuck.

She had the opportunity to make a clean break, and she's smart enough to know it. But she didn't run.

My prognosis is good. There was nothing of note on the CT scan. Tylenol, good nutrition and hydration, and rest are all I need.

Since I used an alias and didn't expound on the details of my injury, there was no mention of returning to practice. That'll be on me.

I have every intention of disclosing my health status to my coach. But only to my coach. Face to face. In the privacy of his office. And we'll go from there.

It's unconventional, but it's necessary, given the circumstances.

There are very few people in this world I can trust. Try as he might to keep things locked down, Kylian still hasn't been able to ensure our texts and emails are completely encrypted. More than once, information from a private conversation has been leaked to the media. Hell, pictures of the X-rays of my ankle found their way online when I was twelve. *Twelve.*

I stopped reacting to it years ago. After Mom, there's no fucking point. I'm not human in their eyes. There's no decency or concern for football protégés. Most people assume my life is charmed and easy, that I owe my fans and the general public their due. They have no problem taking their payment in private moments and personal information.

This week is a bye week—one of two this season—so although the situation is shitty, the timing couldn't be better.

I'm grateful for it. Almost as grateful as I am for her.

I peer over at where she's perched in the driver's seat, letting myself drink her in. Her beauty hit me full force the moment we met in the parking lot, but I haven't allowed myself the privilege of really seeing her until now.

Her hair is a warm halo of brown and cinnamon, loose down her back. She's still dolled up from the game, impossibly long lashes framing her gorgeous blue eyes, and her nails are a different color today: Crusaders red. I'm almost certain her custom Walsh jersey is under the hoodie I let her borrow.

Can't say it doesn't irk me every time I see my best friend's name across her back. But tonight, she's wearing something of mine, too. Something she asked for. A hoodie she's practically drowning in because it's so big.

My focus shifts to her legs, where her shorts are hidden by the hem of my sweatshirt. Those little white shorts make me feral. Every time I look over at the bench during a game, I'm distracted. In a sea of players, coaches, interns, trainers, and Kylian, there's Josephine. Long, tan legs crossed in front of her. Eyes set on the field, or sometimes on Kylian, as she takes it all in.

She must feel my eyes on her now, because she peeks over with a small smile that quickly morphs into concern.

"You okay? Do you need me to stop?" she offers.

Despite the pain that intensifies with every movement, I shake my head. I just want to get home. Get in my bed. Get her back to the mansion. Feel the sense of calm and ease that only comes when I know everyone I care about is warm, safe, and happy under my roof.

"Thank you," I grit out, clearing my throat when the words come out gravelly.

I close my eyes as the headlights of a semitruck going the opposite direction light up the night.

"For everything," I continue when the truck has passed. "For being cool about this. For helping me. For treating me with far more decency and respect than what I've shown you."

Her sharp intake of breath gives me pause.

She glances my way again, then quickly refocuses on the road. I didn't plan to recite a grand speech or make a big deal out of this, but now that I've started down this path, I need her to know just how much this means to me.

"Josephine, I—"

"Don't. Not tonight, Cap." She taps the brakes, slowing the SUV slightly. "Whatever you want to say, it'll keep. We're less than an hour from home. Just sit back and relax. You need rest."

Frustrated, I recline my seat even farther and blow out a big breath. I don't understand her dismissal. I don't understand a lot of things about this girl.

It's not worth arguing with her. Not tonight.

My thoughts are a jumbled mess anyway. I'm certain of how I feel—certain of what I want and what feels inevitable between us—but I don't know how to explain it. It's better she shut me down. She'd probably misconstrue my words as a side effect of the concussion.

Things have changed. I need her to believe me when I tell her my truth.

Admittedly, it's not just the concussion giving me pause. I have no idea whether she feels the way I do.

Or where things stand with her and Locke. Or her and Kylian.

Fuck.

I've done nothing but make her life harder since the day she showed up at LCU. She could loathe me for the rest of time, and I wouldn't blame her. I don't know how I can make things up to her. Or if it's even a possibility.

Ironically, the best way to repay her for tonight would be to trust her and to let her go.

Deep down, I do trust her. I can admit that to myself now.

I made a bad call, doubting her story and forcing her to live in the house. But I had to be sure.

She's earned my trust. She wouldn't intentionally hurt Locke or Kylian, although Kendrick may be a different story.

I should let her go. I don't know where she came from, and Kylian never did find information to threaten her with or hold over her head. But I realize now that I don't have to coerce her into keeping secrets. She's not a threat. She hasn't been planted here to hurt me. Even if she has turned my world upside down.

My own bullshit started this mess. Or I guess Kendrick's untrusting bullshit that triggered my paranoia.

I don't believe in coincidences or fate. The lack of dirt Kylian could dig up on her still bothers me.

And yet...

Over the last week, I've gone from worrying that she's a threat to concerned that she could be threatened because of her association with me.

That's a side effect of growing up in the spotlight—of losing one parent because of the fame of the other.

I'm selective about who I let get close. Most people can't hack it. And I don't have the strength to worry about how my life and my future will affect someone else. It's too great a burden to bear.

My boys are in it for the long haul. They've proven their loyalty over and over again. In exchange for their friendship, I do everything I can to provide for them and to make this life worth it.

Because we're in this for life. My brothers. My family. I'll never stop working to protect them from a fate like my mom's.

Is there room for Josephine among us? Is it worth the risk? And if so, where does she fit in?

I should let her go.

Should. Would, even, if I could.

Except tonight complicates things. By helping me, she earned my trust. But by helping me, she also burrowed herself deeper into the shitstorm that is my not-so-private life. Now that she knows about the concussion, the fate of my career and reputation are in her hands.

I'll admit I was wrong: Josephine Meyer wasn't a threat. But given what she experienced tonight and the way she's affected me and each of my brothers over the last few weeks, she's undoubtedly become one.

There's no way I can let her go.

Chapter 40

Locke

"I've never been in this room," Joey singsongs as she practically skips to the couch closest to the TV.

I fight against the urge to chase after her and wrangle her onto my lap.

The vibe between us has been tenuous at best since she moved in. Hot and cold. Tension and ease. But I haven't let that discourage me. I've been playing the long game—biding my time and allowing her to cool off, hoping that she'll eventually come around.

Thank god she has, because my patience has officially expired.

"What'll it be, Hot Girl? Do you have a movie in mind?"

She pops up over the back of the couch as I approach with measured strides. I'm not usually so reserved around women. I know what I like, and I'm not afraid to go after what I want.

But an overwhelming sense of caution tempers my impulses when it comes to Joey.

Probably because I know what it feels like to bask in her affection. She lights up my insides, and I swear she really sees me. On the flip side, I also know the bleakness of being out of her good graces and the pain that comes with having her ire directed at me.

Never. Again.

I'm determined to lock her down and make her mine. In any way she'll let me.

Cohabitation in a mostly platonic situationship for the last few weeks has proven one thing over and over again: I want her. And now I'm determined to do whatever it takes to make that happen.

"Let's watch something funny," she suggests, stretching her arms overhead in a move that puts her T-shirt-clad tits on full display.

She side-eyes me and winks, proving she knows exactly what she's doing. Little minx.

"Stupid funny, rom-com funny, or stoner funny?"

Her face screws up in the cutest way as lets out a hum. "My favorite movie is actually a combo of all three."

My heart rate ticks up a notch, and I prowl closer. "Are you kidding me right now?"

"No," she insists, wearing a puzzled frown as she follows my movements.

Snagging the remote, I plop down on the couch cushion beside her. Like I said: I know what I want, and I'm done waiting.

Without a second's hesitation, I pick up her hand and lace our fingers together. She squeezes in response, making me woozy with anticipation.

I grin. "I can only think of, like, four movies that encapsulate all three of those categories. And one of them just so happens to be *my* favorite movie."

She narrows her eyes and searches my face. "Did it come out in the mid-2000s?"

"Yep."

"Is it set in Hawaii?" she challenges, a smug look on her face like she's bested me.

I can't fight back my smirk.

"It is."

Her eyes practically double in size, and she gives me a slow blink. "You're kidding me. You're kidding, right?" In this moment, she's happier than I've ever seen her.

I love this side of her. I love that I can bring about this kind of reaction.

"There's no way we have the same favorite movie."

"What if we do?" I challenge.

She stares at the blank screen for a moment, contemplating, then shrugs. Turning toward me, she cuddles closer, leaning against my arm until I can smell the sweet floral scent of her shampoo.

Batting her lashes, she looks up at me with big doe eyes and declares, "Then I guess it means we're soul mates."

She's teasing me. I know that. But a little spark of hope still flares inside me, and I swear my heart feels like it's beating double time.

"Say the name of the movie on three," I instruct.

She nods, then we count together:

"One, two, three."

"*50 First Dates*."

"*Forgetting Sarah Marshall*."

"What?"

"Seriously?"

"No!"

Joey bursts into a fit of giggles. "Your favorite movie is *50 First Dates*? Are you serious?"

"It's an incredible story!" I defend.

She clutches her stomach and gasps for breath. "It's just like every other"—another laugh slips out—"Adam Sandler movie ever made!" She tosses her head back. "But set in a tropical location!"

"Um, no. It's a masterpiece. Cinematic perfection. It's funny. Clever. Romantic." I give her a pointed stare. "It's the best stupid stoner rom-com set in Hawaii. Full stop."

She sits up straight and takes a calming breath before turning to me.

"You know what this means, don't you?" she asks.

"We're going to have to watch them both to figure out the truly superior film?"

She shakes her head, looking forlorn. "We're not soul mates. In fact, this might make us mortal enemies."

I pull her until her thigh presses against my leg, just in case she gets any funny ideas about putting space between us. Not. Happening.

Tilting closer, I brush my nose against hers. "We're watching both. End of story." I hold her wrists in my hands and bite down on my lip, desperate to kiss her. We're still nose to nose, but a prickle of insecurity gives me pause.

She's the one who pumped the brakes. She's the one who pushed me away. As silly as it might seem, I want her to choose me. I want her to want me. I want *her* to kiss *me*.

And as if she can read my mind, she presses her lips to mine.

It's a soft, tender kiss. A sweet caress filled with forgiveness.

I pull on her wrists to bring her body closer, and she opens for me. Her lips part, and her tongue teases mine in a slow, sensual caress. I match her pace, absorbing it all, committing this moment to memory and savoring the feel of her in my arms again.

There's nothing hurried about it. Nothing rushed or hidden. Honestly, I think that's what I like most.

After a hot-as-fuck encounter in the pantry, then a massively bad misunderstanding, she's kissing me on the couch, out in the open for everyone to see.

It's a claiming. A claiming *she* initiated. And I fucking love it.

"Forgetful Joey... she's hotter than David Bowie."

Joey snorts, then smacks me in the arm and readjusts herself on my lap. Her hair's a tangled mess, her lips puffy from our make-out session. Sessions? We honestly haven't stopped kissing since the movie started.

"My turn," she declares, sitting up and straddling my lap.

She drapes her body around me and ghosts her lips along my neck.

"Forgetful Nicky... he really wants a hickey."

Before I can react, she latches on, biting hard and sucking the skin on my neck until my hips take control and buck from below her.

"You're trouble," I laugh, craning back ever so slightly in a feeble attempt to get away.

I don't care if she marks me. Hell, I welcome it. I'm already dreaming up a design to represent her somehow. Bite marks or the shape of her mouth would be so fucking hot inked into my skin.

"Speaking of trouble." She leans back with a salacious grin. "Do you have any weed? We could smoke before we watch Sarah Marshall."

With a low groan, I cuddle her closer. "You're like all my wet dreams come to life, Hot Girl." I bury my face in her tits, which are barely restrained by the thin bralette she revealed when she stripped off her T-shirt. "We have to raincheck the toke up, though. Just until football season is over."

Her brows shoot into her hairline, and she dismounts. After a quick readjustment of her top, she sits beside me instead.

"You'll use illegal injectables and have Kylian alter your drug tests for those, but you draw the line at marijuana?"

I shrug and offer up the truth. "I don't get peptide therapy to intentionally defy the rules or because I think I'm the exception. It honestly helps so much."

Her expression softens, and she takes my hand in hers. She doesn't lace our fingers together, but instead cradles it, tracing the ink and gently massaging each knuckle.

"How long have you had arthritis?"

Good question.

"I don't really know. Forever, I think? I don't remember ever not being in pain..."

I trail off and dip my chin. I'm not interested in getting into the sob story that is my early childhood. The words are true; there was always pain. Pain in my joints and limbs. Pain from the beatings. I sustained multiple injuries that went untreated for years. Bones that were never set. Ligaments and tendons that were probably torn. A holistic doctor once told me the trauma I suffered as a child caused my rheumatoid arthritis.

I don't completely buy into that theory. But it sure as fuck didn't help.

Realizing I'm in my own head, I offer her an apologetic smile.

"I've had it as far back as I can remember. Once I was placed with Gary and Brenda, things got better. It still took a while to figure out the combination of foods, exercise, medications, and therapies that worked best. I wouldn't always tell them when the pain was really bad," I admit. "I was worried that if they had to take me to too many appointments or if I complained too much, they would decide I wasn't worth it."

She doesn't push. She continues tracing my ink, sitting with the admission and letting me feel it. After a minute, she interlaces our fingers, then lifts our hands to kiss my knuckles.

"I don't know much about arthritis, so my questions might be annoying..."

"You're fine," I assure her.

"Is the pain constant? Or is it worse at certain times?"

"It's always there, but it definitely flares. Sometimes it's predictable—after a game, during a storm. Other times, it flares up for no damn reason. Those are the hardest."

"Yet you still play football."

It's not meant as an insult. It probably seems odd to someone who doesn't deal with chronic pain—that I'd willingly submit myself to an activity guaranteed to make things worse.

"There's power in choosing," I explain. "Putting my body through the wringer and leaving it all out on the field makes me feel alive. I'm gonna hurt either way. I might as well have fun doing it."

Her sharp inhale catches me off guard.

"I'm trying to do more of that," she whispers.

I survey our hands as I gently nudge her. "Of what? Leaving it all out on the field?"

She scoffs and side-eyes me, obviously aware that I'm teasing her. But then her expression softens, and she audibly swallows before answering, "Feeling alive."

She doesn't let her confession linger or leave space for me to follow up before directing the conversation back to me.

"I like that you're doing it on your terms and not letting the thing you love be ruined by an illness you can't control."

"Exactly."

She cuddles closer and nuzzles my arm. With one fingernail, she traces up and down my bicep in a featherlight trail that almost tickles.

"Does the same line of thinking apply to your tattoos?"I nod, pressing my lips together. I hadn't considered that before, but it makes sense.

"The process is a great distraction. It's hypnotic when the needle is buzzing against my skin and the pain on the outside matches the ache on the inside."

"So no weed until after the season," she repeats, her voice laced with understanding this time.

I'm reaching for her again when a noise from the doorway snags my attention.

"There you two are," Kylian declares, plopping down on the other side of Joey.

I huff out a little sigh of frustration. I knew I wouldn't be able to keep her to myself for long. Not this afternoon. Not ever.

"Nicky, can you—"

"Yeah, I got you," I assure him before he can even finish that thought. I reach for the remote and click on the subtitles.

"Hi, Jo," he murmurs, his voice so uncharacteristically not Kylian I have to hold back a snicker.

Damn. He's got it bad. We all do, in our own way, I guess.

I watch the pair of them as they exchange a silent greeting. It's intimate, but neither of them is trying to hide it from me.

Theoretically, this is bonkers.

But as I sit here with the girl of my dreams wedged between me and my childhood best friend, I'm surprisingly okay with it.

A few more seconds pass before Kylian stops making heart eyes at Joey and finally looks up at the screen.

"*Oh, 50 First Dates*. Good movie," he notes, placing his hand on Joey's thigh. "It's light-years behind *Forgetting Sarah Marshall* in terms of satire and campiness, of course, but not bad, as far as Hawaii-based stoner films go."

Joey stifles a laugh but reaches out to squeeze my hand. She doesn't pull away when I interlace our fingers and rest our joined hands on her other thigh.

Chapter 41

Josephine

I never expected to spend a Thursday afternoon surrounded by a sea of red and white in the middle of an athletic shoe store, but here we are.

When Decker asked me to accompany him to this event, I didn't hesitate. He's been a surprisingly compliant patient over the last few days.

He talked to his coach on Tuesday, and he'll have to pass a series of tests to work through the NCAA's concussion protocol starting tomorrow. He still has more than a week to fully recover since the Crusaders don't have a game this weekend.

Since it's a bye week, the guys have more NIL obligations than usual. Decker is the only one required to attend this one. It's some sort of exclusive VIP experience aimed at preteens who are eager to talk to him and have him sign everything from footballs to T-shirts to shoes.

Misty is here, flitting around with a clipboard and scolding kids who hold up the line with too many pictures. I guess that's part of her job, but she could stand to be a bit kinder to the kids whose parents no doubt shelled out big bucks to meet Decker Crusade.

Decker is on in a way he usually reserves for the field. He's charming and warm, taking time to ask each person's name. He always asks the kids what they like to do for fun. Not what sports they participate in or what position they play. There's blatant disregard for how into football a kid might be. If anything, he seems to give more attention to the shy, reserved kids who approach his table.

He's so good with all of them. It's surprising and legitimately heartwarming to watch.

I'm leaning against a display of toe shoes—so creepy—trying to fade into the background as I take it all in. The store is a madhouse, with a checkout line half as long as the queue to meet the man of the hour. Despite the chaotic energy and sheer volume of hundreds of parents and kids waiting for their turn, my attention is drawn back to Decker over and over again.

He's enigmatically good looking. It should be a crime to be that talented, wealthy, and naturally handsome. I'd almost describe him as pretty, if not for the hard set of his jaw. I could watch him for hours. His movements are fluid, and his smile, something it took weeks for me to get a glimpse of, now comes so easily. He's quick to laugh when interacting with the kids and totally at ease as he jokes around and slings a huge arm over their shoulders for the photo op.

I watch him for far longer than I should, captivated by the same magic that's put every other person here under his spell.

But as time goes on, he deflates. It's subtle at first. Just a hint of tension in his shoulders. Between groups, he stretches his neck from side to side. Eventually, his jaw ticks in an erratic rhythm, almost as if he can't control it.

It's loud in here. Loud and exceptionally bright thanks to the ring lights set up for the photo op. Concerned, I scan the store and take stock. The line is still out the door. But Decker looks like he could use a break.

Of course, Misty doesn't notice the change in his demeanor. As long as he's still sitting upright and forcing a smile, she likely doesn't care about how he feels.

Kylian was set to come with him today but got pulled into a coaching meeting this afternoon that went on for more than three hours. It may be a bye week for the players, but the coaches and support staff are in full-on planning mode.

Decker and I came to the same conclusion without discussion. Kylian was exhausted when he got home, and he needed time to unwind. Especially since there are even more parties and events to attend as Shore Week approaches.

I suggested Kylian stay behind. Decker asked me to tag along. We never discussed how this would go or what my role would actually be.

Decker doesn't need saving.

But that doesn't stop me from feeling compelled to help.

He's saying goodbye to an adorable freckle-faced kid missing his four front teeth when I slip around the back of the table and brush my hand along his shoulders.

Bending low, I whisper, "It looks like you could use a break. Want to go find somewhere dark and quiet to recharge for a bit?"

He turns, and onyx eyes meet mine. He gives me a skeptical frown, which I'm learning is his default reaction in most situations. From here, he looks even more wiped. The skin around his eyes is pulled tight, and his cheeks droop just a little. Eventually, he nods, exhaling in what I think is relief, before he turns back to assess the crowd.

"The line..." he mumbles, jutting his chin toward the dozens of families still waiting.

"Believe me, Cap. You look pained at this point. You won't like what you see in the pictures if you keep pushing it. They won't mind waiting a bit longer."

"Yeah, okay," he relents, rising to his feet and stretching his arms behind his back.

He waves, and Misty click-clacks across the store and comes to stand close enough that her arm brushes against his.

Taking a step back, he gives her a pointed look. "I'm going to get some air. I'll be back in twenty."

Panic flares behind her eyes. "You can't just walk out!" Her head snaps in my direction, and she hits me with a look full of accusation. She holds up a file and turns back to Decker. "We didn't negotiate breaks in the contract, and this is a sold-out event. What am I supposed to tell everyone?"

"Isn't that your job to figure out?" I quip. Honestly. It's not like he's asking her to cancel or leave early.

Decker nods once. "I'm not ditching out. I just need a break. You can handle this, Misty."

He looks toward the next family in line, who heard the entire exchange. With a pained smile, he holds up one finger. "I'll be back. I promise. Just need a little break."

They grin at him and nod like bobbleheads, obviously unbothered by having to wait a little while longer.

Decker steps out from behind the table and heads toward the back of the store. I follow, and once we've put some space between us and the crowd, he reaches back for my hand.

A thrill zings through me when he interlaces our fingers. I suck in a breath and remind myself that it doesn't mean anything. He's concussed and probably dizzy. He's just using me to steady himself.

I quicken my pace to take the lead, pushing through the back entrance. There are several doors along a narrow hallway, but the buzzing fluorescent lights are almost as intense here as they are out on the floor. The first door reveals a stock room. The next is an office. Then we come upon the equivalent of a janitor's closet.

"In here."

There are empty milk crates stacked against one wall. The distinct scent of lemon cleaner permeates the air. But at least it's quiet. And dark.

I procure a water bottle I stashed in my bag before we left the house, and Decker groans appreciatively as he accepts it.

He heaves out a breath, then plops onto a short stack of crates. With his eyes closed, he rests his skull against the wall and holds the cool water to his forehead.

Now that he's settled, I don't know what to do with myself, and I awkwardly adjust my weight from hip to hip and scan the contents of the closet. Tight spaces don't bother me, but there's barely enough room for Decker among all the stuff crammed in here. I should give him some room.

"How long do you think you need? Fifteen or twenty minutes?" My hand is already resting on the door handle as I wait for him to respond.

It's dark in here, but not so dark that I don't see when he opens his eyes and looks from my face to the door handle.

He reaches out, but I shift, evading his touch. Even so, he snags my free hand and slowly, surely, interlaces our fingers.

"Stay."

His Adam's apple bobs as he swallows. And a lump of uncertainty forms in the pit of my stomach. Confusion swirls with desire as I try to work out what this means.

He clears his throat, then repeats himself, as if he knows I'm doubting what I heard. "Stay with me, Josephine."

My head is swimming. Anxiety churns in my gut, and my whole being is off-kilter. Literally.

One second, my hand is pressing down on the door handle, and in the next, I'm stumbling farther into the closet.

Decker catches me as I trip over my own feet, and he doesn't let go.

Big hands smooth up my legs, grazing over my hips and connecting along my low back. He spreads his legs and pulls me in. I have no choice but to go where he guides me. My body is so close that my knees bump against the milk crates he's sitting on.

I feel him—the heat of his fingers splayed on my low back, his forehead resting against my stomach. I smell him—sea salt and amber. His scent wafts over me, coming on just as strong as when I'm swathed in the hoodie I've been secretly sleeping in all week.

Pushing away all thought of the consequences, I lean in closer and drape my arms over his shoulders. Then I get to work massaging the back of his skull in the way I know he likes.

He groans, so I press harder.

I tell myself I'm trying to relieve his headache. I pointedly ignore the part of my brain that accuses me of wanting to run my fingers through his hair and scrape my nails against his skin.

We stand like that for several minutes. Him holding me. Me holding him.

In increments, the comfort of him against me transforms into heavy tension.

The care and concern of thirty seconds ago has suddenly morphed into need.

A pang of desire. An itch that burns with how desperately it wants to be scratched.

I run my hands through his hair mindlessly, letting my fingertips skim down his neck and trace his throat. In turn, he rubs up and down my back, his touch more pointed and exploratory as it crosses the invisible boundaries it maintained a moment ago.

The darkness makes us bold. We're both guilty of lingering touches and brave caresses we'd never allow in the light. Every time I push the limits, he responds with a more brazen caress.

We've been stripped away of all excuses, reduced to nothing but sensation.

I skirt my hands up his chest, tracing up his neck until my fingertips find his lips. He covers my hand with his, flattening it to his mouth and exhaling before placing the softest kiss on my palm.

"Josephine."

My name is a caress, warming my skin and sinking into the marrow of my bones.

It has to be the darkness. The sensory deprivation. No light. Nothing but silence. It heightens the intensity of every touch. I would stand to forget my own damn name in this moment if he hadn't just whispered it in reverence.

The way he's holding me against his body fills a need I didn't know existed until now.

The way I'm desperate for him to never let go scares the shit out of me.

I startle when his breath ghosts over my lips. I wasn't even aware I was bending down. It didn't take much, given our height difference. Decker cranes his neck, his mouth so close to mine, the tip of his tongue teasing me as he licks his bottom lip.

The door flies open, and light floods in, blinding us. I jump back, then instantly regret it when light hits Decker right in the face.

He holds both hands up and winces on reflex. Shit. I'm sure that did wonders for his headache.

Misty stands in the doorway, hands planted on her hips. "There you are! They're getting restless. And the next time you want to take a break in the middle of an engagement, we need to discuss it beforehand so I can..."

She drones on as she hurries down the hall, confident we'll follow. I step fully into the light, peering over my shoulder to gauge Decker's reaction to that near miss.

He's still seated on the milk crate, half his face cast in shadow. The heated look he gives me with the single eye I can see is all the answer I need.

He doesn't move. Neither do I. We face off for several seconds until a shrill voice rings out down the hall.

"Decker. Let's go!" And with that, the spell is broken.

Chapter 42

Josephine

Another Friday night. Another family dinner.

I wasn't sure what to expect, considering there isn't a game tomorrow. But when I asked Locke if we were still having dinner, he scoffed and looked at me like I was crazy.

Maybe I am. Maybe that's why I'm casually sitting around the table with the guys long after we've finished eating, simply because I'm enjoying their company.

That, or this spiked lemonade has gone to my head.

Kylian glances up from his iPad and flicks his attention to each of us. "Everyone's good with the itineraries I sent out for Shore Week? We all know where we need to be and when?"

I thought a bye week meant things would be more laid back around here. Clearly, I was wrong.

There's no game tomorrow, but there's still a party. An all-day event, it seems. The team doesn't have anywhere to be, so they'll arrive after lunch and go all day and night. Decker has extra security coming to the house since the crowd will be larger than usual.

Sunday marks the official start of Shore Week.

I've been hearing about this stupid rivalry for weeks, so I'm more than a little curious about how it'll all play out.

I gawked when I saw all the events on the schedule Kylian emailed me this morning. But when I FaceTimed with Hunter this afternoon, she promised she'd be at most of them, too. Apparently, it's a whole thing around here. The Lake Chapel vs. South Chapel game is a huge deal. People from all over the state and beyond will travel to watch it.

There's the charter cruise on Sunday night. A bonfire on Monday. The guys have NIL appearances Tuesday through Friday. There's even a parade on Saturday morning.

Locke mentioned a team prank during dinner, but Kylian already explained to me that the four of them don't mess with those anymore. Decker likes to be in the know in terms of what the players are planning, but otherwise, he leaves it to the underclassmen to figure out.

Rapping his knuckles on the table, Kendrick nods at Kylian, then looks to Decker. "I'm good. We're done here?"

Of course he wants to dip out as soon as possible. Typical.

At Decker's nod, Kendrick pushes to his feet and strolls into the house.

"He's agitated," Kylian remarks. Not a question. Just an observation.

"He is," Decker confirms, blowing out a long breath. He pinches the bridge of his nose.

Instinctively, I track the movement, looking for other signs of discomfort.

As if he can sense my concern, he taps his foot against mine twice under the table to get my attention. When our eyes meet, he shakes his head and mouths, "I'm fine."

I offer him a tight smile. I'm glad he's okay, but I'm annoyed with Kendrick. Is it that hard to act like an adult and sit at the table with all of us for more than five minutes after finishing a meal?

"I cooked. You two are on cleanup." Locke yawns, stretching his arms overhead and leaning as far back as his chair will allow.

Mrs. Lansbury prepares most of their meals throughout the week, but one of the guys typically cooks for Friday night family dinner.

He stands, catching my gaze and smiling.

"You want to watch another movie tonight, Hot Girl?"

I return his smile but wrinkle my nose. "Sorry," I apologize. "I already have plans." I side-eye Decker, still unsure of whether things are going to come together. I've got to figure it out fast. It's almost eight, and Hunter might already be on her way.

Decker sits up, regarding the guys. "I'll wash if you want to clear, Kyl." Then he turns to Locke. "You still up for fishing tomorrow morning?"

Locke grins, then pulls out his phone. "Hell yeah. We haven't done that since before two-a-days started in July. Is six too early?"

"How about eight?" Decker counters. "When do we ever get to sleep in on a Saturday?"

Once he sets his alarm, Locke gives us a nod and heads into the house. Kylian stands and gathers up plates, and after a few trips to the kitchen, he leaves us alone, too.

Decker's focus is locked on me, his eyes glinting with promise as he sips his drink.

It's now or never.

"Um, so, I wanted to ask you something," I hedge.

"Did you now?"

A week ago, I would have rolled my eyes. Tonight, his words tickle down my spine and inspire goose bumps on my thighs.

"Hunter and I were planning to hang out tonight. She said she could use her stepdad's boat to get here. I was thinking she could stay the night..."

Decker's face falls, but he schools his expression quickly and leans forward until he's close enough to trace a line down my forearm with the back of his knuckles.

"Are you asking my permission to have a sleepover, Josephine?" His words drip with sarcasm. He's trying to get a rise out of me, and I have no problem calling him on his bullshit.

"I'm asking you not to be a dick to my friend. And I'm ensuring we don't have any problems, Cap." I pull my arm away. "I'm here. I'm not going anywhere. So I'd like to go on and live my life, which includes having a friend over to hang out."

Decker's eyes widen, and I congratulate myself for catching him off guard. I raise my eyebrows as he cocks his head and considers me.

"Hunter is good people," he relents. "I've known her since middle school. I don't have any problem with her coming over any time."

Good. I hide any indication of relief, but internally, I'm elated that he's not making a big deal out of this.

"And it's cool if she stays the night?" I confirm, pulling out my phone and tapping out a quick text to Hunter. I'm almost positive she's already on her way, since I couldn't exactly explain to her that I needed permission before making plans.

"You'll both be sleeping in your room, I presume?"

I hadn't exactly figured that out myself yet.

I shrug but meet his gaze. "She knows I..." I trail off.

How much am I willing to admit to Decker about where things stand between me and his best friends? Deciding I won't be shamed for my sex life—never again—I sit up straighter and hold my head high.

"Hunter knows Kylian and I are involved. And that I hooked up with Locke."

He scrutinizes me with narrowed eyes, but he remains silent. Almost as if he's waiting for me to continue.

After several seconds, I sigh and heave myself out of my seat. Smoothing my hands down the front of my sundress, I straighten my spine and pull my shoulders back.

"Look, I've accepted that this is where I'll be for the next several weeks. I trust Hunter, and I—"

"It's fine. Have fun."

He doesn't even try to hide the bitterness in his tone.

"Decker..."

"I said it's *fine*," he grits out.

"Okay. Thanks," I mumble. This is so painfully awkward. "So... we're good here?" I ask, making my way around the table and heading for the door.

He scoffs and mutters, "We are so far from good, Josephine."

I falter and spin back toward him. I don't want to fight with him, but I won't take his shit, either.

"What's that supposed to mean?" I demand.

He rises from his seat and plants his hands wide on the table. He hangs his head for a moment, then snaps up and gives me a haughty look.

"It's a bye week. There's a party tomorrow night. We've got all the bullshit Shore Week traditions starting on Sunday." He pins me with a glare so intense, I hold my breath. "Did it ever occur to you that maybe I wanted you to myself tonight?"

Shit on a crumbly cracker.

I thought he was being intentionally obstinate. His typical alphahole self. Itching to prod at me and pick a fight.

It never even crossed my mind that he wanted to spend time together.

"Decker, I—"

Locke pokes his head out onto the deck, interrupting me. I cringe at the very idea that he may have of overheard our exchange. I have absolutely no interest in sorting through my feelings for not one, not two, but three guys who happen to be best friends and reside in the house that I'm still being sort of forced to live in. At least not yet.

"A boat just pulled up. Are we expecting company?"

"Is that her?" Decker asks, one brow cocked in question. I peek down at my phone just as the text comes in.

Hunter: The fun has arrived! Do I need to say a secret password to the grumpy dude standing on the dock?

I smile at her ridiculousness. "It's Hunter," I confirm.

Decker nods toward Locke. "Can you call down to the dock and tell them to let her up?"

He takes just about everything seriously. But Decker really doesn't fuck around when it comes to privacy and security.

When Locke ducks back into the house, I watch Decker. Hunter's given me the perfect out, and I'm going to take it for now.

I approach slowly, alarm bells blaring in my head as he tracks my movements with a predatory gaze.

With a weak smile, I wrap my hand around his bicep. "We'll talk later," I murmur, locking eyes with him so he knows my intentions are true. I'm beyond eager to explore things between us. But not with an audience. And not until I get my own wits about me.

He nods once, pressing his lips together, reluctantly accepting that he's not going to get his way right now.

I give his arm a squeeze, then scurry down the deck steps and head in the direction of the beach.

I pass Hunter the drink, which she eyes skeptically.

"What is this?"

I shrug, more than a little eager to tie one on after my conversation with Decker. "It's supposed to be a Tom Collins, but the fridge doesn't get restocked until tomorrow, and we're out of soda water, so technically it's just gin and lemonade."

She cocks one brow at me. "I thought you didn't drink."

"I drink. I just don't drink at parties."

Closing my eyes, I take a big sip, delighting in the way the sweet and sour flavors balance out the sharp woodsy taste of the gin.

"This is weird. You're kind of freaking me out. But when in Rome..." Hunter shrugs and follows suit, taking a big swig. She gulps and practically chokes. Her eyes bug out and she tumbles into a coughing fit.

"Oh my gosh! You could have warned me! That's *so* strong! Why does it taste like Pine-Sol?"

I balk. "Have you never had gin before?"

"Maybe in, like, a jungle juice or something. What twenty-one-year-old willingly drinks gin?"

I giggle and point a finger at my own face. Then I take another drink, grateful it's just the two of us in the kitchen. The guys are obviously trying to give us a wide berth, which I appreciate.

"Okay. Have you had enough to drink to give me some answers?"

"Such as?" I hedge. Bringing my glass to my lips, I take another sip to avoid making eye contact. I know what she's getting at, but I haven't figured out how to explain, well, any of it.

"Really, girl?" she deadpans. "Fine. We can play it that way. Why don't we start with why we're standing in the kitchen of the Crusade Mansion instead of your uncle's place?"

I scrunch my nose and accept my fate. Setting my cup on the island, I make my way around it and hook my arm through Hunter's. "Come on. There's something I need to show you."

She's quiet as I lead her through the house and climb the stairs, which is out of character for Hunter.

When we reach my room, I turn the handle and hold an arm out, gesturing for her to step inside ahead of me. Flipping on the lights, I watch her face as she takes it all in.

"*Oh*, this is pretty," she remarks, panning from one side of the room to the other. "I've never been up here before. Whose room is this?"

I cover my face with my hands.

"Joey... Seriously. Whose room is this?" she asks again, spinning to face me.

Peeking out between my fingers, I mumble, "Um, mine? I sort of live here now."

Her eyes go wide, and she's silent for all of two seconds.

Then she shrieks.

"Holy *shit*! Josephine oh-my-god-I don't-know-your-middle-name Meyer! What do you mean you *sort of live here now*?"

"I don't actually have a middle name," I quip, choosing to ignore the more pertinent question.

"Really? I have two. What sort of person doesn't give their kid a middle name?"

"Someone who doesn't really give a shit about their kid," I gripe.

Hunter's face falls, then her eyes widen in horror. "Ugh. I'm sorry. I wasn't thinking. I didn't mean—"

"It's fine," I insist, making my way farther into the room.

"Okay, okay. Don't try to distract me. You have a whole lot of explaining to do."

I flop onto the bed, then prop my head on my hand when she sits beside me.

"My uncle had to go out of town a few weeks ago, so the guys thought—"

"*Weeks*? You've been living here for *weeks*, and I didn't know?" She grips my arm. "Does this mean you're officially dating? And is it weird that I have to ask which one?"

"Hunter." I groan. Though I'm grateful she accepted my half-assed explanation at face value. "It's weird, yes. But fair. And the honest answer is I don't really know."

"*You don't know?*"

Oh god. I'm afraid her brain is going to implode. She's confused as hell, but she's radiating excitement and giddiness, too. She's smiling so hard I can't help but match her grin.

"Kylian and I... we haven't exactly defined it. Locke and I had a falling out after the first party of the year, but we're trying to move past that now. Then there's Decker..."

"Josephine Meyer! You saucy minx." She shoves my shoulder. "Look at you moving into town and starting your own little reverse harem. And what happened to 'never Crusade'?"

Rolling to my side, I shove her back. "My own *what*?"

"You know. A reverse harem? Like, a girl with a whole bunch of boyfriends? Polyamory? It's a thing. They all love her. She loves all of them. And sometimes, they all love each other together." She wags her eyebrows and scoots to the middle of the bed. "Oh my god." She clasps her hands in front of her chest. "Is there sword crossing in your relationship? You have to tell me who! Wait, wait. No. Let me guess. It's Decker and Kendrick, isn't it? No! It's Kylian. He's got soft dom vibes written *all* over him."

"You're ridiculous. I don't even know what you're talking about. And Kendrick hates me," I remind her, covering my face with my hands once again. I should have brought my drink with me. I'll need it if she keeps up with this line of questioning.

"Um, hello?" She runs her fingers through my hair affectionately. "Haven't you ever heard of enemies to lovers? It's one of the most popular romance tropes."

"Real talk." I peer up at her.

She schools her expression and nods, dutifully slipping back into friend mode when she sees the forlorn look on my face.

"I honestly don't know what's going on. With *any* of them. I'm afraid I'm in too deep."

"What do you need?" she asks, still playing with my hair.

"Probably another drink."

She boops me on the nose. "Silly goose. Seriously. Anything I can do to help?"

Pressing my lips together, I give her question honest consideration. I need to talk to Kylian, Locke, and Decker. Ideally one on one. I need to be honest with them *and* with myself. But Hunter can't help me with any of that.

"I probably need to have a few conversations," I grumble.

"You do," she confirms with a nod. "And until then?"

I grin. "I need an outfit for the party tomorrow. And I have nothing to wear for the charter cruise. Help me?"

"Now *that* I can do." She hops off the bed with a squeal. "I'm assuming all your clothes are in there?" she asks, pointing to the walk-in closet.

Nibbling my lip, I nod.

"Come on," she urges, pulling me upright. "Let's see what we're working with."

"You're the best," I tell her, peeling myself off the bed.

"You know it," she quips over her shoulder as I follow her across the room. "Just promise me you'll tell me when you have your first three-way. Or four-way. Or five—"

"Hunter!" I scold as she cackles and scurries into my closet.

Chapter 43

Josephine

Hunter deemed everything in my closet too basic for this weekend's events. So naturally, we spent most of Saturday shopping.

Kylian whipped his credit card out of his wallet and held it out to me when I told him about my plans for the day, which annoyed me as much as it thrilled me. I guess I've never put much thought into what he does for money. He doesn't have NIL deals like the other guys, but I assume he earns a stipend from the team.

I turned him down, even though it pained me to have to transfer money from my savings account to my checking account when Hunter insisted I *had* to have three of the outfits she styled. Leave it to her to turn me into her own personal Lake Chapel Barbie.

Tonight I'm rocking an off-the-shoulder body-con bandage dress in vibrant Crusader red. The look screams for attention, which is so not me, but it fits my mood tonight.

We make our way down the stairs together—Hunter spent the night last night, and between shopping and party prep, she's been with me ever since—and pause so Corbin and the other security bro can unhook the velvet rope to let us through.

As soon as we step into the kitchen, I sense eyes on me. I scan the room until I meet Kendrick's intense, angry gaze.

"What's his problem?" Hunter scoffs.

Based on the way Kendrick's scowl deepens, her comment carried across the room.

"Ignore him," I murmur, looping my arm through hers and guiding her out of the kitchen.

It's early yet, but people have been partying for hours. I talked to Kylian this morning, and texted with Locke a bit, but haven't really kept up with the guys for most of the day.

I don't intentionally set out in search of him, but I once again find myself scanning the party for Decker. It doesn't take long to track him down.

Hunter and I step out onto the upper deck and make our way to the rail to look down on the beach and across the water. It's clear why Decker favors this spot. Almost the entire beach is visible from up here, and it's easy to see the ferries coming and going.

Control. Power. Dominance.

Everything I used to hate about him makes more sense now. His need to protect his people makes him who he is. He has legitimate excuses for being unreasonable. At least some of the time.

I turn in time to catch him staring. He's surrounded by teammates—a few guys I recognize and several more I don't. He's leaning against the opposite side of the deck instead of lounging on the love seat like usual. To my relief, the women who usually surround him are absent tonight.

I raise one brow, and his onyx eyes darken at the challenge. He wants me to come to him. He's willing me to his side without a word. I have to fight my body's natural urge to obey. The tension between us is palpable.

He cocks his head, and that's all it takes to make my willpower slip a fraction. I want to be closer. I want to know what he'll say or do in front of his teammates. I straighten my spine and lift my chin, readying myself to step toward him.

But I'm stopped by a strong arm that wraps around me from behind.

"Hot Girl," Locke grunts into my ear, his embrace tightening as he sidles up behind me. "You are living up to your name tonight."

I smile, then melt in his arms without a second thought.

Hunter mutters something about a refill and heads back inside, obviously trying to give us a modicum of privacy.

Except there's nothing private about the way Locke is wrapping his arms around me and folding his body over mine. It's a claiming. Half the team is out here on the deck with us.

Unease washes over me as I remember where we are and who I was just eye fucking.

Shit.

I dig my fingernails into Locke's forearms, silently pleading with him to ease up when I look over and confirm that Decker's focus is still fixed on me.

"He wants you, you know," Locke murmurs in my ear, sending a shiver coursing down my spine when his lips brush against my skin. "Decker's used to getting what he wants."

Chest heaving, I swallow thickly. I'm so wrapped up in all things Locke—literally—I can't catch my breath. Damn this ridiculously tight bandage dress.

"But tonight, you're mine." He nips at my earlobe and grunts in approval when a shudder racks my body in response. One of his arms loosens, and for a moment, I think that maybe he's going to let me go. Instead, he slides that arm up between my breasts and gently grips my throat in a clear show of possession.

"Locke—"

"Joey," he growls with a squeeze. My name vibrates through his chest and reverberates to my core.

I clasp my thighs together, desperate to ease the ache as he runs his hands over my body while Decker looks on.

"I want you. He wants you. The only question now is, what do *you* want?"

Him.

Them.

I want it all.

My body hums with need. My clit has its own pulse as it aches with desire. But even as I try to focus on his words, I can't tear my eyes away from Decker's.

"Tell me you want me, too."

There's a quiver to his words that gives me pause. Reality barrels into me like a freight train as I wrap my head around the gravity of this moment.

I want him. I want him so badly I ache. And he deserves to know that. To be picked first. To know without a doubt where things stand between us as we try to make our way back to what we shared that first night.

"I want you," I hum, closing my eyes and letting my head loll back against his chest.

I'm done fighting this. I'm done punishing him. I'm ready to begin again.

"Yeah?" He squeezes my throat slightly, and my eyes shoot open to land on Decker.

I nod, not trusting myself to speak.

"Show me," he challenges with another caress along the column of my throat. "My room. Now."

"Pantry?" I counter, breathless and so worked up I'm not sure I can make it up the stairs.

"No way, Hot Girl. We need a bed for what I want to do to you."

He releases me and stalks off the deck and out of sight.

I stand there, stunned, my hand instinctively gripping my throat to replicate the heat of his skin pressed to mine.

I blink once, then again, willing Decker to look away. Wishing it was less obvious what I'm about to do.

But he never drops my gaze.

His eyes bore into me still when I turn and follow Locke into the house.

The door is cracked open for me, but I knock softly anyway.

His scent overwhelms me within seconds of entering the space. Fresh mint and sugar cane: clean, sweet, and so deliciously Locke.

My desire surges at the sight of him. He's already removed his shirt, because he knows damn well what tats do to me. Joke's on him, though, if he thinks I need some sort of preamble to what's about to happen. I already drenched my panties when he was touching me as Decker looked on.

"You came," he rasps, rising from the bed.

"Not yet," I tease, sauntering closer.

He laughs, and it's the most joyful sound. His presence alone makes me feel lighter—like his very essence has the power to unlock this carefree, playful side of me I rarely feel safe enough to access.

Locke wraps his arms around me and brushes the gentlest of kisses over my lips. The barely there connection is enough to make me shudder. "You will. I told you that first night I wasn't anywhere done with you. Time to make good on that promise."

Big hands cup my ass, then we're moving. He carries me to the bed but doesn't let me go right away. Instead, he shifts me in his arms as he peppers kisses up and down my neck.

"What do you want?" he asks, his voice low and dripping with desire. There's no question he's into this, but those simple words have a meaning far deeper than they convey on the surface.

"I want you," I assert, acknowledging my reciprocated desire because I know he needs the verbal affirmation. And in case I'm not making myself abundantly clear, I clench my thighs around his waist and rub my core against him.

He pulls back, watching me with hooded eyes.

"Say it again."

I pushed him away. Hard. Then I held him at arm's length for weeks. Given what I know about his past and his upbringing...

I cup his face with both hands and look him in the eye.

"I want you, Nicholas Lockewood. I want you so bad I ache. I want you buried deep inside me. I want you to make me forget my own name."

"Fuck yeah." He lowers me onto his bed and follows me down. "What are you gonna scream when I make you come, Hot Girl?" He sits back on his knees and works his way out of his pants while I eye fuck him to within an inch of his life.

His gauges and eyebrow piercing. The tats. He's my every punk-rock fantasy come to life. Hard and jaded on the outside but so damn sweet underneath it all.

"Nicky," I guess.

His eyes blow out. He looks absolutely feral.

Pushing down his boxer briefs, he reveals his gorgeous cock, hard and leaking at the tip below the glimmer of his pubic piercing. He fists himself and regards me on his bed, grinning the most devilish grin.

"Wait—" I rise up to sit and put one hand on his chest. "I want you to use a condom."

"Absolutely," he promises, reaching toward the nightstand.

"And one more thing..." I breathe out, second-guessing myself. It's stupid. But my anxiety won't allow me to focus unless I'm sure.

"Anything," Locke replies as he tears open the condom wrapper.

"This might sound weird..."

"Joey." He captures my chin between his thumb and forefinger, tilting my face until I'm forced to look him in the eye. "*Anything*."

I know him. I trust him. And if I'm lucky, he won't push for details.

Pulling in a shaky breath, I search his face. "Are there any cameras in here?"

He narrows his eyes and frowns.

"Like, surveillance or security cameras?" I push.

He shakes his head resolutely. "No. There's a security camera in the hall, and more throughout the house, but none in the bedrooms."

"And where's your phone?"

His eyes widen in surprise at that question, but he responds quickly and earnestly. "Plugged in by my computer." He tips his chin toward his desk.

I follow his line of sight and confirm he's telling the truth.

Closing my eyes, I let out a sigh of relief. Then I kiss him. Just a soft, grateful kiss to ease the tension I created.

He reads my body language perfectly, deepening the kiss and weaving a hand through my hair. "Any other requests, Hot Girl?" he teases, biting down on my bottom lip.

"Yeah, actually." I tilt my hips up just enough to connect our lower halves. "Can I be on top so I can feel your pubic piercing?"

He gives me the most swoon-worthy grin. "Abso-fucking-lutely."

Locke flips over and scoots back. As he settles in against the headboard, I climb onto his lap.

I spread my knees wide enough that when I straddle him, we both groan on contact. The heat of his erection instantly seeps through my thong.

I'm practically clawing at my dress as we kiss, but I can't find the hidden zipper along the side. Dammit. This thing's impossible to get off.

We're both frantic, almost clumsy, all hands and groans, kisses and thrusts.

We've worked ourselves into a tizzy, and neither one of us will be able to focus until I can sink down on his dick.

"Fuck," I pant against Locke's mouth. "It'll take ten minutes to get me out of this thing. I'll just pull it down under my tits and take my panties off."

Locke claws at my panties, and fabric pulls taut around my torso as I wiggle out of the top of this dress.

"Not good enough," he grits out against my chest. "I want you naked in my bed."

A second later, seams are popping. Then suddenly, I hear a telling rip, and the bandage dress falls in a heap behind me.

"Fuck yeah," he murmurs, hoisting me up so he can bury his face in my tits. He catches a nipple between his teeth, and I mewl at the tugging sensation. Kissing and sucking and licking, he worships. Our naked bodies grind together as I ache to feel him everywhere.

I kiss the ink along his throat, biting him hard as he sucks my other nipple into his mouth. "You owe me a dress, Emo Boy."

He shifts back on the bed, pulls me onto his lap, and gives me that bright, wide, enigmatic smile I love.

"I owe you a ride."

He holds the condom deftly between two fingers, showing it off, then he maintains eye contact as he rolls it down his erect length.

Once sheathed, he juts his chin, encouraging me to line him up at my entrance.

"Get on my dick. I need to be inside you."

The feeling is mutual.

"I might need a minute to adjust," I warn, teasing him between the lips of my pussy. I'm so gone for him—hot, horny, and soaked—but he's impressively large, and I'm only human.

I tease him by lowering just an inch, then lifting up and off.

His hands roam over my chest and stomach, his fingers gripping my hips as he blows out slow, measured breaths.

When I finally sink down and take him fully, we moan in unison.

The angle is exquisite against my inner walls. He feels even better on my clit.

His pubic piercing lines up perfectly, as if our bodies were made to fit together like this. My eyes are fixed on the spot where we connect as I shift my weight forward to see how it feels.

"Holy shit," I murmur, loving the way the press of the warm metal amplifies all sensation. I don't know which pleasure point to focus on first. I'm so full, yet I'm desperate to take him even deeper and get as close to his piercing as possible.

"You like that, Hot Girl?"

He's wearing a grin that tells me he already knows the answer.

As much as I love his smile, I've learned that sometimes he wears it like a mask. I don't want to downplay the significance of this moment: what it means to me, and what I hope it means to him.

"Did I mention how much I want you?" I whisper, scraping my nails through his hair before wrapping my arms around his neck. I rest my forehead on his, holding him close, just savoring the way he feels inside me.

"You may have mentioned it," he murmurs, his smile softer. His kisses slow as he relaxes back into my touch. His mouth savors my skin as he moves along my collarbone in reverent strokes.

There's heat and desire thrumming between us. But there's also this deep sense of ease. I've never been so comfortable with another person—so willing to open up and so eager to know more. I want to know him. I want to discover what he likes, what he fears; his dreams and goals; what he envisions for his future.

I want to know everything. And in a surprising twist, I want him to know me.

"I want you, Nicky," I repeat. "I want to ride you and come all over your cock. Tell me if anything hurts, okay?"

He grunts in acknowledgment, grazing his hands along my inner thighs. His thumbs caress higher, and we both watch, transfixed, as he spreads me open. The contrast between my needy pink pussy and his trimmed dark hair is mesmerizing.

I've never seen anything so erotic—the way he's holding me open, exposing my clit, then thrusting up and grinding against me so the warm metal of his piercing rubs me just right.

"Look at that perfect fucking fit," he grunts, fixated on his cock as I take him on another thrust. "Look how pretty you look riding me like you own me."

I smirk down at him, inexplicably turned on by the way he submits and lets me take the lead. Sometimes I want to be claimed and fucked hard. Other times, I want to do the claiming.

"You feel so good," I pant, running my hands through my hair as I roll my hips forward again. "I can't believe how deep you are right now."

"Yes, you can. You were made for this cock. You're doing so good, baby. *Fuck*. Grind that pussy all over me."

I find my rhythm, but the sensation of his piercing keeps distracting me in the best possible way. It's not long before I'm shamelessly grinding back and forth, chasing my own pleasure.

He digs his thumbs into my hips, guiding my body as I thrust hard and lean forward.

"Locke... Fuck... Locke, I'm going to..."

"Do it. Come on my dick. Give it to me, Joey. I want to feel you drip all the way down to my balls."

I rock back and forth as he thrusts up into me, matching my pace. The tingles are right there. All it takes is a final glance at the way he spears me, and I'm detonating.

"Nicky," I cry as a powerful, mind-melding warmth blossoms from my core and radiates throughout every limb. I'm lost to the world as I relish it all, consumed by a pulsing that just won't quit.

Another shockwave hits, pulling a moan from deep inside me. The intensity of each ripple is just as strong as the last. I open my eyes in time to see Locke crane his head back, wearing a look of pure ecstasy as he growls out his own release.

After we come down, a peaceful silence settles around us as I catch his mouth in a kiss. We stay like that, me in his lap, him buried inside me, naked and sated and so damn happy. The ease I so often feel in his presence descends, and I'm hit with the earnest need to make him feel as desired and seen as he makes me.

"Best ride I've had in ages," I quip, biting down on his bottom lip.

He smooths his hands up my bare thighs, bringing his thumbs together on top of my overly sensitive clit.

Beneath hooded lids, he peers up at me, then rests his sweat-slicked forehead on my chest and wraps me in an embrace.

"This wasn't a one-time thing for me."

He delivers it like a statement. But there's a question hidden under the surface, and I want nothing more than to ease his concern.

Gripping the back of his head, I tug until he meets my gaze.

Solemnly, I shake my head, then clench around his cock for extra emphasis.

"I'm not a one-time kind of girl," I assure him, leaning lower to seal my promise with a kiss.

Chapter 44

Josephine

I leave Locke's room after a few hours, closing the door behind me as he gently snores. It doesn't count as sneaking out if I know I'll see him in the morning, right?

My head's fuzzy, like I'm still drifting in a post-orgasm haze, even though it's been hours since he made me come. This week has just been... a lot. I need to figure my shit out, and fast.

Being with Locke felt so good and so right. We click. Every touch lights me up, and from the moment we met, we've had no trouble falling into a rhythm with one another. He's effervescent happiness. There's a brightness to him that I swear makes me feel lighter.

As I creep down the quiet hallway, I have every intention of going to my room, but my feet carry me past the door and to the end of the hall. And without conscious thought, I find myself climbing the stairs to the Nest.

I knock quietly, but there's no response from the inside. I think it's okay that I'm here. He would lock the door if he wanted privacy, right?

I enter the now familiar space and scan the dark room. The LEDs smoothly transition from red to blue to purple, the changing colors soothing in an inexplicable way. The Nest has become my comfort. An escape. It's peaceful in a way no place has ever felt before.

When my eyes land on Kylian, where he's lying on his bed, it hits me. It's not the physical space that feels like a balm to my soul; it's him.

"I've been waiting for you," he tells me without preamble.

That's Kylian. He says what he means, and he means what he says. I never have to guess or decode his words. He is who he is. And because of that, I can be the realest version of myself when I'm with him.

He shifts over and holds out an arm, inviting me to join him.

I shuffle closer, then climb up and cuddle into his side. We both wiggle and rearrange until we're comfortable. Without prompting, Kylian holds out noise-canceling earbuds.

I used his during the storm after the first game a few weeks ago. A few days later, a second pair appeared. This man. He anticipated that there may be a time we both need them. He expects that I'll be a regular visitor in his private space.

I don't want to be trapped in silence with my own thoughts right now, though, so I shake my head at his offer. He rolls over and stretches out, and when he settles again, he offers me a different kind of earbud instead.

The song he cues up is slow and sultry. A duet I've never heard before. He's got it on repeat, and by the third time through, I hum along with the chorus.

My body settles, and my brain slows. Comfort and ease cocoon me. I reach for him, rolling to my side and nestling my head into the space between his arm and his chest.

He plays with my hair as I listen to the song and watch him breathe. His touch is methodical and repetitive. Soft strokes that soothe me until I'm half asleep in his arms.

"You look guilty and you smell like sex."

It's not a question. It's not an accusation, either. It's just the facts.

"Kylian, I..."

Fuck. Should I apologize? For what, exactly? For having sex with his childhood best friend? For crawling into his bed a few hours later? For not having the gumption to figure out where things stand between us?

Stop it, I silently admonish. I'm not going to slut shame myself. I love sex. We used protection. I don't have to ask permission to have consensual relations with another adult.

Taking a deep breath, I change course.

"Is that a problem for you?"

He doesn't respond right away, and the silence impels me to ask another question in hopes of a response.

"I can go back downstairs if you'd like."

"Based on my research, most females don't have a refractory period. Is that the case for you?"

I choke in surprise, then prop up on my elbow to get a look at his face.

There's no doubt he's serious. His eyes are full of heat. Of wanton, carnal desire.

"Why do you—"

"Answer me, Jo." He tips my chin up with the touch of two fingers. "Can you orgasm multiple times in one night?"

"I can," I answer tentatively, my heart in my throat.

"Good. Because I've been dreaming about making you come again. Except this time there'll be far less clothing between us, and I plan to use my mouth instead of a toy."

Before I can even reply, he pounces. Flipping our positions and cradling my head, Kylian kisses along my chest.

He's been dreaming? I'm living in a dream state right now. Except it isn't right to let him continue without being explicitly clear.

"Kylian," I pant, gripping the hair at his nape to pull him off.

But then he sucks on the skin below my ear, and all lucid thoughts leave my brain.

On a groan, I remember what I needed to say.

"Just so we're clear," I breathe, "I had sex with someone else a few hours ago."

"I know," he says evenly, running his nose along my neck and dipping his head low enough to lick my cleavage. He inhales deeply, then he moans. "Locke, by the smell of it."

Holy shit. He can smell him on me? And how does he know what Locke smells like?

"You got to experience his pubic piercing, didn't you, baby?" he whispers in my ear. "I bet your clit's so swollen and tender now. Engorged and needy and ready for me."

Sitting back on his knees abruptly, he waves a hand at my torso.

"Take that off," he demands, clearly referring to the oversized T-shirt and shorts I stole from his friend. With one hand, he pulls his shirt over his head in a fluid motion that's so sexy it should be illegal. I squirm just from the sight of him as my cunt pulses with need.

I'm naked a moment later.

Kylian situates himself so that my bent legs rest on his bare stomach.

"Spread your legs and let me see you, Jo."

I do as he says, pulling in a deep breath when he smooths both hands along my inner thighs.

He murmurs, "Good girl," and my hips buck up as if my cunt has a mind of her own.

"I can't wait to taste you," he says as he lowers his mouth toward my center.

"Wait." I don't want him to stop. But I have to make sure he understands. "I-I didn't shower or clean up yet. We used a condom, but you might...taste him... down there. That doesn't bother you?"

Kylian hitches one eyebrow and smirks. "Baby, tasting him on you makes this even hotter. Stop worrying and let me work. No more talking. Unless you want to scream my name or tell me you're coming."

And that's that. There's no room for doubt where Kylian's concerned.

I banish all errant worries and prickles of shame from my mind, settling into his sheets and letting the safety and warmth of the Nest cocoon me.

Another kind of warmth very quickly builds.

"How many times did he make you come?" Kylian asks, flicking his tongue over my clit, then licking me from my taint to my pubic bone.

He latches on to my clit and sucks so hard my toes dig into the mattress.

"Once," I pant, barely able to get the word out as I writhe on the edge of orgasm.

A moment later, there's tension coursing up my legs, and a tightness furling in my core.

Another lick, and I'm done.

Spasms of pleasure roll through me like shock waves as I cry out and thrust against Kylian's face. My pussy can't get enough of him; I crave more pressure.

"That's one," he mutters, nipping at my clit with his teeth before spearing me with his tongue and swirling it around my opening to lap up my pleasure.

I don't have time to process his words—or even stop pulsating from my orgasm—before he slips a finger inside and curls it upward.

His mouth is back on my clit a moment later, the combined sensations both overstimulating and somehow not enough.

"More," I pant, clawing at his sheets, desperate to gain traction against his face.

Fuck. He feels so good. I want to get lost in him. I want to get him off, too.

"Kylian," I beg, staving off the pleasure that's coiling down my spine. "I want more."

He peers up at me from between my legs—fuck, that's so hot—and gives me the most wicked smirk.

"I'm not fucking you tonight," he declares. With anyone else, I would argue. Mouth off. Demand explanation.

But Kylian is black and white. I don't have to doubt anything or try to read between the lines. His dissent is clear. I can accept that.

"Harder, then," I counter. "Rougher."

"You want more, baby?"

His voice is pure sex.

I eagerly nod.

"My girl wants it hard." He thrusts two fingers into me. "And rough." He bites down on my clit, causing pleasure and pain to swirl into the perfect storm of tension.

"Yes," I moan, writhing against his hand and face. "Please, Kylian."

He hums against my center. "You're so needy. Such a filthy, needy girl, getting fucked by my best friend, then coming up here begging for me to give you more."

He licks me again, adds a third finger, then somehow adds a thumb to the mix to create the perfect amount of pressure against my clit.

Holy. Shit.

"Yes," I mewl. "Please, Daddy. Please."

Oh. Holy shit. For real this time. *Where the hell did that come from?*

Kylian pauses and sits back on his knees, but his fingers remain firmly on their target.

"Say it again," he demands.

"Daddy," I whimper without overthinking. "Please, Daddy. I need you."

He whistles. "Yep. That'll do it. New kink unlocked." Then he dives back down between my legs, closes his mouth around my pussy and clit, and sucks so hard I buck up and almost dislodge him.

Without missing a beat, he wraps his free arm around my waist, positioning me perfectly.

He alternates sucking and biting, each graze of his teeth against my clit growing harder in intensity. I can hear my arousal as he works his fingers in and out of my body. He hums against me, and that's all it takes. I explode into a million little fragments. Each piece scatters across the universe as he laps at me.

Kylian kisses my pussy, my belly, my thighs—worshipping my body as I come down from my post-orgasm daze.

Eventually, he crawls up the bed and flops down beside me, turning and hitting me with a shit-eating grin. Or would it be a pussy-eating grin?

"And that's two," he declares.

Victorious.

I snuggle up and nuzzle into his chest, sated and boneless in all the best ways.

"I didn't know you were so competitive," I tease, kissing his chest and melting into him. I know he doesn't sleep well if I'm draped all over him, but I can't resist a good post-orgasm cuddle.

He strokes my hair, then snags a water bottle from the nightstand and hands it to me. "Just because I sit on the sidelines at the games doesn't mean I'm not going to play to win in the bedroom, Jo."

There's a hint of teasing in his tone. But there's a bite to his words, too.

And that bite makes me go rigid. Because maybe there's more truth to his declaration than I previously considered.

"Is that how this is going to end?" I ask, slightly panicked. "Between you and Locke... or whoever," I add, wincing. "Someone will be declared the winner?"

Kylian is quiet, and when I tip my head back to search his face, he's wearing a slight frown that's more thoughtful than upset. He meets my gaze and goes back to stroking my head.

"I think that's up to you. As weird as it sounds, we work well together. We've always been a team. I don't know how this'll play out; I just know I'm in."

Chapter 45

Josephine

I wake up basking in an aura of crimson as sunlight filters through one of the stained-glass panels of the cupola.

I swear I sleep better here than anywhere else. It's the safety of this space, the security Kylian's presence gives me. The soundproofing and lack of windows don't hurt either.

Kylian stirs, pulling me close and kissing my hair before throwing his arm over his eyes.

"Can you hand me my glasses?" he asks, his voice scratchy and sexy from sleep. It sends flashes of last night racing through my mind immediately. The echoes of all the delicious, dirty things he whispered send shivers through me.

I snag his glasses off the side table, inspecting the thick lenses for a moment before handing them over.

"How bad is your vision?" I ask on a yawn.

"Awful. My prescription's 20/80."

"Why don't you wear contacts?" I ask.

His body stiffens, almost as if I've hit a nerve. Which doesn't ever happen with Kylian. I lift my head, hoping I can read his thoughts in his expression, but he's staring, straight-faced, at the patterns created by the sun and the stained-glass on the ceiling. I wait a few more seconds, then eventually accept his discomfort in the topic and rest my head on his chest.

He wraps his arms around me and pulls me in tighter. "Have you ever worn contacts?"

I shake my head. I've never been to an actual eye doctor, but in elementary school, the school nurse administered eye examines and said I had perfect vision.

"They're the worst. I can see them. I can see them, and I can feel them. And it's all I can think about when they're resting against my eye." He twitches and shudders. "Most people get used to it. But I can't. It's a tactile defensiveness thing. I just can't deal."

"I was just curious," I say, stroking a hand up and down his chest in an attempt to soothe him. Even if I don't understand what's wrong, he's obviously agitated.

"That's what I do, Jo. I fixate," he whispers.

I don't stop my movements and I don't respond. I leave him be while he remains lost in thought.

"I want to tell you something. Promise you won't get weird."

I still. That's... quite the lead in. But I trust him. And there's nothing he could say to change what's grown between us.

"I'm on the spectrum," he whispers hoarsely.

"Meaning?" I ask plainly.

"I'm autistic."

I nod against his chest. I know he's neurodivergent. I didn't know his preference for how he likes to refer to it, but now I do. I'm grateful he shared it with me in his own way.

I love how his mind works. I love the focus and the clarity. There's safety of being with him, because he takes the guesswork out of things for me. And knowing he feels close enough, safe enough, to open up to me makes my chest ache and my heart beat a little faster.

"Okay. Thanks for telling me." I kiss his stomach and snuggle closer.

He lets out a loud scoff. "No, not *okay*, Jo."

"Why not okay?" I laugh uneasily as dread bubbles in my stomach. I turn my head and tilt my chin to look at him, and he hits me with a steely gaze.

"Because that's not the appropriate response," he counters.

"Wait. Is this a test? You told me not to make it weird." I laugh again, because now I'm really uncomfortable, and I don't know what he wants me to say.

"It doesn't bother you?" he pushes, a frown marring his face and accusation in his voice.

"Doesn't *what* bother me?"

"That you hooked up with a freak?"

I bolt upright, anger coursing through my veins. "Kylian," I grit out. I wait until he looks at me before continuing. "Don't ever say that about yourself again. And of course it doesn't bother me."

He holds my gaze but doesn't reply, so I continue.

"I guess I thought what we were doing was more than just hooking up," I challenge.

He swallows, his Adam's apple bobbing, and a look of dismay replaces his frown. "It *is*. Shit. I'm fucking this up. Come here. Let me hold you."

He opens his arms, and I cuddle into his embrace.

"I appreciate your transparency, but knowing the details changes nothing," I assure him.

He doesn't reply right away. Instead, he arranges my limbs so he's got me where he wants me. Until our bodies come together at a hundred different touch points. Finally, when I'm draped over him exactly to his liking, he asks, "When you say what we're doing is more than hooking up..."

He lets the idea linger between us. He's been open and vulnerable with me. I take a deep breath, mentally rallying my courage to do the same.

"I feel connected to you. You're my safe space. The first one to be kind to me when I moved in. The first to view me as more than a liability. You're the person I crave when the world feels like too much."

He hums contentedly, but the moment is still charged. He may not expect anything more than what I've already shared, but I'm tired of holding back. Keeping secrets. Not trusting anyone fully. Not letting anyone know the real me.

"I want to tell you something now," I offer. "The panic thing—"

"It's okay. You don't have to do that."

"Do what?"

"Share something about yourself just because I shared."

I smile against the warmth of his skin, peeking up to meet his gaze.

"How do you know that's what I'm doing?" I tease.

He lifts one shoulder in a shrug. "There's a discernible pattern to intimacy. Back and forth. Ebb and flow. Conversation should be reciprocal whenever possible."

It sounds like he's reciting some sort of dating manual or advice guide, which galvanizes me in a way I wasn't expecting. Because everything we're doing—this connection, both physical and emotional—takes concerted, intentional effort on Kylian's part. He's gone to extreme lengths to care for me and to please me.

He's putting in the work. He thinks I'm worth the effort. That realization compels me to keep going.

"I *want* to tell you. Not because I'm obligated, but because I want you to know."

He shifts, arranging me in a new position but still holding me close. From here, I can't quite see his eyes. But I do see his Adam's apple bob as he swallows, then nods.

"I panic when it rains. Sometimes a little. Sometimes a lot. The more intense the storm, the deeper and longer I feel it. My official diagnosis is conversion disorder... but that's just a catchall for the way I physically shut down when it gets really bad."

His chest rises beneath me, and I close my eyes to savor the feeling.

The feeling of this moment.

The feeling before I say it.

The feeling before he knows.

"There's more."

I haven't even decided how much more I want to tell him, nor am I sure how much I can articulate. So I focus on the stained-glass panels of the cupola, staring for so long my eyes water. Hues of crimson, sapphire, and amethyst swirl together in a blurry oil slick before I finally blink away the tears.

"There was... this time. In high school. I was outside, in the middle of the night, stranded in a thunderstorm. I was on the side of the road, lying in a gutter. I passed out eventually, but before that..."

Anxiety claws at my throat as I fight to keep my breathing steady.

I wish I could tell him more. Tell him everything. But my sense of self-preservation has a vise grip on the details of what happened that night.

"I was out there until the next day. Left for dead. The panic became part of me that night," I admit in a whisper. "It always happens like that. I feel overwhelmed, then panic takes over. Every storm. Every time."

His abs crunch below my now-damp cheek as he rises up slightly and pulls me higher. He kisses my hair, then circles both arms around me in an embrace that feels just as safe as it did a few minutes ago.

I hold my breath, waiting for the follow-up questions. The judgment. Knowing Kylian, we're just getting started. He'll push for details and need more information.

He tightens his arms around me, as if to warn me it's coming. Then he speaks.

"What did you think about between the lightning and the thunder?"

There's a hushed reverence to his tone that soothes my fretful thoughts. It's such an odd question—typical Kylian—and yet it's one I'm fully capable of answering.

The expansiveness of that night stretched on for lifetimes. So much of it I don't remember. But this I do.

"I begged the sky to crack open and swallow me up for good."

Fingers catch under my chin, tilting my head until I'm looking him in the eye.

"I'm really glad it didn't," he whispers. And then he captures my lips in a slow, sensual kiss that washes away every lingering bit of tension in my body.

Safe.

With Kylian, in this moment, in this room, on this isle, *I'm safe.*

Chapter 46

Josephine

Aside from the usual breakfast spread, it's anything but a typical Sunday at the Crusade Mansion.

The house is buzzing with caterers and waitstaff. There are people unloading and staging décor down on the beach, too.

I've spent most of the day holed up in my room, getting ahead on my reading for class since it's going to be a busy week. I FaceTimed Hunter for a bit, and we chatted while we got ready. We agreed it didn't make sense for her to come over any earlier. The dock is full of smaller boats called tenders, each one manned with crew and security personnel.

I'm not totally confident about my outfit for tonight, seeing as how I've never attended a yacht party, but Hunter swears it's perfect. I've paired bright red hot pants with an oversized white oxford. The gauzy linen fabric drapes beautifully and leaves little to the imagination. I completed the look with the perfect shade of Crusaders red lipstick.

Decker told us to be ready to head out by five, so I make my way downstairs a few minutes prior.

When I walk into the kitchen, the guys are all standing around, sipping drinks.

Conversation ceases as each of them assesses me.

Kendrick takes one look at me and stalks toward the back door. Whatever.

Locke can't get to me fast enough.

"Hot Girl," he groans reverently. "How the hell do you look even better than last night?" He takes my hand and leads me farther into the kitchen, then lifts his arm to encourage me to twirl.

I spin out of his arms and laugh, only to be caught around the waist by Kylian.

"Hi," he murmurs, lowering his forehead to mine.

Tension I didn't even know existed evaporates from my body, and I'm instantly at ease.

Smiling, he brings his mouth to my ear. "You look good enough to eat."

My pussy flutters at the memories his words elicit. As if I needed a reminder. Sheesh.

He tilts my chin and kisses me in a bold move in front of the other guys.

I'm dizzy by the time he releases me and have to grip the counter to keep my balance.

I chance a glance at Decker but am completely unprepared for what I see.

Heat. Hunger. And maybe even a subtle hint of frustration.

He stares right at me—always staring—then beckons me with one finger.

As I approach, he pulls me close, almost as if he wants to hug me. His hands work their way into my hair, which I've curled into big waves for the party. He weaves his fingers through the strands, then tilts my head back where he wants it and pulls. Hard.

I gasp, and he smirks.

"I missed you at the party last night," he says coolly.

"I saw you at the party," I remind him.

He pulls on my hair again and all but growls, "It wasn't enough."

His attention dips to my lips, then quickly travels back up. He repeats the movement, puzzlement clouding his expression.

"What's wrong?" I worry, concerned that maybe he has a headache or is dealing with another side effect from the concussion. He's been doing really well over the last few days—avoiding screens and resting as much as he can. I didn't even think about checking on him earlier. When he doesn't respond right away, I double down.

"Decker. Talk to me. Are you okay?"

"Your lipstick," he murmurs. "It didn't smear when Kylian kissed you."

That's what he's concerned about?

I hold back a snort. "You were watching?"

"Always watching, siren."

My heart trips over itself in delight. He's never called me that before. He's never called me anything other than Josephine. Blushing, I lick my lips, and his eyes track the movement.

"It's waterproof. Smudge proof. Kiss proof, too, I suspect. It's not budging."

He runs his thumb over my bottom lip, his eyes alight with mischief. "I might have to test that theory tonight."

A foghorn sounds in the distance, breaking the spell we're under. I take a big step back to put distance between us, then remember where I am and spin. Locke and Kylian are both watching. There's no way they missed that interaction.

"Here's the deal," Decker announces.

Every eye snaps to him. Kendrick has slipped back into the room for the debrief, too.

"There are four boats anchored out there tonight. You guys know the drill. Tenders bring guests to the yachts, between the boats, or back to the parking lot. No one comes back to the house without unanimous agreement in the group text. And no one comes aboard without proper ID."

The guys are all nodding, as if this is a normal Sunday evening for a group of college students.

"Be smart," Decker continues. "Stay safe. Keep your phone on you at all times, just in case."

Then he turns to me. "Tell me if you're switching boats."

My gut instinct is to argue. No one else has limitations. And why do I have to report to him? But going toe to toe with Decker just for the sake of arguing doesn't have the same appeal it once did.

Instead, I accept him at his word, choosing to heed the concern I see in his eyes. He's not just a bossy asshole. Being in control is his way of protecting his people.

Does this mean I'm one of his people now?

It thrills me to realize it does.

Chapter 47

Josephine

I end up on the emerald boat with Locke and Kendrick. Although the latter wasn't intentional. I had no idea this was "his boat" until we got off the tender and saw him at the bar.

It was easy enough for Hunter to find us. Each boat is decorated in either crimson, sapphire, emerald, or amethyst. The uplighting and specialty drinks are all themed. Even the waitstaff on each vessel match the décor.

The boats are identical otherwise. Sleek and expensive in an understated way. I can't even begin to wrap my head around the cost.

We had to take off our shoes, which, again, didn't surprise Hunter. She humored me and tagged along as I explored every inch of the boat, though she was less impressed.

Security is tight. And I understand now why Decker was so concerned about people coming and going. There's a limit of forty people on each boat to start, operating under the assumption that several people will ship hop each hour.

Rumor has it there's a standby line curving around the marina.

Being out on the water is incredible. Hunter and I ate our fill from the buffet, then we watched the sun set. Each yacht really came to life when the individual DJs synced up the sound systems and the lights contrasted against the sky.

Hunter is caught up chatting with another prelaw major by the bar, so I've spent the last ten minutes wandering around and people watching.

One of the downsides to being on a seventy-foot yacht? It's only seventy feet long. Meaning it's hard to completely avoid the attention of a certain someone who despises me.

I've felt Kendrick's eyes on me more than once tonight. He hasn't said a single word to me since he raged against me on the sidelines of the football game last weekend.

Haughtily, I look up and watch him without shame. He stares back, challenging me to look away. I don't. I'm tired of being intimidated by him. I'm tired of accepting his bad behavior. So I lift my water bottle his way in a mock toast, offering him a saccharine smile. His expression darkens, and I swear if I didn't know how he really felt about me, I would think there's more than vitriol behind the intensity of his emotions.

Eventually, someone calls his name, and he's forced to look their way.

I smile and silently congratulate myself on my victory, no matter how minor.

My phone vibrates in my pocket.

Kylian: You should come find me on the sapphire boat.

Jo: Should I now?

Kylian: Are you being cheeky? Or do you want a list of reasons?

I grin at his candor. Of course he'd offer to list out all the reasons I should seek him out. But it's unnecessary. I'm more than willing to come when he calls.

Jo: Give me half an hour. Locke and Hunter are on this boat with me. I want to see what they want to do.

I stash my phone, intent on finding Locke, but I don't have to look far.

"Hot Girl," he croons, wrapping his big arms around me from behind before I've taken a single step. "Come dance with me," he whispers in my ear.

I nod, barely holding back the excited squeal threatening to spill out as he leads me to the dance floor.

We dance. And we laugh. We make the most of the crowd, boldly touching and even kissing as we get lost in the music and work up a sweat.

Eventually and reluctantly, I duck out of Locke's hold. He cocks his head in question, and I motion to him that I need water.

He nods in understanding but grabs me before I can leave the dance floor and pulls me close, pressing his very hard erection into my hip.

"I want another dance later, Joey. On this boat or in my bed tonight. Your pick."

I swoon on the inside and give him a coquettish smile in return.

"I'm going to look for Hunter. I'll find you later," I yell over the pulse of the music.

I stop by the bathroom first. After taking care of business, I crack open a bottle of cold water and find a quiet spot to look out at the other boats, enjoying the breeze off the lake. I want to hop over and find Kylian sooner rather than later. I also wouldn't mind bumping into Decker. If I'm lucky, maybe they're on the same boat. Kylian is on the blue yacht, but something in my gut tells me Decker is on the red one.

"Excuse me, are you Joey?"

The crew member on one of the tenders smiles when I look his way. We're on the opposite side of where guests are loading and unloading, but there's a hatch near where I'm standing, too.

"Oh, yeah, I am. Hi."

Awkward. But the guy gives me a reassuring smile.

"Hey. Nice to meet you. Decker sent us to come get you. Says he wants you to join him over on his boat now." He inclines his head toward the other yachts.

I fight back a smirk and an eye roll. "He does, does he?" I muse.

The guy looks at me with his brows raised expectantly, and I consider making Crusade sweat this one out. I glance down at my phone, confirming he didn't text before he sent an errand boy to fetch me. Bossy asshole. But then I remember the concern he showed earlier.

And wasn't I already planning to find him?

A surge of excitement rushes through me. Decker requested me. Sought me out. Albeit using his lackeys, but still. I let my giddiness bubble up for all of two seconds, then I steel my spine and look the crew member in the eye.

"Let's go."

He offers me a hand and helps me onto the transport boat, and I smile at the two other guys on the tender who are dressed in matching white polos and khakis.

The motor whirs to life before I have a chance to ask the driver which yacht we're heading toward. We glide past Amethyst and Sapphire, so it must be the far ship. Crimson. I knew it.

As we approach the glowing ruby vessel, we don't slow. If I'm not mistaken, we actually speed up. And then we're passing the intended boat at a speed similar to that we use when heading off the isle.

One of the guys seated across from me hollers, excitement radiating off him.

My heart drops into my stomach as fear prickles through my veins.

"Fuck yeah! I can't believe that actually worked! Too fucking easy."

"Smile, princess," the third guy sneers, snapping a picture of me with his phone.

I'm blinded by the flash, and blood whooshes in my ears. I whip my head back and blink at the charter cruise yachts as they shrink in the distance.

We're not going to a boat.

We're not going to a boat?

Chapter 48

Josephine

Anxiety roils through me as my stomach riots. I'm either going to puke or piss my pants. Maybe both.

As I look between the boats shrinking on the horizon, the frantic energy of indecision swamps me. I don't know what to do. How to react. How to get myself out of this situation. The world feels a little hazy around the edges. Like my brain is shutting down and trying to protect me from the reality of the situation.

No. Stop. I have to stay alert.

I'm snapped back to reality when one of the guys starts narrating as if we're in a film documentary.

"Here she is. Queen of the Crusaders. QB1's girl. Decker Crusade's pet." Their laughs are cruel, laced with contempt. "Doesn't she look pretty setting sail across the waves of Lake Chapel, heading away from the charter cruise yachts?"

He's filming me with his phone. He has the camera pointed right at me, taking a video without my consent. They're going to show someone. They're going to show *everyone*.

That's the tipping point.

I lose it.

As if my consciousness is hovering above the tender, I watch myself thrash about like a wild animal trapped in a cage. I grip the edge of the boat and scream. The sound travels to my ears, the frequency and pitch startling me, even though it's coming from my body. I scream and I scream and I scream. My throat will be ripped right open at this rate.

Never let them get you to the second location.

That's the advice. That's one of the safety tidbits drilled into young girls about kidnapping and assault.

Carry your keys in your hand.

Take down your ponytail when you walk alone at night.

Always tell someone where you're going.

Never let them get you to the second location.

It's my worst nightmare. And one I've already lived.

Another picture is snapped. A sequence of synapses fires off in my brain.

My grasp on reality slips.

I feel it. I'm going under. I can't let them take me. I won't go back there again.

My instincts take over, and it isn't until the douchebag sneering at me says it out loud that my actions register.

"Oh, shit. Fuck. Grab her! She's going to jump!"

I'm halfway over the side when I feel hands—hands *everywhere.*

Touching. Grabbing. Groping. Pulling.

Don't fucking touch me!

I don't know whether I think it or say it. Feel it or sob it. It doesn't matter. They'll do what they want. They always do.

Hands grope and pull until my toes no longer skim the water.

Arms brace around my torso as I thrash and scream.

I relive.

I regret.

The edges of my vision go hazy. My sobs turn to laughter, I think.

That's when I know they've won. When the sobs stop. When my body stills.

I fought as hard as I could. It wasn't enough. It never is.

I crave the rush of water as my vision blurs, my hearing wavers, and my body finally, mercifully, gives up the fight.

Chapter 49

Decker

Tracing the outline of my phone in my pocket, I nod as if I'm actually following the conversation.

I'm trying to play it cool. But I can't hold out much longer.

The way she looks tonight—in those tiny red shorts and those perfect red lips?

I want her on this boat. *Now.*

I pull out my phone to tell her as much, but before I unlock the screen, I pause, considering how to play this.

I'm not used to doing the pursuing. Women are usually lined up and waiting for me. Ready and willing. Repetitive and boring.

Not Josephine. *Not my siren.*

She's unlike any woman I've ever met.

Her prickly exterior is such a contrast to the caring warmth and softness she hides. She's infuriatingly independent. She's also wicked funny and too smart for her own good. She doesn't give a single shit about who I am or who I'm destined to be.

That just might be what I like most. She didn't like me at first. Hated me, in fact. So what's happening between us? It's hard fought and worthwhile. It's candid and real.

I drop my chin and focus on my phone's screen, prepared to ask nicely and even grovel if that's what it takes to get her onto this boat and into my arms.

When the screen lights up again, a notification is waiting for me. It's from an unknown number with a South Chapel area code.

Unknown: Happy Shore Week, Lake Chapel bitches! We're breaking in our new team mascot before the big game.

There's a picture of a woman.

She's shellshocked. Her panicked eyes are wide, as if the camera caught her by surprise. She's a deer in the headlights, frozen in place the moment before the car hits at full speed and snuffs out her life.

Josephine.

The look on her face tells me everything I need to know. She isn't with them willingly. She couldn't. *Wouldn't.*

"Kylian!" I roar, the urgency in my voice carrying across the water to the Sapphire yacht. His head snaps up, and he scans the boat until his eyes lock on me. I don't have to say another word to know he's on his way.

I'm scrolling through my contacts a moment later and hitting the name of the person I know without a shadow of a doubt is behind this.

He lets the phone ring once, twice, then a third time.

When Greedy finally answers, I bark out, "Where the fuck's my girl?"

Afterword

"Where the fuck's my girl?"

Not "the" girl. Or "our" girl. **MY** girl.

Oh Decker. You haven't even started to truly suffer. Sorry, Cap.

Beloved reader! Thank you so much for reading Too Safe! Sorry about that cliffhanger. I promise what happens next will be worth the heartache and angst of this moment.

This story has been in my head and on my heart for more than two years. It feels absolute incredible to finally be able to share it with you, even though Josephine and her guys put me through it, too.

If you loved this story, consider leaving a review on Amazon or Goodreads to show your support. I would also highly recommend signing up for my email newsletter. I'll be sharing extended excerpts and lots of updates about the Boys of Lake Chapel in the coming months.

Acknowledgments

This book has been years in the making, but it wasn't ready to be written until everyone and everything was in the right place at the right time.

To everyone who cheered me on and supported me through the process of making this book a reality, I'll be forever grateful. Special shoutouts to the following people who lifted me up in so many ways over the last several months:

David, my husband, partner, and anchor in the tumultuous waves of this season of life. Thank you for always rising to the challenges before us, and for inspiring me to do the same. You are my own personal brand of premium fuel.

Beth, for listening to a million voice messages yet never tiring of hearing me whine about the challenges of nursing and childrearing and smut writing. You're so much more than the keeper of my medical records and the wrangler of my words. This book wouldn't exist (heck, my career probably wouldn't exist!) without you.

Mel, for being the kindest, most empathetic friend who always knows just what to say. Every message from you is a gift. I'm so thankful for your guidance: in writing, in life, in motherhood, and beyond! Not a day goes by that I don't feel intensely grateful to know you.

Silver, for taking the fragments of ideas and vibes for this series and creating literal masterpieces. The covers and brand for this series are the stuff of dreams (even if we did have to change the titles to make it all possible!).

Jessi, Kelly, and Alina, for beta reading an early version of this book, and providing the feedback and support to make it the best it can be!

Ashley, for beta reading and letting me send ridiculous DMs and helping me brainstorm my wackiest ideas. Thank you for always being there!

Jen, Angela, and Krystal, for saying SEND IT TO ME when I needed last-minute help on the tightest of deadlines. I'm so grateful to have you in my corner!

To my ARC + Promo team members, for reading and raving about my work. I am so appreciative of you, and couldn't imagine doing this without your support.

And finally, to Vicki, who will probably never read this. Thank you for letting me spend half my therapy sessions showing you TikToks of lumberjacks and hockey players, while also teaching me about radical acceptance. You're everything I never knew I needed in a counselor.

Also by Abby Millsaps

presented in order of publication

When You're Home

While You're There

When You're Home for the Holidays

When You're Gone

Rowdy Boy

Mr. Brightside

Fourth Wheel

Full Out Fiend

Hampton Holiday Collective

About The Author

Abby Millsaps lives for the thrill of inflicting emotional damage by writing unapologetically angsty romance. Her characters are relatable, lovable, and occasionally confused about the distinction between right and wrong. Her books are set in picturesque settings that feel like home.

Abby started writing romance in 7th grade. Then in 8th grade, she failed to qualify for the Power of the Pen State Championships because, according to the acclaimed panel of judges, "all her submissions contained the same theme: young people falling in love." #LookAtHerNow

Abby met her husband at a house party the summer before her freshman year of college. He had a secret pizza stashed in the trunk of his car that he was saving for a midnight snack— how was she supposed to resist?

Connect with Abby

Website: www.authorabbymillsaps.com

Instagram: @abbymillsaps

TikTok: @authorabbymillsaps

Email: authorabbymillsaps@gmail.com

Newsletter: https://geni.us/AuthorAbbyNewsletter

Facebook Reader Group: Abby's Full Out Fiends

Printed in Great Britain
by Amazon